We See a Different Frontier

A Postcolonial Speculative Fiction Anthology

edited by

Fabio Fernandes
&
Djibril al-Ayad

Futurefire.net Publishing

We See a Different Frontier
First published 2013 by Futurefire.net Publishing
All stories © 2013 the authors
Cover illustration © 2013 Carmen Moran

Joyce Chng's "Lotus", Fabio Fernandes's "The Gambiarra Method", Ernest Hogan's "Pancho Villa's Flying Circus", Rahul Kanakia's "Droplet", Rochita Loenen-Ruiz's "What Really Happened in Ficandula", Sandra McDonald's "Fleet", Sunny Moraine's "A Heap of Broken Images", Silvia Moreno-Garcia's "Them Ships", Gabriel Murray's "Forests of the Night", Shweta Narayan's "The Arrangement of Their Parts", Dinesh Rao's "A Bridge of Words", N.A. Ratnayake's "Remembering Turinam", Sofia Samatar's "I Stole the D.C.'s Eyeglass", Benjanun Sriduangkaew's "Vector", Lavie Tidhar's "Dark Continents", J.Y. Yang's "Old Domes", Aliette de Bodard's Preface, the editors' Introduction and Ekaterina Sedia's Afterword are all published here for the first time, and are © the authors, 2013.

ISBN-print: 978-0-9573975-2-1
ISBN-electronic: 978-0-9573975-3-8

Contact:
editor@futurefire.net
http://futurefire.net/

Contents

Acknowledgements

Gratitude is due to our generous copy-editors and proofreaders, Paul Graham Raven, Maureen Kincaid Speller and Valeria Vitale.

Our eternal thanks to the many people who supported the fundraiser which enabled this anthology to happen at all, especially:

Kathryn Allan, Barbara Baker, Jacques Barcia, Ryan Baumann, Jennifer Marie Brissett, Nathalie Boisard-Beudin, Tobias Buckell, Regina de Búrca, Karen Burnham, Sharon Carr, Siobhan Carroll, Caroline-Isabelle Caron, Paolo Chikiamco, John Chu, Alicia Cole, Pedro Dobbin, Regis Donovan, Rudi Dornemann, Berit Ellingsen, Kate Elliott, Tom Elliott, Micaiah Evans, Matthew Farrer, Suzanne Fischer, Fish, Sjef van Gaalen, Juan Garcés, David Haddock, Rebecca Harbison, Dr. M.J. Hardman, Sarah Heile, Sandra Heinen, Peter Hollo, L.S. Johnson, Serge K. Keller, Angela Korra'ti, William Kimeria, Alex Lambert, Nathan Lea, Ann Leckie, Rochita Loenen-Ruiz, K.L. Maund, Rory McCann, Kirstyn McDermott, Martin McGrath, Todd Meister, Anil Menon, China Miéville, Rafael Monteiro, Samuel Montgomery-Blinn, Catie Murphy, Next Friday, Patrick Nielsen Hayden, Siobhan NiLoughlin, W. Olin-Ammentorp, Colum Paget, Richard Palmer, Kathryn E. Piquette, Rrain Prior, Giseli Ramos, Paul Graham Raven, Ian Sales, Elizabeth Sanford, Gabriel Squailia, Tricia Sullivan, Rachel Swirsky, Sam Tayag, Kevin G. Toth, Cheryl Trooskin-Zoller, Genevieve Valentine, Jetse de Vries, Nikki Walters, Frances Watson, Mark Webb, Rob Weber, Cel West, Helen Wickham, J.Y. Yang, Zeborah, Stephanie Zvan...

...and the astonishingly generous, beautiful and mighty Hiran Patel.

Preface
Aliette de Bodard

"Colonialism" is one of those words that has a sharp divergence of meaning. In the West, it mostly refers to some vague exactions Western countries might have committed in the past (but at the same time lifting other countries out of barbarism and handing them SCIENCE!); said exactions having no bearing on anything but dusty corners of history that no one else is much interested in. In short, a page that has been turned—and that everyone does their best to forget ever happened.

Outside of the West, the word, of course, takes on another meaning. It is a painful legacy that has destroyed and shaped entire countries; that has ignited painful and divisive wars of independence; and that still holds sway today. For those of us with connections to the world outside the West, we know that colonialism is not dead; that the expatriates coming to Asia or other developing countries and living like kings are just new iterations of the colonists; that the worldwide dominance of English as spoken in the US or in the UK, the vast reach of Hollywood movies and US/UK books like *Twilight, Harry Potter* or *Fifty Shades of Grey*, is another instance of cultural imperialism, recalling times when children were sent to English, American or French schools and made to feel ashamed of their own ancestors' achievements.

When we read science fiction stories where colonists leave their home and hearth, and make first contact with funny-looking aliens, we are uncomfortably reminded of the days where English or French or Dutch colonists came to foreign shores, marvelled at odd and weird customs, and gradually took over everything under the pretence of "civilizing" barbarians. Colonialism is, to an extent, embedded in modern science fiction; and it is no coincidence that most SF is produced by Western Anglophones and fails to concern itself with the point of view of people outside of the dominant sphere—or, if it does, it speaks in their name without regard for what they really think. Depictions of developing countries tend to be produced by Western Anglophones, and to focus on abject poverty, corruption, or any other negative sides that apparently make living in a developing country unbearable. This is not the voice of a country's inhabitants; of those who have pride in where and how they live.

The stories in this anthology are not this kind of science fiction. They are the voices of the invaded; of the colonized; of the erased and the oppressed; of those whom others would make into aliens and blithely ignore or conquer or enlighten. I hope you enjoy reading them, and that they will make a different world and a different viewpoint take centre-stage for you.

Introduction
Fabio Fernandes & Djibril al-Ayad

The new is terrifying. Not because it is this way and not another way, but because it is new.
—Vilem Flusser

A specter haunts a world. This is not a misquotation of Marx; there is a specter, but an infinity of worlds, as all of us who write and read science fiction know too well.

The specter in question, as the epigraph from Czech-Brazilian philosopher Vilem Flusser reflects, is the *new*. Flusser, a disciple of Martin Heidegger, wasn't afraid of new experiences. He couldn't afford to be: having lost all his family in the German concentration camps at the beginning of World War II, he emigrated to Brazil, where he stayed for thirty years, first working at a Czech import/export company, and later entering the Brazilian intellectual community, publishing, teaching at several schools, and finally becoming Lecturer for Philosophy of Science at the Escola Politécnica of the University of São Paulo. He stayed in Brazil until 1972, when he moved to France after the Brazilian military *coup d'etat*, dying in a car crash in 1991 on the way to his native Prague to give a lecture.

Flusser's case was and is still being replicated all over the world, not only by Jewish refugees, but by millions of immigrants who cross borders every day: according to the NGO Rescue.org, there are right now (as of February 2013) about 42 million displaced people in the world. One in every 170 persons in the world has been uprooted by war. This is the largest category of vulnerable people in the world. About one third of them are officially recognized refugees because they have crossed an international border. The other two thirds are so-called internally displaced persons, or IDPs, because they are still within their own country.

❧❦❧

The Future Fire, as a magazine, has long sought to publish speculative fiction at the inclusive and progressive end of the social and political spectrum. In 2010 there was an active push in the direction of including more marginalized voices by advertising and publishing two themed issues of the magazine, on feminist science fiction and queer science fiction respectively. An agenda and focus on political content and underrepresented themes should never be at the expense of quality; the magazine publishes only the very best stories it can. In other words, *TFF* will never try to increase the proportion of minority authors in the publication by being less demanding than one would be with works by straight, white, cis, male, Anglophone writers, but rather by actively seeking out and encouraging authors of the kinds of stories one is looking for; Claire Light's polemical online article "Editorial Work Is HARD, Asshole!" makes this point both powerfully and usefully.[1]

After a year-long hiatus in 2011, therefore, *TFF* advertised for two guest editors to help produce themed issues and reach new communities of authors as well as readers. From nearly a dozen proposals, the team selected Lori Selke (whose *Outlaw Bodies* anthology appeared in late 2012) and of course Fabio, whose proposal for an issue on the theme of colonialism, focusing on the voices of real colonized peoples, struck so many chords with what *TFF* was trying to do.

Fabio wanted to talk about something that, if not exactly new, is still far from being considered normal within the Anglo-American SF sphere of influence: alien cultures. As in *us*, the aliens from Earth. Foreigners. Strangers to the current dominant culture.

The project was as yet untitled, but Fabio already had the title of a story that he just couldn't get out of his mind: Bruce Sterling's "We See Things Differently". A decade ago, this story was translated and published in Brazil and he remembered the powerful impression that it caused when he first read it. We (Fabio and Djibril) remixed this title in the spirit of the cyberpunks (and how better than to use the name of a story written by one of the leaders of the Movement? A tip of the hat to you, Bruce), mashing it up with the other idea that kept coming back to us: that canard of science fiction cliché, "The Final Frontier". We wanted to turn this colonial image on its head, hence the combination of the two titles: *We See a Different Frontier*.

In a world crisscrossed by electronic leylines, we can't afford to let ourselves be guided by old geopolitics. Not in our business. To quote another philosopher (the last one!), Ludwig Wittgenstein, "The limits of my language means the limits of my world." The emergence of a new science fiction around the world which is not restrained by the borders of First World countries, or even by the English language, means the limits of our world are being shattered. There is still a long way to go, but honorable predecessors like *Cosmos Latinos* and *So*

---

[1] <http://clairelight.typepad.com/seelight/2009/08/editorial-work-is-hard-asshole.html>

Long Been Dreaming have proved that we can make this world smaller and richer.

We felt that this issue needed to attract the very best stories, and in particular to pay the authors fairly for their work (*TFF* is a non-profit making magazine, and pays only $20 per story). This was especially important since we hoped to hear from many voices who are often unheard in Anglo-American mainstream science fiction, and paying a fair rate for this fiction was essential if we wanted to be consistent with our social and political stance. We therefore set up a Peerbacker project, which allowed supporters to pre-order copies of the print issue and/or contribute larger quantities to help us pay professional rates for fiction. The support from the speculative fiction community was incredible.

We calculated that with $3,000 we could pay a professional rate of $0.05 per word for an average of 7-8 stories (after paying for all the rewards and administrative costs of the fundraiser). Dozens of people, including some big names in speculative fiction, helped to spread the word about the appeal, wrote guest blog posts for us, allowed us to write guest posts for their sometimes large readerships, donated books and other goodies for giveaways and contests or helped in so many other ways, in addition to contributing generously to the fund. As well as being astonishingly generous and profoundly moving, this is clearly a sign that the theme of colonialism and the exposure of under-represented voices in speculative fiction are things that many people care deeply about. Within six weeks we had so far exceeded our target that we were able to pay professional rates for the fifteen stories you see in this volume.

The call for submissions summarized what we were looking for in this anthology:

> It is impossible to consider the history, politics or culture of the modern world without taking into account our colonial past. Most violent conflicts and financial inequalities in some sense result from the social-political-economic matrix imposed by European powers since the seventeenth century—even powerful countries such as the BRICS (Brazil, Russia, India, China, South Africa) have to be viewed through the filter of our history to fully appreciate their current circumstances. The same is true of art and literature, including science fiction; as Rochita Loenen-Ruiz eloquently explained,[2] "it is impossible to discuss non-Western SF without considering the effects of colonialism." Cultural imperialism erases many native traditions and literatures, exoticizes colonized and other non-European countries

---

[2] <http://djibrilalayad.blogspot.co.uk/2012/05/decolonizing-as-sf-writer.html>

and peoples, and drowns native voices in the clamour of Western stories set in their world. Utopian themes like "The Final Frontier", "Discovering New Worlds" and "Settling the Stars" appeal to a colonial romanticism, especially recalling the American West. But what is romantic and exciting to the privileged, white, anglophone reader is a reminder of exploitation, slavery, rape, genocide and other crimes of colonialism to the rest of the world.

We See a Different Frontier will publish new speculative fiction stories in which the viewpoint is that of the colonized, not the invader. We want to see stories that remind us that neither readers nor writers are a homogeneous club of white, male, Christian, hetero, cis, monoglot anglophone, able-bodied Westerners. We want the cultures, languages and literatures of colonized peoples and recombocultural[3] individuals to be heard, not to show the White Man learning the error of his ways, or Anglos defending the world from colonizing extraterrestrials. We want stories that neither exoticize nor culturally appropriate the non-western settings and characters in them.

❦

We received many wonderful stories in the four months of the submissions period, and even after we had applied the filtering criteria—the story had to be on theme, it had to be beautifully written, and at least one of the editors had to absolutely love it—we had more than twice as many words as we could use. The process of whittling these down to the table of contents you see before you was not a straightforward one. For every story we rejoiced to buy, there was at least one story we wept to let go. There were stories that we both agreed instantly we had to have, but there were also stories that one or other of us hated and had to be talked into: in some cases these are the most interesting stories, the ones that push the boundaries, that tell a story that isn't obvious, that were uncomfortable to our limited perspectives. For an editor seeking to diversify, to include under-represented voices, especially voices that are not her own, this is one of the most valuable lessons to learn: a story that you start out hating (or even just thinking, *meh*) might be the most exciting story you buy. Your instincts do not serve you well; they need to be tempered with reason, with surprise, and with the opinions of others, especially those who have experienced colonialisms and discriminations that you have not.

The stories that appear in this anthology are all brilliant excoriations of one or another element of colonialism, racism,

---

[3] <http://djibrilalayad.blogspot.co.uk/2012/05/guest-post-i-didnt-know-i-was-alien-or.html>

imperialism, cultural appropriation or exploitation. They range in tone from the cynically satirical, via charmingly fantastic and cheerfully brutal, to violently furious and vengeful. There are stories about repelling the invader from a foreign land, about dealing with the aftermath of abuse and atrocity, about making sure history does not repeat itself. There are protagonists who are rebels, terrorists or freedom fighters; antagonists who are patronising scholars, brutal soldiers, white-guilty children of colonists, businessmen and moguls. There are hard science-fictional pieces, alternative realities, steampunk, dark fantasies, mundane SF, social observation and blistering biopunk adventures. We are reminded that the roles and rights of women, the poor, queer and trans folk intersect inseparably with issues of race and colonialism. That suppression of culture and especially language are common tactics in the repression of a people, and as effective as violence itself. That a colonized people is not necessarily defeated, its culture is not inferior or weaker or more backward or scientifically ignorant than that of the invaders. That our (Western) history need not dictate our future, but there are other narratives, other possibilities, other voices and other stories to tell. These stories need to be heard. These stories need to be read.

The Arrangement of Their Parts

Shweta Narayan

Surat, 1076 AH / 1665 AD

The Englishman's workshop nestled close to his people's fortified factory, outside its walls but well within its influence. A night guard watched over it—if keeping to the doorway, eyeing the street from his puddle of lantern light, and turning occasionally to spit *paan* could really be called watching.

The guard had reason for complacency; plastered walls offered no handhold, and the workshop's windows, set into the sloping roof, were too high and small for human reach. But the Artificer Devi had not worn human form in many years. She cut the wooden trellis out from one window, spread her tailfeathers for balance, and telescoped her neck to peer into the room.

It could as well have been a butchery. The air was rank with stale machine oil. Moonlight spread flat on tile and whitewash, caught on gears laid out in disconnected imitation of their proper form. Inked and labelled diagrams, pinned to walls and tables, recorded the workings of legs, eyes, boilers; and on the main workbench a half-dismembered voicebox stood ready to play one cylinder of its speech. Its other cylinders stood in rows beside it, sorted by size instead of tone. Dead husks shaped the shadows: a soldier's head pried open; pieces of a half-golden mongoose; the ungeared skeleton of a large cat, frozen before it could pounce.

The trail ended here. Of course. Anything might be found in Surat, greatest port in the world, for a price.

She landed with barely a whirr on the main bench, next to the voicebox, and reached for three heartsprings coiled naked on a sheaf of papers. Paused. The springs' thin metal had ripped in places; the pattern of dents said they had been flattened out, then rolled back up. Well, that could all be repaired. But—she held one up to the moonlight, then checked the others, shivering. Every graven word was gone. Scratched over, rubbed down to a lifeless blur.

Not even she could bring someone back once their heartspring was destroyed.

A prayer for her dead, then, gone to power that great mechanism marked by stars; and three more notches in her own spring. There was only metal left here. And paper, rubbed over with wax to make imprints of each ruined heartspring.

But remains could, at need, become parts. The hunting cat's

skeleton was still fully articulated. The soldier's head still held his steam boiler, though the ruby lens that heated it was gone. And for the rest—she shredded the paper into a crucible, set the springs gently on their bed of copied words, and turned to build up the fire.

❧✝☙

Four brahmins met in a village one day and, in the way of learned men everywhere, got to talking about their learning. Now, each believed his own knowledge to be the most essential; but brahmins value humility and non-attachment, so none were willing to admit it. In consequence each one heaped praises on the rest, and so they all became great friends and decided to travel through the jungle together.

On the way they came across new bones scattered by the side of the road. "My dear friends!" cried the first brahmin. "While my knowledge is a drop to your monsoon clouds, yet I believe it would reveal the mystery of these bones."

"Do please show us," said the second, "for we have nothing but awe of your mastery of form, and virtue can only increase when learning is shared." For he was hoping to overhear his new friend's mantra and steal its power for himself.

So the first mouthed his sacred words and scattered water from the three holy rivers onto the bones, and they rose from the ground and arranged themselves into the skeleton of a tiger.

❧✝☙

The sun was risen when the workshop door squeaked open, letting in the day's dust on a rush of muggy air. The Englishman glanced in, then turned to give his guard a low-voiced command before stepping inside.

All but one of the windows cast trellis-shadows on the far wall. From that one, the Artificer raised her wings. The Englishman wiped his forehead with a handkerchief, smirked at her shadow, and said in passable Hindustani, "Well, isn't this curious." Behind him, the door pulled shut. The outer bar dropped with a thump.

She tucked her wings neatly back, keeping her good eye fixed on him. His skin showed red through his light muslin *jama*, and it sat oddly with his English hat and boots, but there was nothing silly about the pistol at his hip. "You seem, Sir James," she said, "to find a great many things curious."

"With all Creation so full of wonder, how could I not?" He looked up at her directly, then, shading his face; his eyes gleamed in appreciation. He said, "And I would be loath to damage so lovely a mechanism before even seeing it fly."

9

"Am I to be grateful?"

"Another man might choose revenge." He gestured from the cooling crucible to his disturbed mallets and gravers. His hand drifted down to the gun, jerked away from it again. "Or use this violation to cause trouble for your Emperor. I am a natural philosopher, and prefer understanding."

By Imperial edict, the British could not be touched. Much the bird cared. "Understand this, then," she said. "The usurper Aurangzeb is not my Emperor. And you murdered my own."

"Oh, murdered, is it now?" The Englishman sounded only amused.

"You think your studies justify their deaths?"

"Well said. One would almost think there was meaning to it. But it was Man, after all, whom God made in His image, not clockwork; so clockwork cannot be murdered."

She rattled her feathers. "Ah? Then mere clockwork could hardly violate your workshop."

"Argued like a native! And indeed you may be right despite yourself." He grinned. "For I have discovered that it takes only Descartes' four principles of inanimate form to explain you."

"So you need only know—" She shifted into French. "—*the motion, size, shape, and arrangement of my parts*." Back to Hindustani. "What's left to understand?"

His mouth opened. Shut. "'s Blood, you're a saucy one," he said. "I wish to know *why*, of course."

"We have our last rites, as you do yours." Sunlight crept down the far wall, towards the skeletal forms, reaching lower now than the man's head. "We do not leave our dead unmelted. You've had your dismantlement and your diagramming. Trade me for what is left, and I shall take no further action."

He glanced along the row of windows; then, gaze calculating, back at the bird. "And what is it you offer?"

"A tale of our own natural philosophers, whose understanding might inform yours."

⛝

The second brahmin was impressed, which irritated him because he hadn't managed to hear the mantra. So he said, "That is very clever!"

Such meager praise drew a thin smile to the first brahmin's lips. "You are far too kind, my brother," he said. "But indeed, I don't aspire to cleverness. Only to knowledge of Truth within the world."

"As do we all," said the second, "though we cannot all achieve it."

The third brahmin said hurriedly, "Still, enlightened company can only add to our learning."

"That's so," said the second. "And feeble as my own learning is, such a base does call out to be built upon."

"Yes, and as you so wisely said, our lives will be richer for sharing," said the third. And so the second brahmin mumbled over the skeleton, shaking neem and mango leaves as he spoke; and muscles built themselves over bone, each one the perfect size for its place.

"Why," the third marveled, hiding his own chagrin, "The animal's bulk is clear now. Even so does philosophy grow around a fundamental knowledge of the Vedas. And as art grows up around philosophy, I shall add my own grains of knowledge to give it shape, if this pleases my dear friends." Nothing, of course, could please his dear friends more. So he anointed each muscle with clove oil and camphor, spoke into his cupped hands, and clapped twice; and striped skin grew over the whole, its orange glowing like sunrise.

The fourth brahmin said, "Truly, this is a wonder. Perhaps I can add to it a little, though I admit myself surprised that I might know anything my learned friends do not!" So saying, he breathed dust from the four great mountains into the tiger's mouth and eyes, and he whispered his own words.

The tiger sprang into motion, then, and ate them all.

❧

The Englishman laughed. "If you want someone who takes tales of heathen chanting and anointments seriously," he said loudly, "find a Papist. This explains nothing—"

A shadow loomed behind the bird, silent on bare feet. She dropped from the window, spread her wings, and settled on the main bench. Above her, rain shutters slammed shut.

The Englishman's smile was edged, now. "Though it kept you occupied," he said, drifting closer. The pistol was in his hand, aimed at the floor. "My guard's a native, after all; too superstitious to see why the fire burned all night, but clever as a monkey on the roof. Now, there's no need to *damage* you—" She turned, and he recoiled. "What happened to your eye?"

"Eyes break," she said. "They are mere lenses, and can be replaced." They could also be pulled out whole and set atop a steam boiler, angled to catch sunlight, to wind a new-forged heartspring. Once that sunlight slanted down far enough into the workshop. "And your guard closed the wrong window."

"What? No, no, you'll not make me look away so easily." He circled around till he could watch the windows without losing sight of her, then glanced warily up.

Behind him, a lens flared. Yellow eyes eased open. Golden claws came out with a click from skeletal tiger paws.

Pancho Villa's Flying Circus

Ernest Hogan

General Villa tore the bottle from my hands, gulped down some tequila, then slapped my shoulder.

"Look! Look, Sahagún! Alejandro! See how well Tesla's death ray works!"

Beneath the airship *Cucaracha*, the Chihuahuan Desert was littered with burning, crashed American aeroplanes on both sides of the border between the United States and Mexico. Smoke rose into a sky that turned blood red as the sun set.

"Quite effective, General," I said.

"Effective?" He tapped the bullet-proof glass. "It's magnificent! Beautiful! They thought they were invincible, but look at them now!"

The door to the gondola's cramped observation pod burst open. It was Tesla. He looked paler and more wild-haired than usual.

"Come, Tesla, my friend!" General Villa had not taken his eyes away from the carnage. "Come see what we have done!"

"Yes." Tesla held up a device like a gun, but also like one of his electrical machines. "What have we done?"

"It's wonderful!" General Villa beamed.

"It's horrible!" said Tesla.

"Yes! Horrible! Terrible! Wonderful!"

"I did not make the death ray for this!" Tesla's hands shook.

I didn't like the look of that device. I kept my hand close to my revolver.

"What?" General Villa turned, saw Tesla and the device. "It's a *death* ray! What did you think we were going to do with it?"

Tesla waved the device at the carnage. "I wanted to make war impossible!"

"You of all people," said General Villa, "should know that nothing is impossible."

A spark leapt from the device—like the beam of the death ray, only smaller. General Villa exploded into a foul-smelling dust-cloud.

I put a bullet through Tesla's fantastic brain, then coughed, choking on what was left of General Villa.

Holding my breath, I picked up the device—a death ray pistol—and tucked it into my belt.

This was my big chance. I decided to take it. It's all about seeing opportunities and having the guts to take them. Or, as General Villa once said, "Without huevos—cojones!—brains are nothing."

❧❦❧

The death of General Villa shocked my crew, Cháirez, the copilot in the control pod, and Holguín, the gunner in the death ray blister. I didn't give them time to think about it. I had them toss Tesla's body overboard, then said:

"There is no time to lose. The Americans are probably assembling all the planes they can muster for counterattack. They do not know of the unfortunate death of General Villa. We must move fast."

"What can we do?" Cháirez said.

"We are stocked with provisions. Tesla's generator for the death ray and the *Cucaracha*'s engine allows us to go immediately."

"But where?" Holguín asked.

"To the very heart of America."

"Washington?" Asked Cháirez.

I laughed. "No. What do we want with Washington? We are going to strike at America's true heart—Hollywood!"

Cháirez looked confused. Holguín uttered some blasphemy. I let it sink in. Cháirez smiled. "Yes! Yes! Hollywood!"

"It will be ours!" I said.

Holguín sneered. "We know what you want, Sahagún!"

I found myself touching the letter I kept in my breast pocket.

"Zee-O-Mara!" said Cháirez.

"It's pronounced Shi-O-Mara!" I had to correct him.

"Hollywood will have the whole world saying it gringo-style soon." Holguín was always such a cynic.

"Not if I can help it." I put my hand on the death ray.

"I want Theda Bara!" Holguín smirked. "Think she'll go for a Mexican death ray airship gunner?"

"Then I'll take Gloria Swanson, or maybe Clara Bow... or Anna May Wong..." Cháirez was dreaming with his eyes wide open.

"Why not take all of them?" I suggested.

"Yes! All the beauties of Hollywood will be ours! Or we'll vaporize the town!" Holguín gestured like he was firing the death rays.

I knew these men well. Not much younger than me, but young. Still boys in a lot of ways. A bit smarter than General Villa's ground troops, but with the same basic spirit. They never had much—show them something desirable, offer a possibility, and they will want it.

I put my hand on the device at my belt. It, plus the *Cucaracha* and its death rays, was better than an entire army. We could take on the world, or at least Hollywood

And now Cháirez and Holguín wanted it.

They probably thought it was their idea.

They didn't need to know that it was my idea, what I wanted.

Being a leader is so easy.

And why did I want to take Hollywood?

Simple. Natural. Hollywood had taken something that belonged to me, and I wanted it back.

🌿🎺🌿

It was just a few years ago. The Revolution was going well and was very popular. Even the Americans liked it, donated money, came down to look at it, take pictures of it, maybe even fire a few gunshots or throw a bomb or two. Americans love a revolution—as long as it doesn't cost them too much.

That was when intellectuals from all over the world came to Mexico, thinking that the Revolution would allow them to take their crazy ideas and make a new world.

I didn't really care about making a new world. I would settle for something I could call my own.

That was also when the scientists and inventors came, eager to impress General Villa. Santos-Dumont came from Brazil to help with the airships—and was killed in an unfortunate accident. Tesla arrived with his electricity, and talk of the death ray.

How General Villa's eyes lit up at that talk!

Even people from Hollywood came. Why not? The Revolution was full of action—the stuff of motion pictures!

And they weren't just movie people, but men in uniforms with guns. They said they were from the Studio Corps.

So they were here with their big shiny cars and fancy American suits, setting up their cameras everywhere. Even in Cuauhtémoc, my home village.

The loved it all. The mountains, the desert, our clothes, our music... our women.

How they loved Xiomara!

I can't really blame them. She's beautiful. Her eyes. Her smile. Her laugh. And the way she sang and danced!

She could look at you, and make you want to do whatever she wanted. There were many times I nearly killed someone because of the look in those eyes.

"Even your name is wonderful," said Raoul, a director. "Zee-o-mara!" he mispronounced it. "You won't need a last name! You won't just be stuck with playing señoritas, you could be an Indian maid, or an Oriental siren. We got some technical boys working on a way to make movies that talk—and sing—and you'll be a natural." Movies that talk?

Ridiculous. I knew what he really wanted. The way he would touch her. And she would smile, laugh.

Xiomara was smarter than most women—or men. She was so good at dealing with people. She could speak English, and even French. Some people in Cuauhtémoc called her La Bruja.

≈ ☤ ☞

"If that pig ever touches you again, I'll kill him!" I later told her.

She laughed, then kissed me. "Alejandro, you know that you are the one I love."

Her smile. That look in her eyes. I believed her.

We lived in Cuauhtémoc all our lives. We were going to be married. We couldn't let the fact that the world was being turned upside down get in our way.

But I could see that Xiomara had desires bigger than our town. I would have to fight—even kill—to keep her.

And I would. That was my big desire.

≈ ☤ ☞

I shouldn't have been surprised when they took her. A big American car, gringo thugs with masks and guns burst into her parents' house. They drove off into the night.

Her family was devastated. I promised her parents that I would bring her back.

But at first all I could do was drink. All the time, I kept my eyes focused northward. Toward Hollywood.

≈ ☤ ☞

Then it happened. A movie came out, and Xiomara was in it. She danced—there was no sound yet—and kissed a gringo. Soon rumors spread of her being the star of a new kind of movie—one with dancing, and singing that could be heard.

It looked like she had forgotten all about me. I would pick up my revolver and think about shooting myself, when I wasn't drinking.

≈ ☤ ☞

Then the letter came. It reeked of perfume. The postman laughed. People gathered around because they saw it had come from Hollywood.

"Read it aloud, Alejandro!" someone said.

I pulled out my revolver. "What Xiomara has to say to me is private."

My darling Alejandro, she wrote:

Please forgive me for not writing you sooner, but I have been so busy since I came to Hollywood, and you know that writing is not an easy thing for me.

It has been wonderful, like a dream that I could never imagine, but I miss you and my family terribly. I keep telling them that I would love to see you, but they say there is much work for me to do here.

They want me to make the singing-dancing picture. It will make me a lot of money. After that I will tell them I want to see you and visit my family. I would like to bring them, and you, up here. Things are possible here that could never happen in Cuauhtémoc.

Maybe you can come up and see me? I know that once you want something, nothing can stop you. If you could come here, you could do anything.

Please take this letter to my parents and read it to them. Tell them that I miss them, and I love them, and someday I would like them to come live with me in Hollywood.

I dream of you, me, and them living here. It want it very much.

I want you very much, Alejandro.

With all of my love,

Xiomara

Next to her signature were red imprints of her lips.

I fought to hold back the tears.

Then one of the boys from the neighborhood stuck his head in my window and asked, "Did she write anything good?"

I fired a shot over his head. He turned white and ran. It felt good.

❧❦❧

Then I went and read the letter to Xiomara's parents. I vowed to them that I would go to Hollywood and reunite them with her or die.

"How will you make it to Hollywood?" asked her mother.

"Yes," said her father. "American troops are guarding the border."

"I will get help from General Villa."

With the letter in my breast pocket, I took off to join General Villa's army.

I've always been good with machines, and a leader. They always said I was smart. I became involved with the airship program. I rose through the ranks.

❧❦❧

Now *I* was the leader. The only thing that could stop us was the American Air Corps, and we had just defeated their finest with our death rays. But the Americans were proud and clever. They would think of something.

"I don't like the way they keep sending planes up, watching us from a distance," said Holguín.

"They are cowards," said Shaguin, "afraid of the death ray."

"Let's keep going," I said, "and keep an eye on them."

≈¶≈

We were getting close to the Grand Canyon when Holguín yelled: "Planes! There's more American aeroplanes coming after us!"

"It figures. Just when I was getting ready to get a good look at this big hole in the ground." said Cháirez.

I checked some gauges. "We're losing helium, having trouble staying up."

"Soon we'll be at the bottom of that hole," said Holguín.

"The generators still working?" I asked.

"Yes."

"Then keep going. As fast as we can."

"At least it's a pretty place to die."

I didn't like Holguín's lack of faith.

"I would rather die in Hollywood with Theda to look at," said Cháirez.

I grabbed my binoculars and scanned the east. No sign of any planes. "Where are they?"

"To the west," said Cháirez.

I turned. There were some planes at the horizon.

"Why wouldn't they be coming from the East, like the others?"

"Don't the Americans have air fields in California?"

"A few, but—this is strange."

"They're between us and Hollywood. Do you think they knew?"

"How would they know?"

"Maybe they have a wireless set that can read minds or something."

"Don't be ridiculous."

Then we dropped. The colorful, jagged walls of the Canyon were higher than us.

"Can't we get any higher?"

"Not without repairing that helium leak."

"Chinga!"

"You said it."

Cháirez had his binoculars, and his mouth fell open. "Chinga!" he said again.

"How could it be worse?"

"More planes. Coming from the east."

"We're boxed in!" Holguín screamed.

"What do we do?"

I though about Xiomara, how far we were from Hollywood, and the prospect of never seeing her again.

"They expect us to keep running, and struggling to stay high. Let's get sneaky. Let's descend further into the canyon."

"This is absolutely insane!" said Holguín.

"I love it!" said Cháirez.

☙❦❧

"How am I supposed to shoot them with the death ray if we're in the canyon?" Holguín was complaining rather than asking. "The ray guns are at the bottom of the *Cucaracha!*"

"I'm just trying to buy us some time. If they get too close, rise and blast them."

"Now you are talking!" Cháirez kept looking straight ahead.

But these planes from the west didn't try to chase us into the canyon. Clever bastards.

"They're heading north!" said Holguín.

"Are they trying to circle us?" Cháirez was showing fear. A bad sign.

I grabbed the binoculars. They were a squadron of ten planes. There was something funny about one of them.

"It's towing something! It's a sign—'*Xiomara is here. She wants to talk to Alejandro Sahagún.*'"

"It's a trap!" Holguín looked like he was going to leap out of gondola.

"We have the death ray. Let's blast them!" Cháirez dared to order.

"No!" I roared. It even hurt my ears. "We might hurt—or even kill, Xiomara."

"You don't actually believe that she's there. It's some kind of trick," Holguín had left the gun blister and had opened the hatch to the control pod. "You know how these Hollywood bastards are!"

"I can't risk losing her! We will slow down, get close to ground level and prepare to land!"

"You're crazy! They'll kill us!" Holguín leaped toward Cháirez, grasping for the controls.

I pulled out the death ray pistol, fired. Soon we were coughing up what was left of Holguín.

"That smell!" said Cháirez. "It's the worst thing in the world."

He looked at me funny. He smiled. Tried to laugh.

I put the death ray pistol in his face. "You know what I want you to do."

☙❦❧

The Hollywood planes escorted us to a flat area just outside the Grand Canyon.

"It looks like a military base," said Cháirez.

There were trucks, machine guns, artillery, and lots of armed men in uniform. Only they were funny uniforms. Not United States Army.

There was also a mooring tower set up for us.

"Looks like they did their homework."

"I don't like this…" said Cháirez.

I held up the death ray.

"…but I think I can learn to live with it."

"Sure. Just think about when you'll be grabbing the behinds of those actresses."

He grinned like an idiot.

They tied the *Cucaracha* up like pros and motioned for us to come down. A lot of them had their rifles, not aimed, but ready.

"I don't know. Maybe we should blast the hell out of something, just show them who's in charge," suggested Cháirez.

Then I saw her—Xiomara, beautiful as ever, dressed in an elegant overcoat with a leather helmet and goggles, a very modern woman ready to ride in an automobile or an aeroplane.

"That won't be necessary," I said.

He opened his mouth, but knew not to say anything.

Then he smiled. Two beautiful blondes were standing next to Xiomara, waving and blowing kisses. They weren't famous movie stars, but they were beautiful and blonde.

Once they had the *Cucaracha* stabilized, we popped the hatch, and rolled down the ladder. I sent Cháirez down first, just in case.

They didn't shoot him. The blondes rushed up, hugged and kissed him.

"Alejandro!"

It was Xiomara's voice. I hurried down, getting tangled in the ladder. She grabbed me and kept me from falling down like Buster Keaton.

I nearly knocked us both over as I turned to embrace her, trying to look into her eyes and kiss her at the same time. Her dark eyes scorched my soul. The kiss was delicious, if a bit crooked.

There were flashes of light. Explosions.

I grabbed the death ray.

"Hey! Alejandro, amigo! No need to go for that gun!" It was a voice that annoyed me.

We were surrounded by uniformed men, some of them had rifles, others had cameras.

"Newsmen?" I tried to hold Xiomara close while looking around.

"Of course, my love. This is news."

There was even a movie camera.

She winked at the cameraman and kissed my cheek. "Smile, Alejandro. You are going to be a star."

"Yes, Alejandro, amigo." I looked at the irritating man. It was Raoul, the pig of a director. His Spanish was good, but he pronounced it like a gringo. "This newsreel is going to go around the world—and make history!"

He rushed up, slapped my back, shook my hand and smiled for the camera.

Then I got a good look at the strange uniforms that the men were wearing. They had patches that read Studio Corps.

"Yeah," said Raoul, "Hollywood is getting more rich and powerful. Our need for security has grown beyond what a private police force can provide, with international tensions being what they are these days. So now we have our own army."

"What? Is Hollywood its own country?"

Raoul laughed. This started everyone else laughing.

Xiomara kissed me again.

"Not quite," said Raoul, his teeth gleaming. "Not yet."

I held Xiomara close, and kept my right hand near the death ray.

"You see, Alejandro, my friend, some of us in Hollywood see moving pictures as the greatest leap forward in the history of communications. This is going to make the invention of movable type look crude. Now we have people from all over the world following the same stories, the same stars. We can change the way they think. How they behave. What they want. Newspapers are lagging behind. Radio is still in its infancy. And when we add sound to our pictures, and with this ship, we could take over California and secede from the Union— and then after that—we could conquer the world."

Xiomara put her lips to my ear, and whispered, in Spanish, "*We* could conquer the world, my love."

"We have an army—and planes—but we won't have to fire a shot. Especially with this death-spitting flying machine of yours! Once we've prepared the people of the world, they will want to be ruled by Hollywood. They probably won't wait to vote us in—they'll kick their governments out and beg us make them subjects of the Hollywood Empire." His eyes glazed over. He was lost in his vision of the future.

"You could be *my* emperor, Alejandro." Xiomara's breath scorched my ear.

"So, what do you say, Alejandro, old boy?" He reached out smiling. "Why don't you let me take a look at that interesting gadget you have there?"

He reached out. His eyes were like a snake's.

Xiomara's hand patted my ass. "You know what to do, my love!" She said it so softly, I could barely hear it.

Of course I knew. I didn't think—I just took the death ray and vaporized Raoul.

When I coughed, I remembered General Villa's words, "Without huevos—cojones!—brains are nothing."

Suddenly, all the Studio Corps troops had their weapons aimed at us. I gripped the death ray.

Xiomara put her hand on mine, and winked at me. Then she smiled like a thousands suns rising. She turned around, looking at all of the men, and down the barrels of their guns.

"Raoul was a fool." Her voice exploded. "He was a dreamer, but he was weak. He lacked the killer instinct. He brought us this far, but now we—I—need more. I need a true warrior at my side if I am to become the Queen of Hollywood and Empress of the World!"

She raised my hand—that was still clutching the death ray—over our heads.

For a moment the men were an army of statues. I wasn't sure if they were going to kill us.

Then one of them yelled, "Hail, Xiomara! Queen of Hollywood and Empress of the World!"

Soon they were all repeating that, roaring, cheering.

Then turned to me. "And would you be my emperor, Alejandro, my love?"

Before I could kiss her, she turned to the cameraman: "We're ready for our closeup!"

I didn't say anything. I just kissed her with passion.

But I did keep one eye open.

Them Ships

Silvia Moreno-Garcia

Leonardo says that the Americans are going to fire some rockets and free us from the tyranny of the aliens and I say: who gives a shit. Lemme tell you something: it wasn't super-awesome around here before the aliens. At least we get three meals every day now.

I used to live in a cardboard house with a tin roof and collected garbage for a living. They called my home a "lost city" but they should've called it "fucked city."

Leonardo talks about regaining our freedom, 'bout fighting and shit. What damn freedom? You think I had freedom in the slums? Leonardo can talk freedom out his ass because he had money before this thing started and he saw too many American movies where they kill the monsters with big guns.

I'm not an idiot. The cops used to do their little "operations" in our neighborhood. They'd come in and arrest everyone, take everything. They weren't Hollywood heroes out to help people. They were fucking assholes and I don't see why they would have changed. As for American soldiers saving the day: you think they give a rat's ass 'bout Mexico City? You think they're going to fly here in their helicopters and save us?

I say fuck that shit. I never had no freedom. Leonardo can go piss himself.

❧❦❧

Leonardo's been going on 'bout freedom fighters again, which means I've been putting on the headphones and listening to my music. The good thing is the aliens let me charge the player. Otherwise I'd kill that little shit.

Well, he ain't that little. Leonardo is pretty tall, probably 'cause he didn't have to eat no garbage when he was growing up. His dad had some sort of fast food franchise and Leonardo was doing really well, studying at the Tec, fucking pretty girls and driving a fancy car 'til the aliens landed and started rounding people up in sectors. And, since the aliens don't classify by social status, Leonardo got put in with me. I'm not sure if he was more dismayed 'bout being a prisoner or 'bout having to share a room with the likes of me. I'd say me.

I don't really care. Our home was a one bedroom which I shared with my three sisters and my parents. Sharing with one person is easy and it's even easier when that person doesn't reek of alcohol-laced coffees, like my dad did. The asshole's probably dead and I'm fucking glad for it and I'm also glad now I only share my room with Leonardo. Got my own bed now. My own desk. I don't write much, except for them diary entries 'cause the aliens say it's healthy.

Leonardo's complaining that they're trying to break our spirits again and I tell him to go fuck himself.

❦

The first time I saw the spaceship I was walking down the ravine, picking garbage. 'Cause that's what I did every day. Get my bags and strap them and go pick around. There's some good shit you can find in the garbage, like my music player.

So there I am looking for soda cans and plastic bottles I can drag to the recycling centre, or a juicy find I can sell, and it gets dark, like a cloud just passed over the sun. I don't look up at first because I'm busy but then there's this weird noise so I raise my head and I see it.

It's like a flying jellyfish, though I've never seen a jellyfish in real life. Just a picture in a magazine. Well, this is kinda like that, except real big. It ripples with lots of colors and I'm not even sure I know all the colors. It's hovering there, in the sky, all shiny and it's the most beautiful thing I've ever seen. And I think if they've come to kill us it's alright 'cause at least they've given us something beautiful.

The truth is I cry 'cause it's so pretty.

❦

Leonardo has nice hair and he fidgets in front of the small mirror. I don't really care what I look like. I wouldn't have even clipped my nails if he hadn't insisted they looked gross. Gross? When we met I'd already had a shower and been disinfected. Imagine if he had met me before, when I lived in the slums.

Of course, he would have never met me. That's what pisses me off about Leonardo. He acts like we are totally partners, should totally engineer some great escape together, but he would've never even looked at me if we'd bumped into each other on the street. A piece of bubble gum stuck to his shoe would've been more appealing than me. Now we're supposed to be friends. Now we should get along because we are both slaves.

See, I don't know where he gets that shit about slaves. The aliens say "specialized personnel" and I do feel like personnel. I don't feel like a slave because they ain't having us do hard labour. They ain't whipping us or chaining us or starving us. Yeah, maybe it is a bit like a prison, but I get three meals a day. There's fresh vegetables and meat. There's the nice bed and there's the uniform with my red jacket.

I happen to like the uniform. It's the first piece of clothing that fits me. I used to wear my sisters' hand-me-downs. I was the youngest so I got the short end of the stick. Holes in my underwear and rips in my trousers. This uniform is brand new and it fits me.

Why does he have to be such a downer?

❦

Leonardo is smarter than me but sometimes he is stupid. I didn't finish secondary school, but for all his big words and knowledge of books, sometimes he acts like he's a little kid.

He doesn't like me learning the alien's language. But the thing is, I'm good at it. I've never been good at anything except picking garbage, and that barely counts. But I'm good at learning what they say. I pick it up real fast. Leonardo was a linguistics student and even he can't do as well as I can. I'm proud of that. I can do stuff.

Leonardo sours it by saying I'm a Malinche. I didn't finish secondary school but I know what he means. So I say "Fuck you."

How does he get off on saying that? And how does he know what it was like for La Malinche? They sold her off to the Spaniards and she worked for them. What was she supposed to do? Spit in their face? You get into a crappy situation and you cope. So she coped. I don't see why we've got to be all insulted when a woman tries to survive.

Yeah, I want to learn to speak what the aliens speak. I want to translate for them. 'Cause it's the smart thing to do. Leonardo looks at me and disapproves. Leonardo is a fool.

❦

When we eat in the big hall, Leonardo always wants to sit next to Fabiola and Mario. I don't like them. They're always whispering and complaining about the aliens. I know they also whisper about me.

Leonardo says they're nice people, but they're not. Mario called me *chola* one time ('cause I have the tattoo on my arm) and another time bitch ('cause he's a scared dickless shit). If I was back in the ravine I could slice the smug smile off his face with a glass bottle. I'm here so I can't do squat. The aliens don't like us fighting.

Today they were sitting together and whispering again. I put on my headphones and listened to my music until they were done. Then we came back to the room and Leonardo was all weird. Something they said must upset him but he wouldn't tell me what.

Fine. It's not like it matters.

❦

Sometimes I like Leonardo. Like, when he explains big words to me like "hyperbole" and "paradoxical." He doesn't explain like he's smug and that's good because I don't like people making fun of me.

They make fun of me, Fabiola and Mario. I got funny music in my player, they say. I tell them to eat shit.

Leonardo just lays out it real clear and he knows I get it. He ain't gotta explain ten times before I understand. I'm real good at languages and I remember words. He looks a bit surprised when I can remember some stuff, real quick, but I tell him I've always been a quick learner.

He says I could've done well in school, if I finished. He asks me if I'd wanted to study anything.

What would I've studied, I ask him. All the women 'round were maids or picked garbage. My dad was a scavenger, I was one too. Sort glass from wood, sort paper from plastic, while aggressive flies buzz 'round your face and stray dogs wag their tails.

I told him my biggest dream was to go to California.

He asked me why I wanted to move so far away.

I told him I meant the restaurant with the buffet.

And he smiled and I felt stupid for telling him that.

❧❦❧

I didn't understand Leonardo's books when we first started sharing a room. It seemed so stupid to hang on to those. They were not even fun books, but the textbooks he'd been carrying in his backpack when he was hauled off by the aliens. But now I guess I kinda see the point. The books are like the music to me. They click in your head like a big puzzle piece and make you whole.

Leonardo doesn't like my music, but he's sat down next to me, on the bed, and we've listened to the same song. For kicks. To starve off the boredom because you can't study the alien language all day long and there are those patches in the day that must be filled.

This feels normal. I've never done normal. It's... kinda fun.

❧❦❧

Leonardo told me the aliens conduct experiments and we are like mice. I told him that's as idiotic as the people who say aliens eat people, 'cause they don't. He says they're parasitical and some of them are going to live inside us. I ask him how something as big as the aliens ('cause they're real tall, real pale) can live inside you. But he says they can.

He watched too many cartoons when he was a kid. I now have access to some of the alien databanks and there, and in our conversations, it's pretty obvious it's not like that. We're too coarse, too violent, too stupid and they are going to help us. I suppose some people would prefer to think they'll cook us for supper. That would be easier to understand. This... well, it's harder to stomach.

Not that I can't stomach it. Alien cops, space cops, whatever you wanna call it... they ain't so different from regular cops. You just gotta talk the right way, act the right way, think the right way, bribe here and there, and we're all friends. We're a nice, happy family.

It's kinda funny that Leonardo doesn't get it. Seems simple to me.

≈†≋

Leonardo's been nicer and quieter lately. That's good. When he's nervous, he makes me nervous. Pisses me off. He's all mellow today, laying on the bed and reading his books. He even asks me how the language is going and I tell him it's real good. I'm going to be a translator. Maybe one day I'll be a section supervisor.

He nods and stares at me. He asks me if I miss my family. I miss my sisters. I don't miss my parents. He asks me "what if they're dead." I tell him if my parents are dead, they got what was coming for them. My sisters... they didn't do nothing, but bad stuff happens to good people. Happens all the time and good people bite a bullet just 'cause it's the way it is.

He tells me he misses his parents. He had a girlfriend. He doesn't know where she is now. I tell him not to think about it. It'll twist you inside.

He says I'm brave.

I laugh at that.

≈†≋

There's no windows in our room (the cell, Leonardo says), but there's windows in the dining hall. While Leonardo, Fabiola and Mario whisper, I splay my fingers against the glass and look at the sky. The jellyfish ships swim in the sky, so pretty against the sinking sun.

I want to be on them ships. I want to be onboard. I hope, I hope I make it.

≈†≋

Leonardo gets scared sometimes, at nights. He dreams they're coming for him again, taking him from his school, taking everyone. I lay down next to him and I pat his head. Yeah, it's done, I say. Yeah, it's over.

He wants to know what I did when they came for me. I shrug. I tell him there were raids all the time where I lived. At first I thought it was just cops. Then I saw it wasn't cops and frankly, it didn't matter.

He wants to know what I dream about. I tell him I don't dream much.

He looks all sad and plants a kiss on my cheek. I let him. I didn't let the other boys, but I let him.

❦

Leonardo thinks we can escape. He's talked about it with Mario and Fabiola. I tell him there's no way and he insists on it. Resistance. Fight. Blah, blah. I put my headphones on and listen to my music. He comes over, all plaintive, and puts a hand on my knee. Don't I want to go with him?

I like it here.

Yeah, but he's springing out of here one way or another with Mario and Fabiola.

What's the catch, I wanna know.

Catch is I've got access to the main terminal. Catch is he needs some info. Catch is this smells like being used. I roll over and stare at the wall.

I get him the info anyway.

❦

I know he's going to betray me but it still stings when it happens. He does spring out, but just with Fabiola and Mario. They don't bother taking me with them.

It's okay because they're caught two days later and brought back. I see them being dragged across the patio in chains. Leonardo's got a wild look in his eyes. He catches sight of me, standing with my alien advisor by a window. He yells. He asks me to convince them that they've made a mistake. Mercy. Intercede.

My advisor glances down at me. I know how to say this, of course. But sticking up for a runaway won't look good. I know it'll go in my file. I won't be able to fly in one of the pretty ships. Maybe they'll even say I was an accomplice (and I was, it would be true) and punish me too.

There's one of them ships going by, iridescent (Leonardo taught me that word). It blocks the sun like a great whale, the shifts and slips away.

Sometimes there are no words, in any language, to construct the proper sentence. I remain quiet as he's dragged away.

I'm brave? I don't know. It's called surviving.

I turn on the music player.

Old Domes

J.Y. Yang

Friday, midnight. A young woman pants in the field in front of the Old Supreme Court, doubled over, as though she has run a long way. She is covered in blood, and in her right hand glints a weapon.

Her name is Jing-Li, and she is a cullmaster of buildings. Of embodiments of brick and stone, locations expressed in forms that humans can deal with, difficult to perceive and even worse to understand. But she does not need understanding to do her job.

The job is in two halves. Two old buildings—pre-WWII colonial edicts, ancient by Singapore's standards—are being repurposed for conservation, their insides ripped out and both buildings combined to become an art museum. The first to go: the City Hall, the senior building that was once the seat of Parliament, whose blood is now making its way down the woman's arms in rivulets. (It is not real blood, and it will fade as soon as the shock of the deed has worn away.) That leaves her with the old Supreme Court on the right.

The old Supreme Court building: Child of the Great Depression, completed in 1939, constructed on the grave of the Grand Hotel de l'Europe, its predecessor in the sequence of colonial buildings that had stood there. Once it lorded over cricket players and rickshaw-pulling men with its massive dome and Ionian columns. It witnessed the Japanese troops marching in, and posed a dramatic backdrop to the first National Day Parade after Singapore's Independence. These days it sits empty, dwarfed by the skyline fleshed by glass and with bones of steel.

Its time has come as well. That is why the cullmaster is here.

❦

Jing-Li entered the old Supreme Court building by a side door, trying to ignore the wet on her hands. It was red, like real blood, and it triggered in her all the associations of fear and revulsion that mortal death entailed. She had not expected it: not the blood, not the soft thud of a body on masonry, not the shallow breaths drawing away to nothing.

None of her teachers had mentioned the hunt would feel like murdering a real person.

The City Hall had reminded Jing-Li of her grandfather, maybe that was why. Hair combed back, starched pressed shirt, glasses precisely set. Perhaps it was a figment of childhood, the archetype of the dutiful public servant instantly associated with a man who had died when she was ten and existed mostly through stories falling from her parents' lips. If he had looked like someone else, maybe she might have felt less uncomfortable swinging the blade.

Who was she kidding?

She gripped her consecrated sword tightly, a cheap plastic thing bought at a sports store, usually sold to seniors taking recreational tai-chi. The air here tasted dusty. Jing-Li's footsteps echoed through a warren of corridors until she entered the main entrance chamber, where the ceiling yawned open far above her head and moonlight poured in from the windows on the second floor. She took a deep breath and thought she smelled London.

London: the place where Jing-Li had gained her culling certification in her undergraduate years, taking a twisty bus route to a poorly-ventilated basement where she'd sit taking notes with a handful of other groundskeepers, young and old. She had been the only non-European there.

In her course application she had written cheerfully about the transient nature of Singapore's geography, where buildings ten years old were considered aged. Surely a local, internationally-certified cullmaster would be invaluable.

After all, this was Singapore, where lacking anything else the land itself became the currency in which the nation was defined. A living corpus carved and recarved, hollowed by tunnels and multibasement carparks, its borders fed with the leftover rock and silicate. It was a young land, supple and stretchy, where the maps a year old were outdated, their lines dancing a seismographic tango. Guardians here lived and died in droves.

Except that this was Jing-Li's first hunt since she'd returned home a year ago, law degree in hand. It turned out that guardians here went away as easily as their physical selves did, connections weak as water. Young locations lacked staying power, and older ones were strangely compliant in fading away. This job, then, existed only because it was unique.

Jing-Li looked at her hands: the blood of the City Hall building was gone.

The old Supreme Court was waiting upstairs, she knew. She tried to muffle her footsteps on the curved staircase as much as possible, as though she could sneak up on it by surprise, like a sleeping animal. It was quiet here, even by the standards of deserted buildings, something stately about the way the air rested amongst the shapes of the masonry. She was very, very cautious.

"I'm here," he said, the moment her foot touched the stones of the second floor. He was waiting against one of the balustrades that overlooked the first floor, arms folded much as she remembered from their first meeting. She was a child then, waiting for her father, and she had tugged on her mother's sleeve to ask her about the "funny man in the hat". Later she would seek out pictures of white men in Victorian garb to point out to her mother. Her first building guardian. Her mother had thought her imaginary friends cute.

The Supreme Court of today would have fit in perfectly in posher parts of the Central Business District. "You updated your look," Jing-Li said.

His shrug seemed particularly dismissive. "In keeping with the times, you know."

"The times have caught up to you. Do you know why I'm here?"

"You must think I'm an idiot." He uncrossed his arms and stood straight. "I felt the other guy go too, the sorry bugger."

"It can't be helped," Jing-Li said. They were nearly toe-to-toe now. Was he ever this tall and thin and white? "If it's any consolation, you will be remembered."

If there's any consolation, she thought to herself, it's that after this I'll be done with the job. The sword felt heavy in her hands, as if it were actually made of metal. She raised it in the direction of the guardian, brought it downwards—

The guardian vanished a split second before contact, and she found herself swinging through empty air.

"Oh, kitten, it's not that easy," the Supreme Court said from behind her, and when she turned around he was sitting on the banister of the curved staircase with a Cheshire cat smile. Chest constricting, she lunged forward again, but like a clever insect he eluded her. When she regained her balance she found him back against his balustrade perch.

She took one step in his direction, and he froze her with a wag of his finger. "Ah-ah." She did not move, scared of spooking him, scared that he would vanish once again.

"Look," she said, as sincerely as she could through the heaviness in her chest, "I don't like it either, but it has to be done. That's the rules."

He leaned vertical, hands slung easily in his pockets. "I don't intend to give up this position. After all, the other chap is gone. Somebody needs to man this station. I've decided that it's going to be me."

The guardian Jing-Li remembered was a stern one, back ram-rod straight, features imposing: a presence that filled the room and commanded absolute attention. Perhaps that was when he still functioned as the nation's highest court. "Sorry, but that can't happen," she said. "We've done the measurements and both existing guardians need to go. Another one will arise for the new art museum." Not to mention that his proposal would be incredibly unfair to the former City Hall, who had seemed a much better candidate for representing the art museum if they had to pick one.

"Ah, but I put no stock in the calculations of your groundskeepers' council. They use their own metrics, which are useless. There's no correspondence with a global standard."

The global standards had been scrapped a decade ago, exactly because they mapped poorly across the globe. These days different towns, different regions, different countries used self-calibrated standards, whatever worked best for them.

Jing-Li felt like pointing this out, but she did not. Somehow, she knew it would be like shouting at walls. Perhaps it was.

"You're out of luck," the City Hall said. "I intend to stay." She looked at him, standing resolute in his place, solid as one of the columns that made up the building's facade, and could not argue. He had beautifully blue eyes, movie-star eyes, which crinkled at the edges before he disappeared. "Don't think of summoning me," his disembodied voice said, by way of parting. "It won't work."

Jing-Li didn't try. It took her several minutes after she exited the building before she realized she was shaking.

⛎

Monday, midday. The young woman, neat and dressed in what is generally accepted to be common office wear, trails a large group of people following a guide leading the way through the City Hall and former Supreme Court buildings. The group consists of civil servants who volunteered to help in the open house taking place in a month's time, and are dressed accordingly. Run by the staff of the museum that has taken over administration of the two buildings, the open house will, for the first and the last time, allow the public into spaces previously reserved for the highest offices in the country. License to gawk and to touch, before the diggers and bulldozers move in to do their reconstructive surgery. Some of the group take notes as the guide points out key features and historical nuggets: this will be crucial information in a few weeks' time when they too will become guides, this time to an adoring public eager to soak up the storied narratives contained within the buildings.

The young woman does not take notes. She merely follows, unnoticed.

The guide, with a knowing smile, leads the group away from the prescribed tour route, up to the roof where the iconic dome sits. The group loses flock coherence, running to various edges to take photographs, taking on the appearance of guppies in a tank. A large number of them gather at the front edge of the building, the only one not obscured by towering modern-day buildings. Eager hands point outwards, gesturing over the expanse of the Padang that lies, treeless and manicured, in front of former Supreme Court. It's the first time any of them have seen it from this angle, and, artificial as it is they find it a wonder.

The young woman stays quietly in the shade of the dome, waiting for them to leave so that she can be alone with the one man on the roof no one else can see.

Across the length of the roof from her, the former Supreme Court watches her silently, expression inscrutable to bystanders.

☙ 🦋 ❧

The last straggler of the group vanished downwards with a clatter, and Jing-Li finally let herself relax. The ability to stay invisible in the confines of a building was entirely dependent on the sufferance of its guardian, and she hadn't been sure the former Supreme Court would be so kind to its assigned executioner. She watched carefully as he strolled across the expanse of the roof, analysing the way he took each step (with confidence), the way his hips swayed (hint of mischief).

"I'm not here to finish the job," she said, hands held up. "See, I didn't bring the weapon."

The former Supreme Court laughed. "I know," he said. "Or you would not have made it this far." As her hands went to her hips in protest, and he said: "This building still has working fire alarms."

"Fire alarms can't keep me out forever."

"If I have my way I won't have to keep you out."

She reached her envelope bag and pulled out a small sealed packet of brown paper, which she offered to him. "Courtesy of the groundskeeper's association," she said. "I ran into a senior on the way here and he thought it might be helpful in getting into your good books." Devon, according to his own account, had conveniently been on his way to buy something nearby and had just happened to bump into her in the two hundred metres between her workplace and the former Supreme Court building. Singapore was small, but not that small—Jing-Li wasn't stupid. The association was getting impatient.

The former Supreme Court wrinkled his nose. "Bribery will get you nowhere."

She returned the packet to her bag. "You don't like sweets anyway. You'd prefer a nice rat or some other small dead animal, right?"

"You know me well." He sounded pleased.

"I've done my research."

She had done more than that. Like anyone with an ounce of self-respect she had gone home and dug into difficult guardian culls, carefully populating her browser with pages from countries bearing historic architecture, where the encrusted hearts of cities pulsed in medieval nerve centres laid over and over by infrastructural palimpsest. Places where guardians clung deeply and stubbornly to their location, fed by nostalgia and notions of heritage. She had come out of that tangle discouraged and confused: every story had different tips on how to get stubborn guardians to give up their guardianship, and most of them were quite location-specific. Her one takeaway was that she was on her own, and therefore in deep shit.

Urgency itched under her skin, in her chest, like hungry parasites. Earlier this week the groundkeepers' association had sent an email: "This is not a game. If we knew you were going to mess around, we would have hired someone to actually do the job." She wondered if they understood that the last time in recorded history an unwilling guardian had been culled, hundreds of deaths had resulted from a building collapse.

"I don't like it," the former Supreme Court said suddenly, leaning over the roof ledge, eyes fixed on the green of the Padang stretched before them.

"What?" The Padang outranked the Supreme Court in age and they had no history of animosity that she could recall. A few years ago the Padang had gone underground, not long after the National Day parades had moved to the Marina Bay floating platform. It had not been seen since then. "You don't like what?"

She followed his gaze. The Padang, hemmed in around all sides by temporary light fixtures, had a festive air about it. Banners hung by the street lights explained why: the Formula One races dropped in on Singapore for their yearly call-by in two weeks' time, and the roads around the Padang became part of a racetrack in their honour.

"The Marina Bay Street Circuit," she said. "You don't like him?"

"He's a brat," the former Supreme Court said with finality, as though passing a sentence on the ephemeral entity that only existed for less than a week each year. "Guardians shouldn't be allowed to come and go. It's unnatural."

Jing-Li followed him in leaning over the ledge, hands in her chin. "You mean places shouldn't be allowed to come and go. But it happens all the time." He turned to interrupt her and she cut him off. "If you're talking about naturalness, none of this is natural. Your existence is entirely man-made, you know. You live on our sufferance."

"If you wanted to get into my good books, you're doing a terrible job of it."

Jing-Li blew out a short breath through her nose. Despite the roar of passing cars, in some other part of the city close by, Singapore seemed quiet, too quiet. "I'm just being honest."

Arms folded, gazing out across the green of the silent Padang, the former Supreme Court said nothing. Jing-Li continued: "If you have such problems with transient guardians how are you going to cope with the construction site deity for the next two years?"

Now he did look at her. "Is that your concession that you've stopped trying to cull me?"

"I'm serious," Jing-Li said. "Accidents at worksites will happen if the construction deity is disturbed. You could get people killed." In case he didn't understand the ramifications of that, she added, "Humans will die on your watch."

"I'm not obliged to keep humans alive," he said.

"You don't believe that, and I know that because you're not a rogue guardian. Just a really stubborn one."

His laugh was soft, burbling, like the sound of engines. "I'm perhaps the most fortunate, to have you chosen as my executioner."

"Chosen," Jing-Li says under her breath, and he doesn't hear.

"I can't think of any of your other compatriots who's known me since childhood. Daughter of a judge..." He looked at her, almost fondly, and Jing-Li stepped back a little from him. "And you're a lawyer now, working just a few buildings down the road."

"Okay, sure."

He tossed something at her and she barely caught it. When she opened her palm she was confronted with something small and copper and intricately carved. "A coin?"

"Not just any coin. That's a Straits Settlement coin."

She turned it over and over in her fingers. It felt odd, strangely solid. "Where did you get it?"

"There is a time capsule buried under the flagstone of the main court. Nothing much to it, just a few coins and the day's papers. But they'll open it in the year 3000. I suppose they won't miss one little coin."

"The year 3000," Jing-Li said. It sounded like the title of a sci-fi movie, something Arthur C. Clarke might have written.

"I'd like to be there when they do that."

"In the year 3000."

"Yes."

"That's nine hundred years in the future." She held the coin out to him. "You have a lot of faith, don't you?"

"Keep the coin," he said, still looking outwards. "Consider it a gift."

And then he was gone.

⛧

Sunday, mid-morning. The air thrums with life and the city is busy, consumed in festival-madness. Roads are closed and speakers pop as sound technicians take them through their paces. A hundred thousand people bustle, working themselves up to the frenzy that will take place when the sun sets. In their pens, at the hub of it all, the racecars that will be the stars of the night's festivities sleep fitfully. Anticipation feels like a breathable, drinkable thing.

Within the madness-in-waiting sits a young woman in a big metal swing set on top of the hill that used to be a fort. Cross-legged quietude surrounds her and the plastic sword resting by her side. Eyes shut, she leans into the movement of the swing, back and forth, back and forth.

Two weeks have passed since she met the former Supreme Court on the roof of the building, and the groundbreaking ceremony is less than a month away. She is no closer to solving her problem. Despite her appearance of immobility her fingers twitch over the coin she holds loosely in her right hand, in her lap.

She whispers to herself, whether consciously or unconsciously, it's hard to tell. It is also hard to hear what she is saying, but it sounds like a prayer.

And then a guardian, whom she thought was dead, appears on the swing beside her.

⛧

Jing-Li sprang into alertness at the unexpected presence beside her, even if the swing continued its back-and-forth unperturbed. Her heart tapped a funny rhythm as she realized who it was. "But you're supposed to be gone."

"Yes, I am gone," said the guardian who used to be the City Hall building. "I'm not connected to my old place anymore."

"You're supposed to disappear," Jing-Li said, as if her first sentence hadn't been clear. "Once a guardian has been disconnected from their location they lose the energy from the place that fed them."

The former City Hall building laughed and shrugged, somehow avuncular when he did so. "That's what they told you in school, right? But I guess it's not true. I spend my days here now, here and there.

41

Talking to my friends." He gestured in the direction of a spreading banyan tree nearby, its hanging roots like sturdy beams.

Jing-Li could not see who he was gesturing to, and she guessed it was a tree spirit, because she had problems seeing them. "But the blood," she said, still refusing to believe this was happening. "The falling over, the vanishing, what was all of that? Were you trying to make me feel bad? What?"

He crossed his legs and leaned back in the chair. He looked like her grandfather, but in demeanour he reminded her of her primary school Chinese language teacher. "I always thought that groundskeepers should appreciate the responsibilities they hold."

Jing-Li let her hands drop into her lap. "You think I don't? Like I don't understand the consequences of my actions? You think I'm doing it this just for fun?"

The former City Hall building said nothing, attention caught by something on the metal grating that formed the floor of the swing. He leaned over and picked it up: it was the coin she had been holding. "Wow, haven't seen this in a long time." He flipped it back and forth. "Did he give it to you?"

When she nodded, he handed it to her. "Typical of him," he said.

"Emotional manipulation?" She flipped the coin back and forth in her fingers. "Like falling over in an explosion of blood wasn't?" Her hand closed around the coin, hard enough to press into the skin. "Yours was the first cull I'd ever done and I was so scared I couldn't do the next one. And I still can't."

"Are you scared?" He looked at her. "Or is it something else?"

Jing-Li put her feet down and the movement stopped the swing's momentum. Crickets sang in the greenery as she thought over the question carefully. Finally, she said: "No, probably not. I won't let fear get in the way. It's that he doesn't want to go, and I don't know how to convince him to. Because..." She gestured in no particular direction. "It's a horrible thing. I can't blame him for not wanting to go through with it."

"Horrible?" The former City Hall huffed. "We are not humans, you know. It's not about life or death, it's about moving on, about becoming different. It's natural." He tapped her on the shoulder, in a teacherly way. "You remember your classes, when they taught you about culling? What did they say?"

"A lot of mumbo-jumbo, most of it was not relevant to Singapore, anyway. Most of it was how to give pep talks about heritage and changing perceptions and how things never really go away. What kind of heritage does Singapore have? Even our national symbols are invented."

The former City Hall just smiled.

Silence settled, uncomfortably, and Jing-Li remembered she had been carrying around the small sacrifice packet from the groundskeepers' association ever since the former Supreme Court refused it. She found it at the bottom of her bag, slightly squashed and with a worn corner, but still sealed. "This talk is getting us nowhere, so you might as well have some of this."

"Oh, thank you," he said, accepting it and breaking packet's little paper seal. "I won't be getting these much anymore, I suppose." He dug in with his fingers and pulled out one of those soft, pink-and-white candies coated in powder that Jing-Li had no name for. "This is very good," he said, and then held the packet out, across to the swing's other bench. "You should try one."

Jing-Li blinked. Seated across them, where there had been no one a moment ago, was a young Malay man in formal wear. A guardian, she realized, but one she did not recognize. "I live here," he said simply, probably in response to her facial expression.

"But you're not Fort Canning," Jing-Li said. The Fort Canning was a moody-looking teenager whom she often found perched on the old display cannons scattered around the park, smoking. He had been in place for slightly more than thirty years, she was told.

"I'm the old dude," he said, reaching into the bag that the former City Hall was holding out. "I've been here a long time. I used to be called Bukit Larangan. The Forbidden Hill, you know?"

"You're the original hill," she said, in slow wonder. "From the 14th century."

"It's been a bit longer than that." He tasted the sweet, gingerly. "This is good. I don't get many of them these days."

"You're still around," she said. "After all these years."

"It's like he said. We stay around long after we're gone."

"See, history remembers us, in a certain way," said the former City Hall.

"And do you remember history?" She leaned forward, her heart pounding, consumed by a sudden eagerness that she hadn't felt since she was a very young schoolchild. She turned to the former Bukit Larangan. "Do you remember the 14th century?"

"Hmm." He leaned back in the swing seat. "I cannot say. I remember what it was like, but I don't really remember it. It was so long ago."

She couldn't understand. "But you were there. Weren't you?"

He leaned backwards into the chair, completely calm. "Yes. But memory is quite difficult." He pointed to a sign, one of many that were scattered around the park, packed with information written in four languages. "See that? That's all anybody remembers. Some days I think of the old kings who used to live here, and I realize that I cannot remember their faces, or I only remember a very vague picture of them. Then I wonder if the Tumasik I remember is the same as it was back then."

"You've told me stories," said the former City Hall. "But I'm sure there was so much more."

"Of course there was much more," the former Bukit Larangan said. "But it's all gone now. Singapore's history started in 1819, that's what the history books say, right?" He gestured at the signs. "That's all left. That's who I became."

Jing-Li shook her head. "But—"

"How much of Singapore's history before the 19th century do you know?" The former City Hall asked.

"A sleepy fishing village," she said softly. "That's what they teach us at school."

"No, it was a lot more than that," said the former Bukit Larangan said. "But I don't remember what it was anymore."

She looked down at the sword in her lap and felt like she was falling outwards. The Straits Settlement coin resting in her hand had taken on immense weight and heat, like it was a burning coal.

"But you were there," she repeated emptily to herself.

❦

Sunday night. Halogen lights of unthinkable wattage sear the air, burning a bright orthogonal circuit into the cityscape, thousands of metres long. Thousands cram into rows of seats, specially erected for the weekend, while thousands more press against wire nettings at odd ends and corners of the circuit, as racecars streak past at 400kmh, blurs of screaming metal tracked by faithless, tireless cameras. The Padang, forcibly crowned with a strobe-lit stage, suffocates under the weight of a sweaty, screaming crowd, while above the city, people in air-conditioned restaurants and bars peer down at the blips of cars blazing, ant-like, around the track.

The young woman runs in the alley behind the former Supreme Court, sealed off to prevent people from getting close to the racetrack. The Marina Bay Street Circuit has given her grace to wander the grounds, even the areas deemed off-limits, but she has more pressing matters on her mind. Her target is the former Supreme Court.

For her, for the both of them, it has to end tonight.

Jing-Li ran up the grand steps of the former Supreme Court, her footsteps sending solid echoes reverberating. She knew where the guardian was, up on the roof where they'd last met. She was sweaty, and her heart raced from shoving through the clamouring, oblivious crowd, but none of that mattered.

The moment she burst out through the stairwell the guardian turned towards her from his spot at the edge of the roof, haloed by the stadium-strength lights surrounding the Padang. "I see you've come."

"Don't think of going anywhere," she said, pulling the plastic sword from its plastic sheath, her voice and breathing harsh. Down on the road the F1 racers screeched and made popping noises as they slowed down for the corner turn, lending the scene the surreal soundtrack of an air raid.

"I would not dream of it," he said, his voice carrying over the melee. "In fact, I was rather hoping to stay here for the long term."

"No," Jing-Li shouted, over the din. "You can't. I've decided. That's not how this country works. You served a purpose, that purpose is done, it's time to move on. Your neighbour has done it. You're no different."

He looked a lot smaller than she seemed to recall, like a lost doll somebody left by the roadside. "But I am different. I thought you might think of me fondly, given your childhood. There's such strong nostalgia…"

"Nostalgia? Whose nostalgia? You can't tell me what to be nostalgic about." The thing that had been sitting uncomfortably in her chest since the first night she had taken up her sword came to a boil. "This building is being preserved. That's a lot more than other past locations in Singapore have had."

He ran his fingers over the worn stone surface of the roof's edge. "This place has such memories…"

"You have to believe me, I'm doing this for you." She took bold steps towards him, and he didn't move away. "Your memories will be rewritten, whether you like it or not. Our Government may like what you are. They like what you represented as the Supreme Court. They like the way you look on the television screens when Grand Prix is beamed to the world."

She waved her sword accusingly at the racetrack. "But that's all you'll ever be, from now on. A pretty picture. A tourist attraction. They could have built something else to house the art museum. But they wanted to use your skin, because your skin is what they think is important." She swung the sword back towards him. "Can you live with that? Can you live with becoming somebody else?"

He seemed to straighten up. "I used to be the Supreme Court," he said, a glint of his former hardness returning to his expression. "Important decisions were made on my watch. What I did used to influence the entire nation."

"And no one will change that for you," she said. She thought of Bukit Larangan, it's history faintly etched, fading into a few neat lines of the country's official narrative. "You are so lucky and you don't even know it."

"Will you remember me, at least?"

"I'll come over for tea," she said. "There's a swingset on top of Fort Canning that seats four. We can hang out with your former neighbour. And the old Forbidden Hill. We could talk about history, or anything you like. I'll even bring a lizard for you, if you want."

He smiled. She could barely see his blue eyes in the mad, harshly shadowed lighting. "I'm still right. I am still fortunate to have you as my executioner."

"You had a good run," Jing-Li said.

"Well. I won't deny that."

She did not blink as she brought the plastic blade down.

❦

Sunday night. It has been a year since the groundbreaking ceremony, and the races are on again. The former Supreme Court stands, its form cloaked in netted black scaffolding on which its façade is projected. Its interior is a mess, gutted masonry like phoenix ash, but the millions around the globe watching the race live do not need to see that.

Across the track sits a grandstand, its rows packed with the chattering masses. They have paid well to be here, even if only for a brief time. Amongst their number one might pick out the shape of a young woman, her back straight, an unreadable smile on her face. From this distance you cannot tell, but she is turning and turning a small object in her hand, which appears to be a coin of some sort.

But she is only one face in the crowd, and as the camera pulls away she becomes invisible, part of the story no one sees.

The black box of the former Supreme Court, drenched in new light, remains impassive. Around it rise skyscrapers—shades of New York, shades of Abu Dhabi—that vanish into the night, the hands of a new city reaching ahead.

How to Make a Time Machine Do Things that Are Not in the Manual
or
The Gambiarra Method

Fabio Fernandes

The elevator fell five decades in three seconds flat.

"We need to calibrate this thing, to synchronize it on a decade-floor basis," Raitek said.

"Is that really necessary?" Jonathan asked.

"Do you even have to ask?"

Patel looked up at both men and sighed almost inaudibly. He was used to the young, eager tech from Ghana, always wanting to know more, to push the envelope further, to suck up every quantum of information as if he were a sponge, a veritable black hole.

But he still wasn't used to this weird manager from Brazil. They had already been working on this project for months when the higher powers saw fit to send this guy all the way from Rio de Janeiro to Accra. All just because he had a top-notch score in project-trimming and problem-solving? The man wasn't even a scientist, for crying out loud!

"Jonathan does have a point, actually," he decided to cut in. "*Why* is it necessary, really?"

Raitek raised his left hand and lifted two fingers.

"Two reasons," he said. "First, the symmetry. The more symmetrical a relationship we can establish, the better we can gauge and calculate the length of the prototype's displacement in time."

Patel considered the fact for a little while, then wobbled his head in agreement. "It stands to reason," he said.

"And the second?" asked Jonathan.

Raitek opened a smile from ear to ear.

"Thought you'd never ask," he said. "Second is the beauty of it."

❧❦❧

Time travel was discovered in 2077.

As happens with many scientific discoveries, it was completely accidental. Sometimes you are looking for one thing when another gets in the way, with results you are most definitely not expecting. Take Viagra. Or antigravity associated with superconductors.

Time travel was discovered during experiments on locative media and augmented reality as applied to elevators.

Anyway, it happened at a very interesting time in history. The human race had suffered a long period of war and disease, which ended on a grim note in the 2060s with the Second American Civil War and the Big European Depression. Even though it was still far from universal peace and understanding, it seemed to be entering a period of relative tranquility. A post-virtual environment embedded in antigravitational elevators—part of an ambiance designed to soothe and distract people during the long risings and falls through the two hundred or so floors of the arcologies—seemed as good a place as any to give this new age a jumpstart.The environment turned out to be not only a virtuality but a time displacement device which took its occupants to a very different set of coordinates from what was expected. Suffice it to say that, when the doors of the elevator opened, the dumbfounded passengers were not in Accra anymore—at least not in 2077 Accra, but in a shabby building in that same city... one with a mere thirteen floors. And, more importantly, according to the ceiling display that showed date and time, in 2011.

After a few minutes of absolute confusion and, in one case, total denial, the temporary denizens of the past—two techs and one project manager—returned to the elevator and told it to get them back to where they had come from. Fortunately, it was able to do so. They got out of the elevator safe and sound, back where—and when—they belonged. Without knowing why it had happened.

But intending to find out.

≈†≈

It took Hiran Patel, the project manager who was aboard the elevator when the "episode" (the only word they used inside the lab and the building to refer to the incident) happened, a couple of days to be sure everything was under wraps, so upper management didn't find out what had really happened. He wanted to reproduce the conditions of the experiment again before he could present it to the board of directors with a new business proposal: *to establish a time agency travel somewhere in the past* (probably 2011 Accra, if the elevator could somehow only go to a fixed point—the mathematics would still have to be worked out) and offer his clients a plus. He could get quite a bonus for that.

Unfortunately, things didn't work out so easily. As soon as the veracity of the time displacement procedure was established, the bureaucrats came.

They had the facilities shut down until further notice. Not only the labs of creation, production and ambiance editing, not even only the lab containing the elevator carriage used to test it, but the entire building, even unrelated areas. Every lab tech, every assistant, even the secretaries and cleaning staff were politely asked to remain inside the premises for as long as it should be needed to debrief everyone.

Everyone's needs, one of the bureaucrats said (Patel couldn't tell who, they all looked the same to him), would be taken care of.

Patel was the head of the software team at the time the discovery was made. This meant that, until the arrival of the bureaucrats, he was in charge of a team of eight people, namely: three programmers, three IE (immersion environment) modeling designers and two WS (world-builder/scriptwriters), most of them from the games industry, seduced by the allure of making money in the glamorous countries of New Western Africa that thrived on software production after the collapse of Europe in the '30s.

Patel was one of them; he had come all the way from Wolverhampton, leaving behind a so-so life developing robotic pets as companions for elderly people in home care facilities. But it wasn't as if England had anything else of significance to offer him, and besides, he had no attachments there, nothing that really mattered. When he first saw the sun glinting on the top of the brand new Nkrumah arcology thrusting up from the middle of Greater Accra, that Solerian dream dwarfing the now obsolete postmodern steel-and-glass buildings, with their mere two or three dozen storeys, he knew he had made the right decision.

When the bureaucrats came, however, he started to have second thoughts.

☙❦❧

Then the man from Brazil arrived. A tall, black, bald, lean man in his mid-thirties, with an easygoing smile that won over most of the team.

Except Patel. He knew better than to trust a suit.

The man walked up to him and extended a big hand.

"Raitek da Silva," he said in a perfect English. "Nice to meet you, Mr Patel."

Patel shook his hand. A surprisingly rough hand, very different from the well-manicured jobs he associated with most bureaucrats.

"Care to show me your research?"

"What can I possibly show you that I haven't already, Mr Da Silva?"

"Please, call me Raitek. Seriously. We're going to work round the clock here, and I won't be wearing this suit for much longer, you feel me? Besides, you may have shown the other executives, but you haven't shown *me* anything. And I am the one you must show things to. So, if you please…"

Patel didn't like the patronizing tone, but he already had his orders from above. He had no choice.

So they went for the Grand Tour of the Little Lab.

"In the beginning," Patel said, "we were simply researching a more high-resolution and cost-effective immersion environment to be used in arcology elevators. Something to pass the time, and to act as a pressure valve for borderline claustrophobic individuals.

"Then something went wrong. During one of the experiments with the prototype, we lost the signal from the car."

He paused, more for dramatic effect than for anything else, and glanced at Raitek. The suit was still listening attentively, hands behind his back. Patel went on.

"Five minutes later, the signal was reestablished. When the car was opened and the three team members aboard it were debriefed, they all said the same thing: that the doors had opened on another place and another time. That they were apparently still in Accra, but, according to the elevator display, in 2011."

Then Raitek raised a hand.

"Can you trust them completely?"

"Mr Da Silva," Patel said. "I was there. I am one of them."

Raitek nodded.

"So I am to assume the lab cameras registered everything? And the car never left the lab?"

"As I have told your men countless times. They have the records."

"They are not my men. So: you all must have traveled, if such a time travel really occurred, in some sort of 'bubble' inside the car?"

"As I'm sure you already know, that is the current theory, yes."

Raitek stopped, straightened himself and looked around. "Do you have a private room, Hiram? May I call you Hiram? And, please, call me Raitek. I really insist."

Patel had to control himself not to huff audibly. "This way. And my name is Hiran, ending with an 'n', not an 'm', if you please... Raitek."

Raitek grimaced.

"Ok. As long as you don't forget to pronounce my name with a guttural 'R'. It's not a weak 'R'. It's more like a roar, if you please, Hiram."

Both went silent the rest of the way. When they entered Patel's office and he closed the door, Raitek turned to him and suddenly changed his tone. He went from that easygoing mode to utter seriousness and delivered the following speech, almost as if in a robotic mode:

"Do you want to know what I do, Hiran? Do you really want to know what I'm here for? I'm going to tell you.

"I compress stories.

"These are times of raw information. Information is not knowledge—at least not until it gets mixed with reference and experience. Then it becomes something else: it gets transmuted, translated into a legible, understandable message.

"Information is pure data being fed to you from every possible source at the same time. People like me act like human filters. In the past, some tried to call us names: Googlists, information curators, Gibsonians. I don't call myself anything. I am what I am. In fact, I don't do anything you don't already do. When you open a book, do you read all its pages at once? No. You read them one by one. Whether on a linear basis or not, it doesn't matter. When you watch a bustling, crowded street at rush hour, are you able to take in every single face in the sea of people who threatens to engulf you from all around? Of course not.

"I just happen to be able to do it a little bit better.

"I take the ancient concept of the memory palace and shrink it down to the size of a 1:72 scale model. A die-cast aircraft toy of a memory palace in my head. All I do then is move the goods in.

"The process is like unloading a removal van. But, instead of big, tidy boxes crammed with info, I picture amorphous masses, not hard stuff, but spongiform ones instead, bouncy buckyballs with tiny spikes all over their surfaces, like weird alternate-Earth Mongol-Raygun-Gothic antennas. I stuff the place with them, and their antennas start telescoping and touching each other. Kinky alien robot sex. I always thought it a bit too cyberpunk-chic-démodé, but it's deeply imprinted in my culture. I'm comfortable with the imagery.

"The balls interconnect and form a rhizome. The information sexes up and creates a wave of mutilation. All the data is cut, cropped, pasted. Measured, compared, verified. After all this processing, I expand the memory palace... and the knowledge is there. Not so simple, but you don't need to know every single step, do you?

"To keep it short: I'm the one you're looking for. I am the one you need to collate all the data you've amassed, to make some sense of all your fucked-up experiences. I came here to salvage your invention, and to save your ass in the process. Is that clear or not, Hiran?"

Patel was impressed with the apparent intelligence of the man, but not with the vulgar display of power. He knew it came with the suit, even if the Brazilian bureaucrat decided to change clothes later.

"It is clear, Raitek."

The easy smile came back to the Brazilian man's face as quickly as it had vanished.

"Good. Good, man. We'll work this out. You will see."

Patel nodded. But he was not amused.

☙ ❦ ❧

The next day began on a lighter note. As promised, Raitek wasn't wearing a suit: to match the hot weather of Ghana, he wore a light blue polo shirt, khaki pants, and flip-flops. Patel noticed the man's feet were well-manicured.

"*Salve, moçada! Tudo beleza?*" he said to everyone in a loud, happy voice. "Let's get to work, shall we?"

As if we haven't already been working our asses off for months, thought a disgruntled Patel, still combing his hair. He missed his flat. He missed his freedom. He was becoming more and more uncomfortable with the increasingly military vibe of this whole lockin. He didn't respond well to authority. That was why he always preferred working for civilian companies. This time, however, he thought he might have made the wrong choice. Maybe there was no right choice at all in this line of work. It was a depressing thought.

"Good morning, Hiran," Raitek said, closing on him like a shark upon its prey. "Shall we begin the mission briefing?"

"What mission?"

"Why, the retrieval mission, of course." Raitek showed his big-toothed smile.

In five minutes the entire team was in the meeting room.

☙ ❦ ❧

"The funny thing," Raitek started the briefing, "is that we never see the elevator disappear at any given moment in time, from our side."

"Yes," a young black man cut in. "This happens because only the environment travels in time."

Raitek stared for just the smallest amount of time at the young man.

"You are Jonathan, right? Jonathan Kufuor? One of the techs who was originally in the carriage when it traveled back?"

The young man smiled.

"Yes, sir. That's me."

"Call me Raitek, please. Same goes to everyone here. No red tape, no ass-kissing. We must do what we must do. The sooner we get this solved, the sooner we get home."

Yes, but we are staying here and you are going to a hotel every night, Patel thought grimly. *Nice try, though.*

"Do we know why that happened, Jonathan?" Raitek asked.

"Not exactly," he answered.

"But we suspect," Patel said.

Raitek nodded. "Pray tell."

"The Faraday cage principle."

Raitek shook his head. "I wouldn't put it that way, but I agree with you that the analogy seems solid enough."

"Why is that?"

"We are not talking about electricity here, but tachyon flow."

"We haven't established this with absolute certainty yet."

"You probably won't," Raitek said. "We don't have the tech for it, nor the necessary measurement tools. Unless we use the Gambiarra Method."

"The *what*?"

"It's just a thing we learn to do in Brazil," Raitek explained. "How to do things with whatever you have at hand."

"Oh, you mean a kludge," Jonathan said.

"No, not a kludge," Raitek corrected him. "Kludges are for electromechanical things. A gambiarra goes for *anything*. Even abstract stuff."

"And how do you propose we use this gambiarra of yours...?" asked Patel, already feeling very uncomfortable. The Brazilian guy was insane.

"First, assuming that everything you experienced was absolutely real, and not an illusion provoked by extreme immersion, what probably happened was that a bubble formed inside the carriage. Not a spherical, topologically perfect bubble, but an extradimensional structure, or better yet, an n-dimensional structure according to the parameters of the Calabi-Yau Manifold.

"Theoretically, a Calabi-Yau space can project itself beyond the borders of our, let's say for lack of a better term, 'traditional' space. Kähler manifolds could also apply, but the calculus involved seems to make it a poorer choice. Right now, it doesn't matter: we should be able to repeat the experiment with no problem at all and no harm to the test subjects."

"Test subjects? What do you mean, test subjects?" said Patel.

"May I go again?" asked Jonathan.

Damn, thought Patel. *This is getting out of control.*

❦

As Raitek explained to them, the Calabi-Yau Manifold (if that was what really formed inside the elevator) opened not a window, but a kind of excrescence, something like a vesicle, a ballooning organ with only one end stretching towards our so-called normal reality. So, one could enter and exit the CYM via this stretch the same way one could use a door—probably, in this case, the elevator doors. Maybe they would not even need to do alignment procedures.

"We'll probably have to do lots of calibrations for years and decades before going for something bigger," Raitek said. "That is, if the mechanism isn't already locked in 2011."

"What makes you think so?" asked Patel.

"Nothing special," said Raitek. "Science fiction stories. And wormhole theories."

"I thought you were pretty sure about the manifold."

"Well, *quem tem dois, tem um. Quem tem um, não tem nenhum.*"

"Come again?"

"It's an old Brazilian saying. If you have two, actually you have only one. If you have one, you have none. Bottom line: you better be prepared and have a spare—a spare tire, a spare sonic screwdriver, a spare condom, a spare of anything you can possibly think of, because you will most probably need it."

"A spare theory as well?"

"Yep. That too."

⛨

In the second controlled experiment, the elevator fell four decades in three seconds.

Naturally, it wasn't the elevator that was really falling, as it was mounted on a spring-based shock absorber structure. But the principle seemed to remain, as Jonathan reported being taken to a different decade each time. They weren't able to calibrate the instruments well enough to account for years.

Another precaution they took this time was securing Jonathan to the carriage by rappelling equipment, harness, static rope attached to the guardrail. It wasn't necessary in the end, but they did it all the same. All that Jonathan did was to get out whenever he happened to be, take a couple of steps, recording every sight and sound for no more than five minutes, then get back to the interior of the carriage, close the doors and pray to return to this own era. Which he did both times.

The only occasion nothing happened was when they decided to turn the immersion environment off.

"Okay, one thing we can be quite sure of," Raitek concluded after the second experiment, "is that the immersion machinery is somehow the key. Now, another question: can we use it *outside* the elevator with the same result? Or can we use another elevator *and* different immersion machinery to the same effect?"

"This last question I can easily answer," Patel said. "No, we cannot. We had two elevators and half a dozen immersion machineries running in parallel. Only this one presented this result."

"Then we could normally say that something is wrong with this particular setting," Raitek said. "Therefore, it's an anomaly."

"We already knew that." This time Patel smiled.

Raitek turned back to him and said, "Hiran, I already know something else: you are a top-notch robotic expert who does not like to have your time wasted and is deeply pissed off by my very presence at what you consider to be *your* lab, even though you've worked for this company for much less time than I have. So I will propose a deal: don't be smug with me and I will tell you what you don't already know. How about that?"

Patel remained unamused. But this time he replied.

"As long as we can reciprocate."

Raitek just nodded. And extended his hand.

❖

What didn't they know? First off, they couldn't ascertain if the bubble inside the car was the byproduct of the Calabi-Yau Manifold or a portal to a wormhole, but the former theory held more water than the latter—issues of mass and gravity pertaining to wormholes made it almost impossible to think of them as a viable option.

The second thing: they never could reproduce the experiment outside the elevator. And the car had to be in motion, if only at a small rate of acceleration.

Acceleration. Raitek wondered if it played a major role in the events after all.

At the end of the day, he took the elevator in the central shaft and pushed the button for the top floor.

Raitek stepped out of the elevator and into the penthouse of the 400th floor. It was a sparsely furnished space, all-white, with very few interior walls. He liked the lofty aspect of the place, its half-spartan, half-samurai cleanliness. It reminded him a bit of his summer refuge in Rio; the concrete-and-woodplank house in the middle of Tijuca National Park was very different structurally, but the silence was almost the same. It gave him freedom to think.

He took a long, hot shower and lay on the queen-size futon in the bedroom. He closed his eyes and initiated the memory palace walkthrough.

The meditation technique took less time and was less cyberpunkish than he'd described it to Patel. Instead of spiky buckyballs, all he could see this time were cubes: cubes fitting inside each other, like an ancient 3D version of Tetris he'd played at his grandpa's house as a kid—only in his vision they penetrated each other, almost as if they were having sex.

Then, suddenly, they all snapped into a giant megacube which started to slide down along an axis, and this axis was a shiny metal cable with no discernible end in sight. Raitek couldn't see the interior of the cube. He did know, however, that the cable ran inside it as well, and *anyone who touched it would be hurt by its speedy passage through the cube.* The faster the cable ran, the bigger the chances someone would be badly cut or burned by the friction.

Acceleration mattered.

It was then that Raitek called Patel and Jonathan for an emergency meeting.

❦

"Are you kidding?" Patel said.

"Is this what you called gambiarra?" Jonathan asked, amazed.

"This is one of its many possible variations, yes," Raitek said. "Are you willing to try?"

"What are the risks?" Patel asked him.

Raitek spread his hands in the air.

"Honestly? No idea. All I know is that acceleration seems to be the key, here. I may be wrong; in which case, nothing out of the ordinary will occur. Hell, the fact the we will be using a different elevator means it probably won't result in anything at all, so why not?"

Patel stopped a bit to consider. Indeed, why not? Wasn't it to get out of the sameness of Old Europe that he had come to Ghana? Deep inside, didn't he want to take chances, to take risks? Indeed, *why the fuck not?*

"Okay, but on one condition."

"Name it."

"*I* will go."

❦

The next day, a teary-eyed Jonathan was beside Raitek in the control room, following the preparation for the third experiment.

They had spent the previous night transferring the whole immersion machinery array to the elevator shaft at the center of the floor. It was a good thing that Raitek had the necessary clearance to bypass the proper channels.

"Too convenient, if you ask me," Patel grumbled as they mounted the wafer-thin screens of the array inside the carriage.

"Hey, it's all in the name of filthy lucre," Raitek said half-jokingly. "They don't want to jeopardize their investment. We live in the Golden Age of Science, blah blah blah."

"You don't believe that?"

"I believe in everything, Hiran," he said. "The world is a big place, and everything you can possibly imagine exists. I've seen many strange things with these eyes."

"Such as...?"

"You don't want to know."

"I do. Really."

Raitek just shrugged. "Nothing that you haven't seen in India."

"I grew up in England."

Raitek went mute for a while. *Wow, that's a first*, Patel thought.

"Sorry," he said after a minute. "I meant no prejudice."

"It's all right."

"No. My grandfather hated it when some guy from the US called us *chicanos* or tried to talk to us in *Spanish*. Same thing, no excuse. Do you drink?"

"Not much. But a beer, occasionally, yes."

"When this is all over, will you let me buy you a pint?"

Patel wobbled his head in a slight amusement. "Yes, sure. Thanks."

"Thank *you*, Hiran. Thank you."

That was then. This was now: a sweaty Patel checking his harness, his wraparound recording glasses and the impromptu emergency kit Raitek had given him at the last minute, checking them two, three, four times. He looked like a man with OCD. He didn't give a fuck. He just wanted to know he was safe.

"All systems go, Hiran," Raitek's voice came over the elevator's intercom. "Ready when you are."

"Okay," he replied. "Wish me luck."

"*Boa sorte, meu camarada*," Raitek said.

Patel breathed deeply and remembered what they had discussed in the last meeting: in the previous experiments, they had been very cautious, pressing buttons for no more than fifty floors, even though the feeling of acceleration wasn't exactly corresponding.

This time, though, what should they do? More of the same could only bring the same results. More floors down could provoke an accident if they jumped to a past when the elevators hadn't been invented yet. More floors up, on the other hand, could mean an incredible future—but what if they ended up in an ecologically improved Earth, one with no arcologies? What then? More importantly, would any of these scenarios affect the bubble and anyone inside it?

They just didn't know.

In the end, they had reached a decision.

Patel pushed the button for one hundred floors up.

It was no big deal. The communication with Raitek was cut up immediately, but that was to be expected. The acceleration was smooth, but noticeable.

Then, full stop. The doors started to open. Patel felt immediately a freezing cold.

And the dark of space.

He was sucked to the void instantly, but felt the tug of the rope just before he could fall into the blackness. The only reason his eyes didn't explode in their orbits was that the glasses were watertight, but he knew they wouldn't resist for long. He gasped; not only he couldn't breathe but he felt his trachea burning cold.

This is it, he thought. *I'm going to die here.*

His hands were already fumbling in the emergency bag.

And found the small oxygen unit there.

He quickly secured it over his mouth, but he couldn't adjust the rubber strap: he started to feel numb, his fingers losing their grip. He should close the doors before he could inhale safely. He closed his eyes for just a second. *Focus, Hiran, Focus.* Then he opened his eyes and caught the rope, starting to pull himself painfully with one hand while still holding the oxygen mask with the other.

Then the mask slipped off; it started to drift away slowly, but by then he had already turned to the inside panel of the car, lifted a hand and pushed the emergency button. The doors closed. The car was a vacuum: would he survive when he got back?

❦

He did.

"We were worried about you, mate," Raitek said to him, sitting by his bed in the building's small medical ward.

"I wonder why." Patel managed a shadow of a smile.

Jonathan looked at him from a distance.

"He won't admit it, but he was scared shitless," Raitek said.

"I know," Patel said. "I was too."

"We all were."

"How did you know?"

"I didn't. It was an educated guess."

"Too educated."

"Here's the thing: it turns out that acceleration wasn't really the issue after all. You have think in systems of *coordinates and geolocation tools*. Later that night, I started wondering, what about the Earth's orbit? Shouldn't we be calculating to compensate the transit of Earth around the Sun? You'd be traveling in space as well as in time, after all, so your bubble would be slingshot towards Mercury, probably."

"Probably."

"I had too much on my mind to do all the math."

"That makes sense."

"Then I figured, hell, it's too late for that, but not too late to take some precautions, just in case."

"In case."

"Exactly."

"Thanks."

"No. Thank *you*. You were the hero."

"Are you fucking kidding me? You conned me into doing it. I won't forget this!"

"We'll discuss it over a beer as soon as you get better, all right? I'm going now," and he started to get out of the room.

"One more thing," Patel said.

"Yes?"

"Is Raitek a common name in Brazil? I must confess I don't know much about your country aside from football, but I've never even heard of such a name before anywhere."

Raitek smiled.

"Say it out loud again. This time slowly, separating the syllables. And don't forget to exaggerate the initial R."

"Like a roar."

"Exactly."

Patel did it.

"Fuck. Fuck." He couldn't help it.

The other man shrugged. "My mother was a sucker for puns. And for hi-tech too, of course. How's that for a geek, huh?"

"One more thing," Raitek said, coming back to the bedside. "I took the liberty of filing the whole project under a FAIL tag. I already had a talk with the rest of the team. They were pretty shaken up after what happened to you, and they all agreed with it."

"Wait, why? After all we did?"

"Because a FAIL tag is better than a DANGEROUS one. A DANGEROUS tag means it's a good project, ready to be revived at a later date with the right team and the right equipment. That is…"

"Not us."

"Exactly."

"But then what? Did I work in vain?"

"Not at all," Raitek said. "I have clearance with failed projects. What would you say if I got you a transfer to Brazil? We have an arcology in São Paulo that's a bit higher than this, and you'd have everything you needed to start working right away—including a better paycheck."

Patel squinted. He could feel a massive headache coming.

"What's the point? What can we do there we can't do here?" he tried to keep his voice down.

"We have a good aerospace agency in Brazil," Raitek said.

"I still don't understand."

Then Raitek smiled again that devious smile of his.

"Why, Hiran, you wanted to open a travel agency, and so does the company. But, after what happened to you, I was thinking of aiming a little higher. Why not the stars, Hiran? *Why not space travel?*"

☜✝☞

Hiran Patel and Raitek da Silva arrived in São Paulo three weeks later—time enough to move the necessary equipment and transfer everyone in the team who wanted to go with them (a condition Patel imposed to close the deal). Jonathan was among the group.

In Brazil, the team doubled in size, as did their workload. They had better working conditions, better equipment, an almost stress-free environment and lots of money.

"We can do better, Hiran," Raitek told him when the lab was finally ready to work. "We can change the game for good."

"The company will back us in this?" Hiran asked him.

"Never mind the company," he said. "I'm applying the gambiarra method here too." Suddenly he stopped smiling and said, "Want to know why?"

Hiran stared at him.

"Why the gambiarra? Of course I do."

"No. The gambiarra goes without saying. I meant why Brazil."

"Oh. Okay, carry on."

"In Ghana, as well as in Europe, Hiram, space exploration is still the domain of the military. Not in Brazil.

"We also had a military space program here in the 20th century, did you know that? No, you didn't. Almost nobody didn't. It was no big secret. It just happened people wasn't that much interested in anything coming from a banana republic then. Until 2003, when a rocket intended to get two satellites in orbit exploded on its launch pad. It killed twenty-one civilian techs.

"After what was considered a thorough military enquiry—to which no civilian had access—the official investigation report said that the explosion was caused by dangerous buildups of volatile gases, deterioration of sensors and electromagnetic interference at the launch site. Nobody could prove if it was true, but after that our space program pretty much stopped. The military one, that is."

"You mean that there are civilian companies working on space exploration now?"

Then Raitek's broad face broke into a smile again. He produced a laminated card from the inner pocket of his jacket. It was a dull grey ultrathin plastic job, featuring his name, an old redundancy QR-code and, most important, the acronym of the company: AIM.

"There is one now," he said.

A Bridge of Words

Dinesh Rao

Once in a while, you'd suddenly see someone, out of the corner of your eye, with the tattooed dots on the forehead and the side, but of course, you'd blink and before you got a better look, the person would disappear into the crowd. It is a hopeless task, thought Riya, as she trudged along the main thoroughfare in the market, unable to keep her eyes from constantly scanning the crowd and yet weary of the necessity to be constantly alert. It didn't help that she drew attention to herself; no matter how much she tried to blend in, something gave her away. It wasn't her face—she could pass for a local any day—nor her clothes, but maybe her stance? The way she walked? Some subtle trait advertised her strangeness to the people around her. Bahsa, the research assistant, was amused by their failure, but even his cheerful explanations of their situation were beginning to grate on her.

"I hate field work," she announced. "Let's just scan through the police database. I can write a script in ten minutes…"

"If we can get hold of it… personally, I don't think they will just give it to us, here, take the camera files, have fun," replied Bahsa.

"But Dr Gudi promised…"

"I know, I know, but in my experience"—Bahsa looked around conspiratorially—"Dr Gudi is a nice man, but sometimes he says things you want to hear. We all do, it's a national failing. Scholars have long lamented this problem. There is no way the police will let us have access to anything."

Riya sighed, and longed once again for the cool of the old library. "Maybe that's how they can tell that there's something off about me— maybe they can sense the sweat rolling off me," she thought.

Bahsa said, "Look let's give this half an hour more. If we don't find anyone by then, let's go back and have a drink." Riya muttered okay, and cheered up grudgingly.

They wandered through the market, dodging shoppers and sellers and pickpockets and beggars, through the byways of the marketplace, constantly scanning people's faces for the telltale dots on the head. Riya's feet were aching and the need for sustained alertness tired her. They stopped to buy some weirdly shaped fruits—even Bahsa had never seen them before. He asked the old lady selling it what they were called, and she said its name in that sing-song accent that Riya remembered so well from her childhood. Bahsa handed one to Riya, and they peeled the flakes off the *Khumba* fruit and munched into it.

Riya pretended not to listen as the woman interrogated Bahsa about her. She could understand most of it but it was the accents that troubled her. She heard the familiar patter that Bahsa used every time it came up—

"Yes, she's from here, but lives abroad. In Krashigar. She was born here, in ThuLadvipa, but her father is a Krashigari. Her mother went there when she was a small child. Yes she speaks ThuLu, yes yes she knows, she's from one of the Old families actually, her mother is a *Sumuka-Vaarta*."

At this last bit of information, the old lady turned to face her. She stared at her intently, and Riya finally acknowledged her with a quick nod.

"What is she doing here?" she asked.

Bahsa, completely oblivious to the change in her tone, continued with his spiel. "We're working on a university project, it's part of a huge nationwide project about the Spaceship (he used the Krashi word) that came looking for our ancestors." Bahsa didn't mind telling everyone he was on this project; he was really proud of it. But Riya found it hard to deal with the inevitable questions. *How could they let a foreigner come and work on the project? Yes of course, I understand that her mother is a Vaarta but it's not like she lived here, and she doesn't even speak ThuLu properly.* On a normal day, Riya would have smiled politely and used one of her twenty-five different ways to Get Out Of This Conversation, but this time she just turned and walked away. Bahsa yelled, "Hey! Wait up," but in a tiny gesture of rebellion, Riya pretended not to hear him and ducked through a stall selling scarves into another section of the market.

She stopped in front of a stall selling spices and prepackaged food, the kind that they would never allow her to put in her luggage on a plane. A small kid came running to the stall holder and asked for *Bamsa* powder, but the guy minding the stall said, "No, I won't sell it to you, go get your parents." Riya moved on to the next stall selling cheap resin reproductions of the Spaceship, side by side with lovingly hand-crafted wooden ones. Riya picked up a model. This one was really good. It used differently tinted inlaid woods to show the various parts of the ship. She asked how much it was, and was pleasantly startled to realize it was affordable. "Ah, why not," she thought, "Everyone else here has a Spaceship idol somewhere or the other. After all, they came looking for the ThuLu people—they came looking for us!"

Riya walked among the stalls till she ended up at one of the entrances and then she called Bahsa on the 'phon. "I'm here," she said, watching the people watch her. "Let's go back to the campus. Today has been a complete waste." Bahsa caught up to her quickly, already a bit guilty that he had let her go off on her own. On the way back to the university, she asked him, "What is *Bamsa*?"

"*Bamsa*? In what context?"

"Some kid came to this shop asking for *Bamsa* powder, but the shop keeper wouldn't sell it to him, asking him for his parents. I assumed it was something like alcohol, you know, like you need to be of a certain age before you can buy it."

"Oh *Bamsa* powder, no, no, it's not age restricted. They sell it in spice shops mostly, it's a powder to dye your hair."

"Then why would the guy refuse to sell it to the kid?"

"Maybe he was orthodox. Some of these shopkeepers are orthodox and won't sell *Bamsa* to kids, because they also use *Bamsa* paste in religious ceremonies. They take *Bamsa* wood and scrape it against a metal plate and this produces a paste. The paste is then used in the ceremonies; you'd dip a special stamp-seal in the paste and then place it on your forehead. The patterns on the stamp seals are unique to lineages. They are usually passed on from mother to daughter. You must have done this yourself; it's very common among the *Vaartas*?"

"No," said Riya. "Or rather, I don't remember any such thing. My mother gave up many things when she left for Krashigar. We hardly celebrated any festivals; she was always too busy in her work. She did try to teach me and my sister many things, but it's never the same when you live away from the island. I know ThuLu better than my sister, and that's only because I learnt it at university rather than at home. Everyday I discover little things like these, things that every islander knows. It's an impossible task."

Bahsa said, "When I was a child, my father made me go to a priest to learn the prayers, you know, the morning prayers, and he was old-school. I am not *Vaarta* but there are many similarities in our traditions. Anyway, I used to fight it every day, I didn't want to wake before dawn and do the whole transfer of night to day pledge, nor the guardian prayer or anything, I just wanted to sleep in. But eventually I'd wake up long enough to mimic the movements of the family priest."

Riya looked at him steadily, barely hearing his words, already lost in a swirl of images and memory. She remembered the prayer box that was the first thing that her mother installed in every house they'd been. And no matter how discreetly she placed them, some guest at every party would always comment on them, "Oh, I didn't realize you were religious, how interesting." And then her mother would make a halting oblique speech of her background and what each object meant, and then politely change the topic. When one lived in the land of the people who ran roughshod over the old ways, every such innocuous comment made her wince. Riya could still see the little altar clearly; it was the first physical sign of connection to her history and so assumed a large significance. The little flute-like tube, the incense holder, the filigreed pyramid, a chunk of wood and the ornate metal plate, and of course the stamp-seals. A chunk of wood with a telltale smell; she remembered it now. She had seen it before.

They reached the university campus after sunset, and as was her habit, she looked west to see the artificial red glint of the patiently waiting Spaceship, no doubt still broadcasting the same key phrase over and over again hoping for a response. Like someone in a darkened room saying hello, hello... hello. At first the new star was a source of terror, a red eye in the sky, but now it comforted her. Riya waved goodbye to Bahsa and headed to her house. It had been a long day and her bed was especially inviting; sleep would ease all disappointment.

🙰 ⚕ 🙰

The next day, at the group meeting, Dr Gudi was incredulous. "How can you come here and tell me that you couldn't find a single Thuri person? What, has there been some nationwide shortage of study subjects? Riya, I can understand if you missed them, but Bahsa, seriously, you should know better. From here it looks like you're slacking on the job. Well, there's nothing to it, go back on the next market day and keep trying till we get someone to talk to."

Riya was disheartened. This project was turning into drudgery. She hooked up her 'phon to the screen and searched the net for a sympathetic ear, but the usual timezone asynchrony denied her this. Instead she got hooked into watching yet another documentary about the Spaceship. This time a team of researchers from Krashigar announced that they'd cracked the message from the ship, and that it was some sort of a countdown, but this theory was dismissed because the message never changed. Then there was news that a gorgeous version of the message was published, in a sort of codex, that one could buy. On a whim, Riya ordered the codex. In paper form, even. Her project was only tangentially related to the ship—Dr Gudi was exploiting the fact that there suddenly was a vast amount of money available if anyone wanted to do anything with the ship and its message. All they knew that the ship had come down before, very very long ago. There were stories in the scriptures. There was no doubt that this was the second visit. The *Vaartas* had compiled extensive records about the first visit. But the sources were secondhand. All the myths and the scriptures were in ThuLu, and the original language, DevfaLa, was lost when Krashigar invaded. Dr Gudi's research was on the origin of language—he focused on tattoos and other body patterning—and he had, with great professional skill, linked the themes of body patterns and the Spaceship's signal in a breathtaking daredevil act of grant writing, and thus financed the department for a few more years. The wolves of disaster were at bay, for now.

A message blinked on her 'phon. Her mother.

She began, "Riya, I have a mission for you. You know I had to leave ThuLadvipa in a hurry, but I had time to store many family heirlooms before they were lost. I left them in the care of very long time family friend in Purja—in fact, we were almost married to each other when I reached the right age. Now that you are there and will possibly be there for a while, it's fitting that these things are in the family's possession once again. I want you go to Purja and get them. I want to come myself to show you our ancestral home, or what is left of it, but work is keeping me tied up here and I don't know when I can get away. But I will feel a lot better when I know that these things are in your hands, it will be a weight off my back."

Riya was annoyed and intrigued. She called Bahsa, and then hung up immediately when she realized how late it was. What could those items be? Probably old photographs and clothes. Her mother always exaggerated things. Her 'phon pinged; it was a message from her mother again, telling her that there was a festival the next day, but Riya already knew that. She had seen people buying the leaves of the *Sugarpa* plant, and preparing for the Sun festival by stringing banners and paper flowers and all manner of activities. Festivals here were quite different than the ones she was used to at home in Krashigar. There the ceremonies were muted; her mother quickly performed some offering in the house, almost furtively, before heading out to work. But here, the whole city celebrated. Riya felt the excitement in the air at the prospect of a day spent engaged in the old ways and dressing in the old style. A thousand years of the effects of Krashigar's brutal insistence on the removal of the old ways had almost vanished with the resurgence.

Bahsa had invited Riya home for the Sun festival. Bahsa's wife GavaNi was a wonderful cook and relished the festivals, and Riya never missed a chance to eat there. Every bite was like a little sensory explosion. Her father, though, often complained that the smell of the cooking gave him allergy attacks, or that he couldn't concentrate. It was always a mystery how he managed to survive ten years in the island. And later, chomping down on the delicacies, she listened to GavaNi telling/singing the story of the Sun festival to her twin girls, hearing the story both as an adult and as a child. As night fell, talk turned inevitably to the project. Riya was worried what she would do if she did not find enough Thuri subjects. Bahsa reassured her. They spoke of the ship and its possible message, unconsciously glancing at the west to see if it was still there. Bahsa said, "I can't believe, if this is the second visit, why didn't they devise a better way to contact us? Surely they must have known that things were going to change here?"

Riya replied, "Maybe they didn't know that. Maybe their society is super stable over millennia."

"That could be it. And another thing: why us? Why not Krashigar? How did they choose us? Ah, so many questions."

"I hope that this is resolved in my lifetime. I would hate to revisit this conversation sixty years later and still have no answers."

"I'm sure those Krashigar scientists will come up with something soon enough. They're sending another rocket."

"Are they?"

"I think so, let me check." Bahsa peered into his 'phon. The steady hum of city traffic filtered their way up to the apartment. "No, the mission is not a Krashigar mission, it's from Partia. Hmm, I didn't know they were interested. It must be an election year there."

"What's the plan this time?"

"Oh, just the usual: try to get close to the ship and try to get them to say something other than the damn key code."

"You know, I think there's nobody on the ship. It must be a robot/artificially controlled ship. Prepared to wait till the end of time for a correct response."

"Yep."

There seemed to be nothing more to say.

❦

A few weeks later, the codex was delivered to her house. Riya had almost forgotten about the order, and it felt like she was getting a surprise present from a secret admirer. She opened the box, and realized instantly that the book was so gorgeous it just didn't belong on her cheap bookshelf. She spent the rest of the evening on the balcony, watching the sunset with its incongruous star, flipping through the book and nursing a glass of hot wine. A series of unbelievably clear photographs of the ship, a section recounting the first approach, the *Vaarta* connection. She was familiar with most of this, and she brushed past the now iconic photos that filled the net and the papers every day. A few personal stories of people involved in the various planetary level projects. But the bulk of the book was devoted to the complex message and the possible interpretations.

She told Dr Gudi about the book during one of their sessions, and got a quizzical look in return, as if he was surprised she was wasting her time with books that were clearly meant for the general public. His mood had definitely taken a turn for the worse in the last few weeks. The high of getting the big grant had finally worn off and he was deep in battle with the university bureaucracy to get started on the project. To add to his woes, an ongoing expensive computer simulation study had ended with no clear results, leaving him with a gigantic bill and not even enough data for a small paper in a low-impact journal. Bahsa and Riya had managed to find a few Thuris willing to be interviewed, but the numbers were nowhere near enough, and the lack of results was causing a tension in the group.

"Have you put out ads?" Dr Gudi asked, for the tenth time.

"Yes, but only three Thuri people responded, and only one of those was tattooed as a child. The other two were modern. Fans, so to speak."

"I hate these modern types. It's so much ethnic pollution. Okay, we'll see what happens. You might have to travel to the small Thuri settlement at Purja, after all. I was trying to avoid that possibility because they are really hostile to strangers. But there may be no other option."

"Purja!" exclaimed Riya.

"Why are you surprised?"

"Hmm, my mother just asked me to go to Purja as well! She wanted to me to revisit our ancestral home, and meet some old family friends."

"Okay, that's settled then. That's fantastic. If you know someone from Purja, it'll make all the difference. I've had three projects die because I didn't have the right introductions. See if Bahsa can go with you. I don't want you to travel there alone. Purja has always been a bit radical against Krashigar, ever since pre-independence times, and I don't want you to get into trouble."

"But I am not Krashigari…"

"Yes, yes, *I* know that, and *you* know that, and I'm just being cautious, you see?"

Riya bit back a retort, and had to be content with merely glaring at Dr Gudi when he turned his back.

☙❦❧

Purja was a surprise. Riya expected a small backwater village, but she didn't expect the calm that comes with being surrounded by backwaters and *Sugarpa* farms. The fields were shiny green, and the deep silence of the fields was broken only by insects buzzing and birds chirping. Time slowed, her breathing slowed, and Riya felt the endless chatter in her mind slow down as well. It felt like she was returning home. Bahsa walked behind her, as they headed towards the village centre. There was a small stone engraving there, proclaiming that this was the origin of the freedom movement, a small act of disobedience from an unlikely hero that somehow caught the imagination of a hitherto hopeless people. The village itself looked as if not even a single house had so much as changed a single tile on the roof in all this time.

They stopped at a house to ask for directions to Paparta's house, and found that they were expected. Riya's mother had already sent word about their arrival. Paparta, a slight balding man clad in white, opened the door and ushered them sedately into a cool room. A shy kid brought a tray with glasses filled with juice of a fruit that Riya didn't recognize. They sipped in silence, as Paparta spoke, "Welcome to Purja. You look so much like your mother that for a minute I thought I was seeing a vision. You look like her, you walk like her; it's only when you talk that the illusion shatters."

"Yes, I know my ThuLu is still not fluent," Riya replied in a flat voice.

"And one cannot miss the Krashigari accent."

"Yes, that too."

"So, anyway, welcome. I know you have never been here, but you know that as a daughter of the *Vaarta* lineage, this is your ancestral home. This very house is where your mother was born, and it remains in her name. We still hope that she will return and take it back, but those hopes are already dim. But we are very happy that her daughter has come back. You are after all a *Sumuka-Vaarta*."

"Thank you," said Riya as they lapsed back into the distinctly uncomfortable silence. "People here seem to speak in spurts," she whispered to Bahsa. They listened to the sounds of the wind and the birds intermixed with the dull sound of a persistent argument somewhere in the background.

Paparta continued, "Your mother says you are studying here?"

"Yes, I'm here on a research project. It's about the ship," said Riya and she pointed upwards.

"Oh, the ship." Paparta sounded interested, despite himself.

"But it's only vaguely related. Actually, that was another thing that I was hoping you could help us with," and Riya nodded to Bahsa. Bahsa explained that they were looking for Thuri people who still tattooed their faces in the old way.

At that Paparta's face turned into a mask. He said, "Why do you want them?"

Riya explained that her project was to study the patterns of the tattoos.

Paparta seemed unconvinced, but all he said was, "You might know that the practice almost died out, but your professor is right: there are still some people left. My cousin knows some Thuris. I will ask him to take you to them."

And after some more interminable minutes of silence, Paparta nodded to a small man who was hovering near the wall, and he brought out a trunk. "This is all your mother left behind. How will you take it?', he said.

"Oh, we brought a vehicle," replied Riya.

Paparta ordered the man to put the trunk in the vehicle, but they could tell that he didn't want to give that order. He watched the trunk leave the house, followed it to the vehicle, and supervised the loading himself. Riya realized with a start that there were lots of people watching her, the neighbours had all come out to stare at her. The man who loaded the trunk introduced himself as the "cousin" and he led them to one corner of the village.

"This is where Shavo, one of the Thuris, lives," he said. "He is very friendly, he will be able to help you in your research."

≈¥☞

Shavo turned out to be very helpful indeed, and the next few weeks flew by in a blitz of work. Documenting the tattoos, copying the patterns, hearing their stories, all these things kept them busy from morning to night. They made frequent trips to the outskirts, and even to a few neighbouring villages, because the tattooed Thuris had spread across the country. Eventually, there were no more new tattoo patterns, and for the first time Riya felt the satisfaction of a field season coming to an end. From now on it would all be a matter of analysis and writing, but at least that would be under her control.

The code was tedious. She had to sift through and schematize the tattoos, hundreds of distinct patterns. Some tattoos were composed of multiple parts, and the code not only had to analyse them as a whole but also consider the parts. Riya had to do a substantial amount of verification to make sure that what the computer said was different was actually different. She hardly left her office these days, and only returned to her house late at night. Her only breaks were when Bahsa invited—well, blackmailed her to go visit him, saying that his daughters missed her and that they always kept asking for her.

On one such dinner visit, the conversation turned to their trip to Purja. Bahsa had never been there before and he was especially pleased to have been able to go to the heartland of the *Vaartas* given their longstanding role in the history of the island. He asked Riya if she'd opened the box yet, and Riya replied with a start.

"Oh no! I just put it in a guest room and forgot about it. My mother will be so mad at me."

"It's probably old clothes, don't worry," teased Bahsa.

"Yes, old heirloom, out-of-fashion clothes, all moth-eaten."

"Paparta really didn't want to give you the box; did you notice that? It was like he *had* to give it to you."

"I saw that. I just assumed it was because I'm half Krashigari. I always seem to generate weird responses in people."

"No, I don't think it was that. I think he was obliged to give it to you, because of your mother. But he didn't want to lose custody of it."

"That's odd."

"It must be treasure," they said simultaneously and laughed out aloud, startling the twins who were watching a movie.

GavaNi came in then with some more snacks, and though Riya protested, she was also glad to eat them. They then settled down on the balcony overlooking the river of traffic.

GavaNi said, "So how is your project coming along? We hardly see you these days. Dr Gudi should give you a holiday."

They smiled, knowing how much Dr Gudi enjoyed giving time off to his students.

"I think I'm close to the end. The coding is mostly done, and basically I see the light at the end of the tunnel. It won't be sensational, but it is very satisfying to finally document such a little-studied practice from ThuLadvipa. It's a bit funny that I ended up using my own heritage to get some progress on my project."

GavaNi said, "But no, it's not that strange. The *Thuris* and the *Vaartas* were one sect for a very long time, but after the teachings of Dapasya, the sect split into two. The *Vaartas* were followers of Dapasya but the *Thuris* rejected his ideas. Sometime during the Krashigari rule, everybody started hiding the old ways, and the tattoos were a lot harder to hide so they became really unpopular, and easy targets as well for Krashigari enforcers. Even now, the ones who are tattooed are from the really old lineages."

"Oh, I didn't know that."

"I don't envy you. Just keeping track of all these sects is a pain," said Bahsa.

❦

A few weeks later, Riya presented her results to Dr Gudi. As the obvious conclusion appeared, he grew excited. He walked back and forth in the little room, rapidly twirling a pencil. Beads of sweat flowed down his bald head. "Riya, this data is fantastic. You have no idea how fantastic. This is a game changer. Do you realize what you have done? We will be famous. Not rich, but famous."

Riya grinned. She'd already realized what the tattoos meant, and had spent several extra weeks checking and rechecking to make sure that her code was okay, and her hypothesis sound.

Dr Gudi continued, "It is obvious that the tattoos are some highly condensed version of the lost language of DevfaLa! It was never lost but hidden! The tattoos are a compressed representation of the language. Reminds me of DNA actually, the packing is so dense. Look at this one, and this one, it is as clear as could be. Did you find any overlaps?"

"Yes, there are some redundancies. Within a single family, for example. There are very strict rules. Brothers share a certain type of tattoo. And male offspring have the same as their father. There are oral records, now transcribed, that show unbroken lineages for hundreds of years."

"This is the smoking gun, Riya. This is not only important from the point of view of DevfaLa, but also in my hypothesis that tattoos are precursors of language. I think that when Krashigar threatened total annihilation of the old ways, the people simply went back to an earlier ancient time when tattoos were a means of communication. Excellent work, Riya. Now let us recheck the data. It's not that I doubt you or your work, but extraordinary claims require extraordinary proof."

Later that night, Riya went back to her house. She needed someone to join her in celebrating the discovery. Bahsa was visiting family on the other side of the island, and all her other colleagues were away on field work. She felt at a loss, and when she sat down, she remembered her mother's box. Now that she had some time on her hands, she decided to open it.

The trunk was densely packed with items all wrapped in silk, everything in perfect condition. There were books and papers, photos and clothes (as she'd expected), small jewellery boxes and other items. At the bottom of the trunk, exquisitely wrapped in silken layers, were the original idols of the family *Vaarta* altar. Riya brought them out one by one and set them up on the table. The last package was a set of items used in the prayers and ceremonies. Riya closed her eyes and distant memories of these objects grew stronger in her mind, the feel, the touch, the smell. And then she saw the set of *bamsa* stamp seals.

She pulled out the *bamsa* wood and scraped it against the plate, adding a little water, till the paste came cleanly. She dipped the seal on the paste and then deliberately pressed it against the side of her forehead. The coolness of the metal. The paste itself. All those submerged memories. She looked at herself in the mirror opposite… and saw for the first time the patterns that were left behind on her forehead, like temporary tattoos. Tattoos. She hurriedly, with increasing impatience, dipped the seals one by one in the *bamsa* paste and pressed them against her skin. The dots and the lines, the swirls and the dashes. The patterns looked familiar. Suspiciously familiar. She remembered GavaNi saying that the *Thuris* and the *Vaartas* were historically connected. And if the *Thuri* tattoos hid the DevfaLa language in one way, then the *Vaartas* must have hidden it as well, but in another way. The seals had been passed down from generation to generation; fossilized within the tradition, surviving secretly during the occupation by Krashigar.

❧ ✝ ❧

Many months later the paper was published to great fanfare. Dr Gudi was attending a conference in the capital, and no doubt being fêted by all the government for "his" remarkable discovery. After the news got out, the priests were really angry, claiming that they had known it all along and that Dr Gudi was betraying his country by exposing a secret tradition to the outsiders. Research was still a Krashigari custom to the priests. Riya also got a fair bit of attention, her story made her irresistible to the journalists, and there were a few profiles of her.

Riya had invited Bahsa and his family to her house. GavaNi had outdone herself, and had brought a series of steaming rich dishes. The twins wandered around oohing and aahing at the stuff that Riya had accumulated during her stay and had propped up on the bookshelves. After dinner, they sat sipping hot wine and reminiscing about the project, and about the future and what Riya would do once she'd received her degree.

Bahsa asked her, "Do you think you will stay here?"

Riya said, "I don't know. I've learnt a lot about life here, largely due to you and GavaNi, but... I miss Krashigar as well. I grew up there, and even though I always felt more like I belong here when I was there, now I feel the other way. I'm stuck between the two worlds."

"You need to find a project that needs you to be here half the year and there the other half."

"YES! That would be the best. But seriously, I need to stay there for a while and figure out what to do next. I thought coming here would clear my head, especially with respect to my identity, find some sense of belonging. And yes, I found that, to a certain extent... but nothing is clear. Now, I feel neither here nor there."

GavaNi said, "No, no, that's not the way to think about it. You are neither here nor there, but that's because you're the bridge. The bridge between Krashigar and ThuLadvipa, the past and the present."

"That's very nice of you to say…"

But she was interrupted by one of the twins who came up to her, and said,

"Riya, can we see your book on the Spaceship?"

And Riya said, "Of course you can, just be careful," and she went to the bookshelf to pull down the codex. She was just about to place it on a coffee table, when it slipped and fell with a thunk. Riya started picking it up, the codex turned to the pages with the visual representation of the code. Riya looked at the alien code; except that this time intuition washed over her, the code, the alien code was suddenly not so alien after all. The patterns were made with components that were the same as the seals from her mother's trunk. It was clear now: the Spaceship was waiting for a response from the *Vaartas* but not just any *Vaarta* family. A particular *Vaarta* lineage. They were waiting for a response from her.

Droplet

Rahul Kanakia

The drive north from the airport took Subhir Joshi's family through the rotting heart of California. From behind the wheel, his American-born father, Rajiv, pointed out boyhood landmarks, while Subhir's mother, Priya, joined in with reminisces from their college days. But Subhir wasn't paying attention to them. He was mesmerized by the "KEA"s and "T-RG-T"s that had been fading away and shedding letters for years, by the empty roads, by the entire overpasses that had been cordoned off or demolished, by the wasteland of miles where there were just the ghosts of towns. This was to be the land of Subhir's exile.

At home, in Bangalore, millions of people would be on the streets by now. Even walking to the market took half an hour, not just because of the traffic, but because Subhir would be stopped three times by friends shouting from street corners, cars, and apartment windows. Those same friends had dutifully broadcast their congratulations at Subhir's acceptance to one of America's top universities, and then privately joked with him about "going to school amongst the ruins". Subhir's nostalgic father had responded to his son's summer of protests by bringing him here two days early to sightsee with old friends.

"Aravind hasn't seen you since you were a baby," Subhir's father said. "You know, your Thanksgiving breaks will be too short to fly all the way back to India. Maybe you could go and stay at his motel, like your mother used to."

"No, I'll come home," Subhir said. "Maybe next time, the U.S. government won't let me re-enter this country." The immigration officials at SFO had spent an hour staring at Subhir's student visa, and making dozens of calls from behind their glass partition, before stamping his passport without an explanation. The Alienation Acts were almost two decades old, but Americans still didn't hesitate to use them against any foreigner who looked out of place.

His mother twisted in her seat. "*Baap re baap*, once when I arrived for the beginning of the term," she said. "I was taken to a room and not allowed to leave. Your father's father had to call some politician just to find me."

The rental car passed into the parched golden hills of Northern California. Abandoned farmhouses and fields lined the sides of the highway, interspersed by flashes of dusty, boarded-up towns. They turned off the highway at the first sign for "Sinclair" and made two left turns, pulling to a stop in the near-empty parking lot of a motel owned by Rajiv's childhood friend, Aravind Patel.

The Holi Inn looked like a setpiece from the Bollywood summer blockbuster of three years ago, *Cowboy Singh*. Subhir remembered the ending of the movie: The turbaned motel owner was sitting behind the front desk, loaded shotgun in hand, waiting for the sheriff to serve the eviction notice, when he looked up and saw the cross he'd put on the wall to ingratiate himself with the whites, the stupid sacrilegious cross that hadn't even worked, and he took it down and smashed it again and again on the counter. After the mob finally burst in, the camera panned up from his body to the bullet-ridden portrait of Guru Nanak on the wall.

Subhir stared at the flaking tan paint of the Holi Inn. Had there been gunshots here? Had Aravind fought to keep his land? Had he signed his business over to a white patsy, some busboy or clerk, and kept the latter in line with gifts and threats? What did Aravind have to give up in order to be allowed to stay?

☙ ❦ ❧

Aravind had loaded down the American desk clerk with their bags and then ushered Subhir's family, past the "closed" sign barring the hotel's restaurant, to a table. He'd bobbed his shiny white hat at them and told them to "Get yourselves comfortable," and then disappeared into the kitchen.

"*Pappa,* why does Uncle speak that way?" Subhir said to his father.

"*Hai Ram,*" Subhir's mother said, "even your father once spoke like that, before university cured him of it. His friends at Stanford used to make such fun of him. But Uncle never left Sinclair district. There was no reason for him to change."

"I can see that," Subhir said. License plates from what looked like all fifty-one states hung on the walls, over a full mural—depicting the length of "Highway 66"—that stretched across all four walls. Aravind exited from a door just below Santa Monica, trailed by a young Indian woman in a red uniform shirt who was balancing a large tray.

"Sit, sit," Aravind said to her. "I told you to let Teresa bring the food."

"You wanted me back for the summer," she said. "If I'm here, I'm working. I won't let them say I'm just a lazy quota brat."

She smiled at the table. Her nose stud and hennaed arms struck Subhir as curiously old-fashioned, like she'd modeled herself on his mother's mother.

"Chicken enchiladas for you, Mr. Joshi. My dad insisted that you'd be hungering for Mexican food. But I have *samosas, aloo tikki, papri chaat, bhel puri*, and *pani puri* for the real Gujuratis."

"My daughter Nisha," Aravind said, "has spent the last three summer breaks teaching our Mexican cook how to whip up Gujarati snacks."

"This table looks like a *chaat*-stand," Subhir's mother said, nodding. "Are you in attendance at Stanford as well?"

"Wouldn't I wish!" Aravind said. "She's been studying computer science at IIT-Bombay. Took the entrance exam without my knowing. I said, 'the world has enough sliderules. All they'll teach you is how to cram for tests and take orders.' Told her to take Yale up on their offer. Or, hell, Berkeley woulda been even better. Major in English and minor in raising Cain. But she ignored me, as usual."

Nisha rolled her eyes. "Six of the world's twenty richest men went to IITs. Even the ranchhands who get trashed in here every Saturday know IITB is the best engineering school in the world. But he wouldn't even take me to visit."

It was Subhir's turn to roll his eyes. Of course she'd gotten into the Indian Institute of Technology. With the quotas for Diasporic Indians, any Brit or American or Australian who got a score above the minimum cutoff could get in, while Subhir—who'd scored in the top decile—had failed to secure a spot. Twice.

She took a seat next to her father, who belatedly said, "Not that computer science has to get in the way of having a little fun, Subhir. Especially at Stanford. Your folks met in that department, after all. I remember the first time your dad brought Priya home. I had to make all the beds for a week while my mom whipped up feasts for them. She was convinced your mom had to be *really* homesick if she'd settled for Ray here."

The table drifted into nostalgic remembrances for the better part of an hour as Nisha poured the whiskey and Subhir stared at the walls. He noticed that all three of them were careful to keep it light, and avoid the topic of his family's final expulsion. Finally, his mother visibly yawned, and the table stood up.

"Have you all seen the old homestead yet?" Aravind said. "The Koreskys—the folks who tried to farm it after you all left—finally packed it in. Place is abandoned now, but lots of it is still standing. We can take the kids tomorrow. They'll get a kick out of it."

❦

"Do you remember this at all?" Subhir's father said.

Their car was parked on the overgrown grass at the edge of a dry irrigation ditch. Nisha and Aravind had retreated towards it, leaving the visitors amongst the wreckage. Subhir and his mother were sitting on the steps to the bungalow's cracking front porch. To their right, the rusting hulk of some sort of farm vehicle was sitting in front of a barn that had fallen in on itself. The next closest building was a silo in the distance, no more than a thumbnail tall.

"Though there would have been more trees when you were a baby," his father said. "And when I was your age, all of this was orchards."

Now there wasn't a tree in sight. The grass had colonized these gently rolling hills where Subhir's grandparents had struggled to eke a living from some of the richest, most fertile land in the world. But the summer droughts kept getting longer. And the water demands from fishermen, ecologists, and the thirsty cities of Southern California kept growing. And every year, his grandparents had to let more of their almond trees die, and let more of this golden poison reclaim the land.

Until, finally, they'd stood out here and watched the water district dam up their sluices. Even after three decades, the dotheads who owned "the Johnsons' plot" were still foreigners. And foreigners had been the first to lose their water rights. That night, they'd packed a few bags and left the rest for the tax assessors. When Subhir's father heard about the court order, he'd left his Silicon Valley job and gone with his wife and newborn son to Bangalore to found a software startup. Subhir's grandparents eventually moved back to India. Even now, they refused to talk about the long evening of their stay in this foreign land.

Subhir's mother was stroking the wood of the porch. "Remember Memorial Day weekend?" she said. She looked up at his father. "We sat out here until dawn, while your mother peered down every fifteen minutes. She stayed up all night too, and fell asleep at the breakfast table."

Subhir stepped up onto the porch. He twisted the knob of the front door and felt something crack inside the mechanism. He took a step back, but no one else had heard. The door creaked open. A short hall led into the living room, where three wooden chairs were still arranged around a plastic folding table; the house smelled clean, like rain and wind, even though the fixtures were thick with mold. Subhir grazed a hand over the pile of pulpy boxes left next to the door. He lost any hope of remembering something. Too much had happened since he'd last crawled through this hallway. The place reeked of a hasty exit: a family packing, resentfully, under the eyes of the sheriff's deputies.

"This is yours, you know," Nisha said. She'd wandered in behind him. "Your dad had my dad buy it at the tax auction three years ago. He swung up from the Bay Area last year and visited it."

Subhir laughed. "He got it back the same way he lost it."

"How do you figure?" Nisha said.

"I mean, when my grandparents left, it must have been sold off at a tax auction too."

"Maybe. I mean, I don't know what happened to the lands," she said. "Maybe they did just abandon it. Place wouldn't have been very valuable with the water rights sold off."

"With the rights taken away, you mean. Under the Alienation Acts."

"What? Your grandparents weren't aliens; they were naturalized citizens. None of that applied to them. But they sold out to a water district in So-Cal. And not just for a year or two, but permanently. Back then, it was a huge deal for the biggest shareholder in the Sinclair County Irrigation District to sell his allocation. Folks broke their windows, cut their fences, even welded their sluices shut…they left in the middle of the night, after getting death threats. My dad refused to speak to your dad for ten years."

"That's not true," Subhir said. "My grandparents loved America. They were driven out."

"Not for being foreign. For having a son who could see what everyone else couldn't," Nisha said. "The rains were failing; the San Joaquin river was a ghost of what it used to be. People still thought the Sacramento would flow forever, but your dad could see that the southern water districts were just waiting to make a grab. He negotiated the deal during his last year in grad school."

"My father would never have sold out his—"

Nisha said, "What does it matter? History proved him right. All the other farmers, they were just slow off the mark. They got wiped out during the reallocation. Nowadays, you can't win a poker game without ending up with a fistful of worthless, superseded water rights. But your dad, he turned that money into capital, and built a business that's lasted a lot longer than this farm would have."

Un-American. Profiteer. Parasite. Those slurs—leveled against all the foreigners—had brought tears to his father's eyes when he told stories about his last years in America. Tears of shame, Subhir realized.

"That's all history," Nisha said. "But your dad thinks he can make it right. My dad owns two million acre-feet of superseded rights that he picked up for next to nothing. They want to use your dad's money to go to court and get those rights reinstated, like the vineyards in Napa did. This trip was supposed to, you know, ease you all into the plan."

Subhir's father came in. "Come on," he said. "I want to show you the creek." His accent was resurfacing. He'd pronounced it "crick".

"Why did you tell me this land was stolen from us?" Subhir said.

"We were…what have you been telling him?" his father said.

"I just…" Nisha retreated back into the living room as Subhir stepped forward.

"You chose to leave," Subhir said. "Why force me to come back?"

Subhir's father turned around and marched out of the house. "Dammit Aravind," he said. "What've you been telling her about me?"

Subhir and Nisha edged towards the door, and saw Subhir's father confront Aravind out by the car.

"Shit," Aravind said. He'd taken off his hat, and now he was twisting at the brim. "I don't know what she said. Anyway, that's all in the past. I'm just glad you decided to make it right. Took you long enough."

Subhir's father said, "Make it right? How can you still think I was wrong? I was the smart one. I left before I was forced to leave. How many of the people we went to high school with have stuck around here?"

"That's different, Ray," Aravind said. "And you know it's different. They went to Los Angeles or Seattle or Sacramento. They didn't run out on their country when it needed them."

❦

The argument continued in the front seat of the car.

"Look, we still going to do business or not?" Aravind said.

"How can I work with someone who's held a grudge against me almost twenty years?" Subhir's father said. "I can't believe you still think I'm a traitor. Do you know how stupid you're being?"

"You did betray us," Aravind said. His voice was quiet. "I don't know whether this county would've turned out the same either way. But you didn't even care what happened to us. You worked on those poor old parents for years while you made deals behind their backs. Told them they could be rich. Spun them stories about the high life. And when you finally broke them down and made them sign, you whisked them away from the land they loved and lived on and spent their lives improving and you shut them up in an apartment in Bangalore, right above the muck of the sewers, while you let this place go to hell."

Subhir's father was quiet for a few minutes. The motel came into view. His mother gripped Subhir's arm and whispered, in Gujarati, "*You* should not be blaming your father—"

Then Subhir's father cleared his throat and said, "Every day, my father sits in a restaurant in Bangalore, reading the English newspapers and loudly mocking your president for his latest blunder. Our cousins stop by and ask him for advice on how to raise their children. He is present for every wedding, funeral, and birthday. Anyone in need just has to ask, and they'll get money for their health or educational expenses. He and his expat cronies sit there for hours, and tea comes to him without asking, and people call him 'sir'. People like your father. He died behind that reception desk, didn't he?"

As soon as Subhir's father stopped the car, Aravind grappled with the door. He stalked into the lobby of his motel and disappeared.

☙❦❧

The door buzzed as Subhir and his parents were packing. When his father answered, a uniformed man said, "Mr. Rajiv Joshi, I'm Sheriff Pereira."

"Joe?" his father said. "I didn't know anyone was still around, besides Aravind."

"Yeah, Ray, I'm afraid I have to ask you to leave."

"I haven't committed any crime," Subhir's father said.

"None that I can arrest you for, anyway. But the hotel's full up. You have to go."

"I know my rights. This is racism. The Civil Rights Act. You can't do this."

"You're not being kicked out over your *color*," the sheriff said. "But I heard tell you gave up your citizenship years ago. Right now Americans need these rooms, and, well, Vin would be breaking the law if he rented to you instead of them."

"That bastard," Subhir's father said. "Fine. We'll be out soon."

"We need these rooms immediately," the sheriff said. He stepped to the side and two deputies walked in. They nodded at Subhir and his mother, who were standing by the beds, and then gathered up armfuls of clothing right out of the open suitcases. One ripped Subhir's laptop from the wall and bundled it up with the rest. Then they headed out and down the hall.

"Dude, this can't be right," said a voice from the hall. "We're not sharing this time?" A teen came by and poked his head into the room. He was wearing an Eastland High football jersey. "Umm," he looked at the sheriff. "Coach said this was my room. Number 308."

"It's all yours," the sheriff said. "Would you three please step out?"

In the lobby, Subhir and his parents sorted through the pile of clothes left by the door while teenagers rampaged around them. The coach said to the sheriff, "Thanks for donating us these rooms. I thought we were going to have to sleep all crowded up on the floor at my sister's place again."

Aravind came in through the door behind the counter and said, "Here's your receipt for the rooms, Joe."

"No problem, Vin," the sheriff said. "And here's the receipt for your contribution to the Sinclair County Police Benevolent Association." He stared at Subhir's father while saying these words, but

Aravind looked away.

"Aravind," Subhir's father said. "How could you do this?"

"What are the regulations on a foreigner owning land in California?" Aravind said. "I hear there's something funny about the titling to the Koresky place."

"I'll have to look into that," the sheriff said.

As they were leaving, Subhir saw Nisha standing in the door to the restaurant, wearing her uniform shirt. She ventured a faint wave at them, but only his mother returned it.

≈†≈

His father spent the four-hour drive in silence, except for a single muttered "Dammit" occasioned by traffic around the Bay Bridge.

"Baseball traffic," his mother said. "You used to check the game schedule to make sure it would not interfere with our drive home."

Shortly after, Subhir said, "You missed the exit for the airport. Or are we flying from San Jose?"

"We're still flying out of SFO," his father said. "The two of us."

"After all this?" Subhir said. "How can you justify leaving me here?"

"This had nothing to do with you," his father said.

"You lied to me," Subhir said. "You weren't driven out. You wanted to leave. Let me make the same choice." He wished that he was in the front seat, where he could speak to a face, instead of just radiating words towards the barren highway unspooling in front of them.

"When I left, it was always meant to be temporary," his father said. "And now it's time to come back. It's time to rebuild."

"Why did you do it?" Subhir said. "You grew up with them. And for them to hate you..."

"You can't understand," his father said. "They didn't understand, not even at Stanford. Things were changing, but they all did the same things in the same way and said everything would turn out fine. And they were so smug about it. Smug enough to call me a traitor, when I did the only sensible thing. I tried to show them... but they drove me away."

"Things did turn out fine," Subhir said. "Aravind seems fine. People are still living. They didn't need you. And even if they did, you didn't try to help them. You just took the money and left."

The car drifted towards the barrier wall and then swerved to the right as Subhir's father overcorrected for the drift. Then they were decelerating and pulling onto the shoulder. When they came to a stop, Subhir's father pressed his head to the steering wheel. The horn rang out an unceasing note.

His mother opened her door and stepped out, then yanked open Subhir's door. "Get out," she said.

His father was still slumped over. A hand grabbed Subhir by the sleeve and pulled him out, onto the grass. His door slammed shut. The car's horn fell silent, but his father wasn't looking up. A truck flew past, screaming sound and air at them, and missing the side of the car by a foot.

After long silent moments, his mother said, in Gujarati, "Can you really hate him for leaving this place?" she said.

"He lied to me," Subhir said. "You both did. America didn't drive him out. He left because he could make more money in India. And before he left, he stole. He took their water and gave it away. He made those people poorer, while he got richer."

His mother shook her head and said, "Do you think it wasn't stealing when your father's father stayed here? A wealthy modern farmer with a master's degree in agronomy? Couldn't India have used him while its people were starving? Couldn't he have saved lives? India, America... they're just places. We all went to where we could find a future. There are plenty willing to stay behind, and sell their lives to a place... to dirt... and they do stay...and they become poor... and those places still prosper or decline as the rains, or the markets, dictate. Because places don't care if you devote your life to them."

Then his mother opened the door and said, "*Challo*, he will be late for moving in."

But his father got off at the next exit, and said, "Use my phone, book another ticket back."

He entered the highway in the other direction: away from Stanford, away from America. Subhir's mother leaned over the seat and glared at her son.

Subhir looked out over the highway. It was just another stretch of the same mile of wasteland that he'd been travelling through for the last four hours. To him, this was America. And Subhir didn't hate it. How could he? It was too hapless to hate.

It was just a place. And he didn't feel anything towards it. Not anymore. He knew that if he said, "Wait," they would happily deposit him here, and he'd sink down into America and serve out his time. He wanted to. Just to make them happy.

He warred with himself for hours over that word. But... how could he repeat his father's mistake? How could anything he learned here ever be relevant to his life? How could even a single moment spent here ever be real? He knew where he belonged, and he wouldn't gamble that away.

Then they were on the plane, and he saw his father, one row up, lean past his mother and slam the window shut. Subhir looked out his own window, and soon those golden hills were receding beneath him and taking the burden of that unspoken word with them. And all that his choice left behind was a tiny residue in his heart as he flew towards a home that he would have to love all the more because of the losses he'd suffered in returning to it.

Lotus

Joyce Chng

Respect the waterway — anon, circa 2100.

It was the smell of burning that woke Cecily up. She got up, wrapped her sleeping robes around her body and padded out. It was still cold, even in this time of morning with the sun shining bright in the sky. She squinted—blue, with white fluffy clouds. It looked like a good day ahead. She adjusted her footing; the boat rocked gently beneath her.

"Good morning," her companion greeted her. He held a plate of burnt fish. She sighed. After all this time, he was still burning fish. And fish and fuel were not easy to obtain. Those little *ikan selar*—she was hit by a pang for home—came from their dwindling supplies. They needed to travel down the Waterways for the barter.

However, the fish was still salvageable, just as things were still salvageable in this day and age. She nibbled at them, grimacing at the bitter taste of carbon in her mouth. The flesh was surprisingly sweet. She used to eat them as a child, deep-fried and accompanying a special coconut rice dish her mother cooked. *On Sundays*, she remembered, *when every family member was home*. But where was home now?

She washed the fish down with water, savoring the taste of it. Sweet. Slightly brackish. Drinkable water was hard to come by too and every boating folk had their private stash, their hoard. So ironic that they were surrounded by water, water, water.

While she was eating, her companion—he called himself Lent, first name Si—went back to repairing Flotsam, their boat. Flotsam was more than just a boat; he was their house, their shelter and their identity. Without Flotsam, a boater was without a name, without a solid tangible background. Yet, Flotsam had suffered from minor ills—his rotors refused to work after a particularly long journey, or his fuel tanks—ethanol, but hard to distill—were empty. He had served them faithfully, loyally.

Si whistled as he fixed the rotors. He was a trained mechanic and he loved working with machines, getting his hands dirty with engine oil and tools. Cecily watched him with a rush of tenderness in her breast. They were all travelers on the Waterways. He came from an old city called New York, she a tiny island by the name of Singapore. These places were now submerged in water—only the skyscrapers served as reminders of their joined pasts. Home, solid terra firma, was gone.

They were all using new names, even though they keenly remembered *who* they were. It was better for the Waterways where names did not matter. *New names, new places, old Earth.* They were still infants when the tsunami and subsequent melting icecaps came and conquered the land. Those who survived the Washing as they called it came out different. Changed. Transformed. And some said "cleansed" and "purified". Those who lived found, salvaged and built boats. There were even large ships, the size of container ships (or were actual container vessels) serving thousands of families crammed together. They traveled the Waterways too—and trade was always good with the large ships.

Once in a while, boaters would congregate, bunched together for protection, for community. Cecily had seen one or two of these villages. Boats, big and small, bobbing with the waves. Cooking fires sending up curls of smoke. They communicated by kayaks and by signal flares. Boater children grew nimble-footed walking on the planks joining the boats. On certain nights, the boaters would gather at one of the larger boats and tell stories about old Earth, when land was still land. Sometimes, they would sing. Sometimes, they would dance. The boating villages were always temporary. After a month or two, the boats would disperse, traveling the Waterways again.

Si cheered. He had fixed the problem. Flotsam was live! She smiled, placed a straw hat on her head and prepared for another journey.

Of course, there were still patches of land here and there. They were occupied, fought over and occupied again. Many still preferred to live on the boats. Much safer, less cut-throat. The landers were vicious and territorial. Much of old Earth's history was filled with lander violence. The landers were so jealous of their land that they even forbade contact with any boater. Ironically, some of the small lander communities still depended on the boaters for essential items like food and clean water.

Flotsam moved forward, Si at the wheel now. Cecily made an offering to Maju, the Goddess of the sea, and then stood beside her companion. It would be a long day.

❦

"Land ho!" What a misnomer! — A common boaters' saying.

It was not long before they sighted the familiar jagged outline of former skyscrapers. Si was suddenly quiet. They seemed to have traveled back to his old home. As Flotsam approached the place where an impressive Statue once stood, he turned sharply to Cecily and said, "Let's make it a short visit. There are many better places to go to."

Cecily wondered about his abrupt change in mood. And "places". What an odd word to use. But she kept her peace and took over the wheel, watching the former buildings, now frameworks of steel and concrete, come closer. It was a sober yet beautiful sight. There were still people occupying the more stable buildings. They welcomed the arrival of the boaters, because they brought much needed barter and gossip.

A hush fell upon both of them as Flotsam slid along former roads, his rotors chopping noisily. The sounds echoed around them, like a steel canyon. Flights of birds, disturbed by Flotsam's noisy presence, took flight, their squawks echoing. Cecily could see nets, very fine nets, erected across certain areas, no doubt to net unsuspecting birds. She'd had fried sparrow before. Goddess knows what kinds of birds were being cooked here.

As it was getting late, they dropped anchor next to a building with a "School" sign swinging crookedly from it. In the slight breeze, the sign made soft rattling sounds. They cooked a small dinner—again with fish and some flatbread made a couple of days earlier—and went back to bed, making love before falling asleep.

❧❦❧

Cecily dreamed. She knew she dreamed because she was back at her grandmother's. There were pictures, photographs and memorabilia hung on the walls. The ancestral altar had lit candles on it. It was the 15th lunar day of the month, for there were fresh lotus blooms—fist-sized pink buds—in the simple porcelain vase.

Her grandmother and her mother were folding paper money into ingots and they were chatting about daily matters. Someone in the family had given birth to a daughter. A relative from so-and-so was getting married. Simple things. Normal things.

Then her grandmother, dressed in a plain light blue kebaya, lifted up her head and beckoned to Cecily who felt as if she was standing in a corner, like some ghost. It was odd, because her grandmother and her mother were now ghosts, people from her past.

"Ci Ci, never forget who you are. Remember your roots, just as the lotus roots dig deep into the soil," her grandmother said, with a gentle smile in her lips and eyes.

Suddenly, inexplicably, as dreams are, Cecily was showered in petals. Pink lotus petals.

❧❦❧

The next morning saw them sailing down boulevards of water. They did some trade with some of the folk living in the buildings. From the tenants (as they called themselves now) came the supplies of water and some vegetables, grown indoors. From Cecily went soft wool shawls, comfortable for chilly mornings. The temperature never seemed to have warmed up ever since. After the trade and some light-hearted gossip, they bade farewell to the tenants and moved on.

Cecily took the wheel again. She felt at ease with the steering of Flotsam. It felt intuitive. As she steered, her mind eased into a semi-meditative state. She went back to the dream and wondered deeply. She was indeed surprised to see her grandmother and her mother in a dream. They had not appeared to her for a while. She pondered on the images.

Afternoon whispered in a brief downpour, forcing them to drop anchor again. This time, it was an abandoned hotel. Si decided to give Flotsam another once-over while Cecily moved lower deck to do some knitting. She was recently given a basketful of homespun yarn by a woman who lived alone on a small sailing boat. She wanted to make good use of the yarn.

Yet something nudged at her. A soft inner voice or some stray thought. She put down her darning needles and wore her poncho (again, from the woman who gave her the yarn).

"I am going to explore the hotel," she announced to an astonished Si who stared at her with worry in his grey eyes.

"There might be unsavory tenants hanging around," he protested as she donned her gumboots. "You know how dangerous this part of the Waterways can be. You know, *ghettos* and the like."

"You are still stuck in old-Earth thinking," Cecily chided him gently. Si could be so sensitive sometimes. She brought along her wooden waster, shaped like a medieval longsword. She had salvaged this a few months ago, straight out from an old store selling military ware.

Si looked at her. "I am just concerned, that's all. You a petite woman and all..."

She laughed. "I have this!" She waved the wooden longsword. "And I know how to use it." *Petite woman?* She chuckled and caught sight of her reflection in one of the cupboards. *Dark hair, dark eyes, swarthy skin bathed by constant sun.* Old-Earth thinking, indeed!

Cecily stepped off the boat and through an open window.

❦

People are so anal-retentive about the concept of wealth. What is wealth? Money? Riches? Resources? — an excerpt from a neo-Marxist chapbook, circa 2040.

She stepped into a dark world.

A dark and dank world, filled with broken beams, broken window shards and broken furniture. Musty curtains still hung from window frames, torn and frayed. Some had been removed, obviously by inventive tenants. She looked around cautiously for any sign of tenant activity. So far, only silence or a silence laced with the sounds of animals roosting somewhere and of water dripping somewhere.

Water. Her ears perked up and she walked on, using her waster to push away debris. She seemed to be in the mezzanine area of the hotel. It was once grand, this hotel. It was now a hollow husk with a skeletal metal frame and fallen beams. She found a baby grand, still intact, the keys yellowed and the cover mildewed. She played a simple tune—it was rusty and the song vibrated around her. It was a familiar tune and she hummed softly to herself. Then she left the baby grand and headed towards the direction of the dripping water.

The hotel had sagged in the middle, much like a failed soufflé. She found her footing gradually precariously and walked, sometimes crawled on all fours, on the ripe carpeting. It was vivid red velvet once.

Just then the world around her plunged. Concaved sharply. She grabbed onto some protruding beams, swung herself onto a ledge—

—and gazed right into a large pool of emerald water.

Sunlight had lanced in from the top half of the building, illuminating the pool of water and a field of... lotus flowers and leaves.

This time she gawked, just gawked, because the lotus flowers were as big as dinner plates and the leaves were huge, circular. The petals glowed, taking her breath away. There was movement in the water, concentric ripples ever widening and criss-crossing; she spied shapes swimming lazily beneath the surface. *Fish.* By the look of it, large carp or koi.

She sat down, overwhelmed. She remembered her dream. She also remembered that all parts of the lotus could be used. And the fish. Fresh food. *Nelumbo nucifera. Cyprinus carpio.* And the pool was *huge*, by the looks of it, ballroom-size and probably larger.

There was wealth in front of her. She reached out, dipped her right hand into the water and scooped out a handful of the cool-warm liquid. Tasted it and gasped with instant pleasure—it was drinkable water!

Wealth.

She flung a worried look upwards. There were no tenants around. The hotel was empty. This pool of water with its wealth was hers.

With some ingenuity, she knew, she could harvest the lotus leaves and roots. The roots could be used for stews, soups and pickles. Even eaten slightly raw, with crisp sweetness. The leaves could be used to wrap rice. The flowers could yield seeds, also delicious roasted or ground into flour. The fish could be caught, salted or fried. So many possibilities, so many...

And the water. *Drinkable*. And when treated, definitely usable for so many things. She felt giddy with joy. *No more barter, no more hoarding. No more worrying.*

⚓

She emerged hurriedly out into the open and clambered back into the boat. Si stood up from the small oven; he was preparing a late lunch. She smelled frying fish and bread. She told herself that they were going to eat much better food now.

"Si!" She called out and he came up to her, his face filled with relief. "You will never believe what I have found…"

"Unsavory tenants?" He teased her, smiling to take the sting out of his words.

"No. Much better."

She brought him through the hotel window, led him down the dark path leading to the pool of lotus flowers and leaves. He stood stock still, eyes open wide, taking in the sight. Drinking it in.

"This is wealth in front of us, Si!" Cecily said excitedly. "And drink the water. It is definitely drinkable water."

He did so and his face lit up with elation, like a child eating candy for the first time. "Unbelievable. Perhaps, this place is being fed by some unknown natural source." He sipped the water again. "Sweet. So sweet."

They both watched the lotus flowers glowing quietly in the sunlight and marveled at the fish flitting through the lotus stems submerged in the water. They held hands, feeling as though they were Adam and Eve, in an abundant Garden of Eden.

Later, they brought in nets and caught two large carp, obviously well-fed by the nutrients in the pool and heavy with much flesh and milt. Cecily collected a handful of lotus roots, covered in rich dark mud. They had a hearty meal that night, of lotus soup and baked fish. They kept the leftovers in the supply box and went to bed with full stomachs.

⚓

They stayed next to the hotel for a few more days, guarding their treasure. Cecily was secretly well pleased that there had been no other claimants to the wealth. They found it. It was *theirs*. Si, ever the mechanic and the scientist, attempted to look for the source of the water but to no avail. It was a mystery and Cecily was glad that it should stay a mystery. *Imagine what would happen if people started finding the source; wars would break out*, she thought darkly.

Cecily harvested some of the large plate-like leaves and wrapped rice with them. The rice came out lightly perfumed and fragrant. Eaten with the fat fish flesh, it was heavenly.

Si created a makeshift mobile of sorts, hung with metal cans, forks and spoons to act as an alarm. If anyone—tenant or otherwise—triggered it, they would know that the pool of lotus flowers had been compromised. Invaded.

It was theirs, and Cecily was determined to keep it that way. It was hard to come by natural sources of food—and such a wealth of it. They both knew sustainable farming, having spent years cultivating their own gardens; they would make sure that the water, the lotuses and the fish remained a permanent fixture.

Cecily had never felt so contented before. Granted that traveling down the Waterways, with its diverse pathways, gave her some satisfaction but this… this wealth was so heartening to the spirit.

She started to nurse thoughts of remaining in the old city, right beside her hotel and its wealth. Not as a tenant per se, but living in their boat and using the wealth. Protecting it from harm's way. She started having fantasies of having children and having them grow up with the lotuses and fish.

It was immensely heartening.

❧❦❧

Live free — an old saying, circa old-Earth period.

She found herself dreaming about her grandmother. Dressed in elegant kebaya with richly embroidered goldfish and a forest-green sarong, she was cooking something in the kitchen. Even in the dream, it smelled gorgeous and the dream-Cecily experienced a strange thing: her mouth watered, at the smell of the cooking. It must be a festival day in the dream because there were plates of festive food on the kitchen counter. And sweetmeats and multi-colored kueh on platters, in mind-boggling variety.

There was laughter coming from the living room and Cecily walked towards the sound. What she saw confused her.

People whom she had met as a traveler of the Waterways were congregating in the living room. Some sat on the sofa. Some lounged on the floor. Everyone was at ease and laughing. There was the woman whom she had traded the yarn with. There were the tenants whom she and Si had met earlier and exchanged gossip, water and vegetables. Some of the people were less familiar but certainly encountered. A family of six—South Indians—chatted animatedly with the yarn woman; she remembered they gave her spices and gave her recipes in exchange for clean water. A single dusky-skinned man with a day's growth of beard massaged another man's back—she had met them at one of the great trading posts. They were big-ship dwellers and were lovers. They taught her how to weave a certain kind of scarf and she gave them two large balls of orange-colored yarn. Even Si was there, chuckling away. He looked much younger, less care-worn. Even handsome.

"Dinner's ready!" Her grandmother's voice startled her and there was soft chatter as all the visitors moved towards the large dining table. There were bowls and containers of food and desserts.

There were also curried fish that looked suspiciously like fat carp and bundles of rice (wrapped in lotus leaf). The scents were intoxicating.

"Come, eat, share." Her grandmother was saying. Cecily watched as the visitors, including Si, approached the table and placed their own contributions on the table. Pakkora. Irish stew. Vegetarian minestrone. Fry bread. Even Si's burnt fish. And everyone ate from the various dishes, their faces happy.

Someone tugged at her arm. She looked around and saw a little Eurasian girl, about four to five. She had Si's eyes and tanned skin. "Mother," the little girl lisped but her words were clear and her eyes bright. "Share."

She woke up then and stared at the roof of the lower deck. Si was snoring softly next to her. She placed a hand on her flat abdomen, realization dawning.

⛚

They managed to harvest more of the lotus roots and bottled the water for further consumption. Their upper deck was laden with food and water. Enough to last a month or even more. Si rigged up the distiller to clean the water and Cecily washed the mud off the roots.

The mobile jangled, breaking the comfortable silence. It was a sharp rude sound shattering a peaceful morning. Si got to his feet and ran to confront the intruder.

A tenant—an old man, hobbled with age, dressed in plain yellow shirt and tattered brown pants—looked up shocked, with eyes wide as if he was caught in the middle of searchlights. His arms held a bundle of lotus flowers and one large fish dangled from his right arm.

"Thief!" Si snarled and leapt over, knocking the man down with a solid punch to the jaw. The lotus flowers fell, scattered. The fish flopped on the unsteady floor, still living, mouth gaping away. It was that fresh. There was a feral look in Si's face, an unwholesome gleam in his eyes. Hunter's eyes. Predator's eyes. "Thief!" And he kicked the old man.

The old man cowered, trembling and terrified. His face was

bruised. His limbs shook.

"Sorry, sir, I was just taking some of the 'looms and 'ish," the old man quavered. He must have been in his late seventies. "It is all out there, free, sir…"

"We found it, old man," Si snapped. Cecily realized how *ugly* he looked like that. What had happened to her quiet and placid companion? "Now, go."

"But sir, I have 'randchildren to feed and my youngest daughter is 'regnant," the old man choked and wept. Cecily's heart clenched.

"It's ours," Si bit out, his eyes dark with rage.

Cecily knelt down, picked the fish up and gave it to the old man. "Here, take it. You need it." The fish was slick and warm, still twitching, in her hands.

The old man looked at her half-fearfully, half-thankfully. Grabbed the fish and scrambled back onto a little run-down kayak. He pedaled away as if he was being chased by a ferocious demon.

"Why did you hit him?" Cecily shot accusing eyes at Si. "He was just an old man."

"He was taking our food," Si answered grimly, color still high in his face.

Mine. Ours. Theirs.

There was a horrible taste in her mouth. It was bile.

It was disgust.

❦

She refused to talk to her companion for the rest of the day, spending more time below deck. She was unable to knit; her thoughts were heavy and sobering. She kept on rewinding the incident in her head: the old man, the old man hit in the face, Si punching him, the lotuses and fish flung onto the floor.

She placed a palm on her belly. She knew that she was pregnant, so they needed the pool of lotus flowers and fish even more. For the nutrients and the protein. For…

The old man quivering with fear, balled up in a fetal position, as Si punched him.

Mine. Ours. Theirs.

There was the taste of bitter bile again in her mouth and she washed it down with clean water.

It was theirs. She wanted to believe that. They found it. However, there were people who needed the water, the lotuses and the fish as well. The pool was theirs too.

Were they indeed living free? Or were they still tied up in old feuds and conflicts driven by need? Should they stake a claim on the lotus pond? Was she turning into a lander?

Her head throbbed. She felt sick to the core.

❦

She spent a sleepless dreamless night and woke up, feeling exhausted. Si was up early and making breakfast. She could smell a sweet fragrance: they had ground the lotus seeds into flour and he was making pancakes from it.

She ate in silence just as Si ate in silence. They were both mulling over the same incident.

"I don't like the way you hit the old man," she began by saying and Si looked at her closely. "He needed the food for his family."

Si swallowed his pancake hard and stared at her. "I just don't like the idea of him taking from the pool."

"The pool is wild. The lotuses and fish are wild. It is a free place, Si." Cecily started to feel angry and knew that her voice was becoming louder. "The water flows free."

"Now you are talking," Si whined, his face sullen. "Just a couple of days ago, you wanted the pool to yourself."

Cecily shut her mouth. The words struck home. *It hurt.* She did want the pool. It felt like hers. It was hers. Or was it?

"I think we should go," she managed to say again, her voice soft. "Take what we need and go. The Waterways will provide for us, I am sure." *And I am pregnant—*

Si's eyes. They were angry, sad and disappointed. "Why? Why should we go? I am tired of being a boater and this place is just perfect."

"If we stay," Cecily said firmly, "there will be disagreements. Quarrels. Fights." She sipped the water. "If we stay, the pool will not be free anyway. It will come with a price. Our price. Their price. We will end up paying."

"Feh," Si spat and stalked out from the upper deck, throwing the half-eaten pancake petulantly onto the floor. It crumbled instantly. Cecily could only stare and feel a dull ache in her heart. Conflict, unpleasant and dangerous, was already starting to creep in like winter chill.

❦

She went to the pool and sat down next to it, beside the musty beams and steel rafters. Sunlight still glowed in the middle. Fish swam peacefully. The lotus flowers tilted their faces towards the sun. It was such an idyllic place. And it could so easily become a place of tension, anger and—

Boaters lived free. It was a code all of them knew, understood and took to heart. With the Washing, the concept of home was removed and the Waterways were created, because Earth was now covered with water. They had taken away the concept of money; barter trade was the lingua franca now. Boaters moved freely. Fluidly. Nobody made rules for them.

Staying next to the hotel, guarding the pool, had begun to engender unspoken rules. If they stayed longer, she was sure that they would start making laws. *When to harvest the lotus plants. How many to harvest? How many fishes to be netted? How many liters of water to be collected?* And penalties would be implemented, if such laws were being transgressed, breached. They would end up behaving no better than the landers. *Perhaps we* are *no better than the landers, because we are all humans*, Cecily pondered, concluding her internal argument with this sad realization.

She buried her face in her hands. She had begun to love this pool and its riches. Yet deep down inside her, she knew that the pool was *free*. The lotus plants were wild and so were the fish. The water was free to everyone who used it. If she stayed, she would put a price on all of them.

The pool was to be shared.

She clambered back up to the boat, only to find Si sitting contemplatively on the upper deck of Flotsam. He had somehow cleared the pancake off the floor.

"Cecily," Si said and his voice was gentle. He came over and held her hands. "I am sorry. I was behaving like a royal jerk."

They hugged each other tightly. When they let go, Si gazed at her. "I have thought it over. We should go. I mean, there are paths in the Waterways less traveled. And I am getting tired of New York anyway." He smiled, trying to lighten the mood. "Never liked the city... Makes me mad all the time."

"Si!" She said. "Oh, Si."

They both made their last trip to the pool and harvested what they needed. They bottled enough water to last until the next Trading Post, netted enough fish to be salted and frozen; and bundled enough lotus plants—flowers, roots and leaves—for a month. Enough for personal consumption and for barter. When they looked back, there were still many lotus plants left, swaying slightly in the breeze. The fish were still plentiful. The water was still sweet to the taste. The pool was wild and free.

Cecily packed everything in the supply box while Si lifted anchor and started the engines. Flotsam sputtered into life once more, sounding as if he was grumbling about the previous inertia.

With not a backward glance, they sailed away and journeyed down the Waterways once more.

❦

Glossary

Ikan selar—Horse mackerel, a fish popular in Malaysia and Singapore.

Kebaya—A traditional blouse worn by women in Indonesia, Malaysia, Brunei and Singapore.

Kueh—Bite-sized sweetmeats, including cakes, pastries and cookies. They are often made with coconut cream. Some of them are savory.

Maju—Also known as Mazu or Matsu, a benevolent Goddess revered in Taiwan, Fujian, Guangdong and Vietnam. Protectress of the sea and sea-farers.

Paper money—Incense or ceremonial paper made for burning rituals. The ingots are made from them, symbolizing wealth, in the afterworld.

Sarong—A tube or wrap of cloth worn by both men and women. It is often covered with intricate designs and vivid colors.

15th lunar day—Full moon.

Dark Continents

Lavie Tidhar

1.

"I contend that we are the first race in the world and that the more of the world we inhabit the better it is for the human race."—Cecil Rhodes

2.

We began to edit, but we were sloppy at first.

3.

Cecil Rhodes marches into the Ndebele stronghold in the Matobo Hills, unarmed, of which it was written:

> *Low-lying clouds rest on the Matobo Hills*
> *precariously balanced*
> *in the stillborn morning air*
> *like the snores of sleeping elephants*

It is 1897 by your count, and the Ndebele people are at war with the British. "Lay down your weapons," he says. He is an imposing figure, a fatherly white man. Standing against him the chiefs are black against night. In the distance the elephants call to each other. A bird cries overhead.

The Ndebele are persuaded to lay down their arms, ending the Second Matabele War.

We began to edit, but we were sloppy at first.

4.

Cecil Rhodes marches into the Ndebele stronghold, unarmed.

His whiteness is startling against the night. His moustache is a bold stroke of black on a white canvas. "Lay down your weapons," he says.

There is a disconcerting silence.

"Hello?" Cecil Rhodes says, into the night. "Hello?"

There are no Ndebele here. What is that moving in the darkness? Rhodes squints into the night. "What—?" he begins to say.

The giant bugs rise out of the ground. The product of a parallel evolution, from a world which never knew a human. A world so close you could touch the membrane of its wall, a world so far you would never see it. The bugs are eight feet in length, armoured and intelligent.

They carry spears which fire a gooey green poison. They swarm over Rhodes. They grab him and hold him captive. He screams. The leader of the bugs approaches the captive. "Go back to your people," he says, in a clear, unaccented English. "And tell them to surrender."

5.

The first Human-Bug War lasted between 1897 until the death of Queen Victoria in 1901.

6.

The bugs evolved in a parallel space. There are many spaces. Only we see them. We are artists, not barbarians. We mix. We remix. We edit.

The bugs invaded southwards, at first. Down through Rhodesia, down to South Africa, crashing the Boers in the Orange Free State and making it all the way to Cape Town without being seriously challenged. They were hungry for resources—we made sure of that. They took hold of the ships in the harbour and turned their compound eyes to Europe.

Their fleet sailed towards England in the winter of 1898.

7.

They had crossed the ocean and sailed all the way up the Thames before they were stopped, and the Thames from Greenwich to London Bridge was filled with the floating corpses of giant bugs.

8.

I remember the fires. The spring of 1899. We had fished them out of the river and piled them in huge heaps by the wharf-side and set them aflame. Their carapace burned drily, they crisped as they burned, translucent wings flew in the air like burning kites. The smell was not unpleasant: they smelled of aniseed.

9.

We were the invaders but also the invaded; we saw through multiple eyes.

We began to remix but we were sloppy at first.

10.

A second wave of bugs emerged from the trans-dimensional gate at the Matobo Hills. The Ndebele, wisely, stayed out of their way. The bugs swarmed South and East, to Mozambique. They overwhelmed the colonial Portuguese forces and gained their ships. They set sail for Europe again.

11.

I once followed the contours of the Thames at low tide. This was in 2011. I had a metal detector. We were looking for coins. We were under Waterloo Bridge when it began to beep. I knelt in the wet sand and dug my fingers into the ground. The river smelled of sewage. My fingers found something cold and hard and I plucked it out and cleaned the sand off it and turned it in my hand, over and over.

"What is it?" she said. I showed her. She took it from me and examined it thoughtfully.

It was a coin. On one side of the coin was the year. 1901. On the other was the profile of the Queen.

But it wasn't human.

It was the face of a bug, an alien thing. What expression it had I could not tell. "What is it?'—it was my turn to ask.

"It's an anomaly," she said.

"A what?"

"It's a Fortean object," she said. "Something that should not exist."

I looked at her. She was very beautiful with the dying sun in her hair. Overhead seagulls cried. "It fell," she said. "Through a time-slip. It's from another when."

"Throw it back in the river," I said, and when she did nothing I shouted, "Throw it back!" and I was afraid, even if I didn't know why. She slipped it into her jeans pocket. "Let's go back," she said. Later, I looked for it in her pocket, but I never saw the coin again.

12.

We were careful but slippages happen. Rather than go forward we went back, instead.

Lake Nyasa, 1859. David Livingstone was resting in the sands of Chembe Village, on the southern shore of the lake, when pain shot up his left arm. I was a boy, then. I had come to stare at the white man when he began to breathe heavily. His face was twisted with pain. He spoke, though I did not understand his words. I had seen such an illness before. I knew that he was dying.

I pointed at the stars, then pointed at the near distance, to Thumbi Island. An unearthly glow rose behind the trees on the island. I saw the white man's eyes follow the direction of my finger but whether he saw or understood the nature of the glow I did not know. There was no time to waste. I helped him up and into the canoe. The moon was up, lighting the bay. It was why we were not fishing that night. I rowed us to the island, worrying all the while that the white man would die, and that I would be blamed. But he did not die and I brought him to the island and there they took him and gave him a new heart, as I knew they would.

13.
It had been a trivial thing to arrange.

14.
In 1861 Livingstone released the boy Chuma from slavers.
"We must fight slavery in all its forms," Livingstone said.
"I understand," Chuma said.

15.
Chuma's army resembled that of Hong Xiuquan, the Heavenly King, who had raised a million men to fight an empire in the Taiping Rebellion. They followed him and his white man across the continent: Yao at first, then Chewas and Ndebele and Shona and Zulus, a rising tide of dark loam becoming the sea. The doctor had been touched by the divine, it was said. His heart glowed in his chest at night, a dull red that penetrated through his pale skin. He was always behind Chuma, Chuma the Brave, Chuma the Fearless. Chuma the divine.

In another timeline he was Livingstone's faithful servant. In this one he was a messiah reborn, a new Hong Xiuquan for another, older continent. He called and they followed, slaves and freedmen, from all across the continent. They had stormed the Swahili nations of the coast and subdued them, and took Zanzibar almost without a fight. From Zanzibar they could go anywhere. Chuma sent diplomats across the old trade networks the Europeans had damaged like the silk of a spider's web. Damaged but not destroyed. He reached out to India. And he set sail, at last, with his captured ships, to the New World, his faithful doctor by his side.

16.
Richmond, Virginia, burned to the ground.

17.
As the Civil War erupted the Southern states were hemmed in by the North on one side and Chuma's forces coming in from the sea. Southern refugees escaped to the North as Chuma's forces landed and former slaves joined the revolt. By 1865 the North and South signed a ceasefire, and Chuma's Confederacy came officially into being.

18.

Or remix, re-edit, fast forward, backtrack.

The way it almost was:

May First, 1873.

In one time-line a retired President Chuma visits David Livingstone's hospital room in New Nyasa, in what used to be called Richmond, Virginia. He sits by his old friend's bed, waiting for the end.

Not in this one:

Ilala. Southeast of Lake Bangweulu. May 1st, 1873. The doctor is lying on the bed, dying. They can both sense it, Susi and Chuma, who had been with the doctor for years. Malaria and internal bleeding is leeching the life out of him. With the last of his power he kneels in prayer by the bed, and it is in that position that they find him.

They take him outside and lay him down gently on the ground. They strip him of his clothes. His body is old and scarred from travel. Susi holds the knife. He cuts the doctor's corpse open as Chuma reaches inside, fingers stained with blood, and carefully removes the doctor's heart that we gave him.

In your history, this is how it had happened.

They buried the heart under a nearby Mvula tree. The body they preserved with herbs. Susi and Chuma carried the body the thousand miles back to the coast, and from there, by ship, to Britain, where he lies to this day, missing his heart, in Westminster Abbey.

We continued to edit. We were getting better.

19.

I remember visiting the graves of the Scottish missionaries near Chembe Village—the place Livingstone had called Cape Maclear, after his friend, the royal astronomer in Cape Town. You were with me, we had just met, it was the summer of 1995 and thunder clouds gathered over the lake in the distance. It began to rain as we looked at the old weathered headstones. Scottish missionaries in Africa, like the punch line to an old joke. Like malaria. The lake had killed them; for seven years they struggled to survive on the Lake of Stars before they abandoned their mission, retreated to Bandawe and then to Khondowe, the lake and the mosquitoes pursuing them, relentlessly.

We ran back through the hot rain. Lightning flashed. In our bamboo hut on the beach we huddled together for warmth. Your skin shone with the lake's tears. "What if—?" you said. The thunder rolled over the lake, magnified like cannon. "What if Livingstone never found the lake?" you said. "What if Stanley never pursued him to Ujiji, never uttered those words, Dr Livingstone, I presume?"

We were in the early stages of love. What if we had never met, there on Lake Malawi, my people and her people couldn't have been any more different.

20.
Three years later, in Ujiji, I played Bao with the descendants of Swahili slave traders and lost. We visited the baobab tree under which they stood, those two white men, Livingstone and Stanley, Stanlivingstone merged into one in our memories. "Dr Livingstone, I presume?" I said, and you smiled, tolerating me. We were living on the hill above Kigoma, Dian Fossey was a neighbour. When we went down into the town we saw nothing but refugees, amputees from Zaire, begging for a change we couldn't offer.

"Forget Livingstone," I said. "What if my people had come to Africa?"

21.
"The goal of our present endeavours must not be the 'Holy Land' but a land of our own. We need nothing but a large piece of land for our poor brothers; a piece of land which shall remain our property from which no foreign master can expel us."—Leo Pinsker, *Auto-Emancipation.* 1882

22.
In 1904 the Zionist Congress sent a three-man expedition to British East Africa, to the Uasin Gishu Plateau. They comprised a British explorer, a Swiss engineer and a Russian Jew. They spent two months exploring the plateau. In your primary reality they went lost, were attacked by hostile tribes, returned at last to Europe and delivered their verdict. Jewish settlement in Africa was voted down overwhelmingly by the Congress.

We edit. We shift and change the parameters.

23.
"[The proposal to settle Jews in East Africa] is monstrous, extravagant, and unconstitutional, and opposed not only to the best interests of Christendom but of civilization at large."—E. Haviland Burke, M.P., parliamentary debate, 1904

24.
If you drive down Lake Victoria today you will see a strip of hotels rising into the sky, at the place called Neve Nitzachon, the Spring of

Victory, and a sign for the weary traveller that here, too, is a shopping mall and a rest stop, with a Mashbir department store and a McDavid branch and even an Egged bus station. The blue-white-and-black flags wave above the buildings, especially on our Independence Day, celebrated every year on the Fifth of Iyar in the Jewish calendar. It was not until 1965—in your calendar—that we were made free from the British, like our neighbours on either side, Uganda and Kenya, with whom we are periodically at war. Our independence was inevitable. We had moved en masse to this land, empty but for its people, granted to us by the power of the British empire and its King and parliament. We fled from German hostility and Russian pogroms, British contempt and the French's frank dislike, fled across land and sea to this land-locked country in the sun.

Palestine forgot us. The British gave us the plateau but it was not enough for us. Our people bought guns across the seas and the ships smuggled them to Mombasa. From there on foot or by train we carried them inland, training in secret in the valleys.

Our land suffices for our needs. We are not without problems, but what country ever is? Our struggle for independence merged with that of the Mau Mau. Jomo Kenyatta and David Ben Gurion met in secret on the shores of the lake and signed an agreement of cooperation. Our own problem materialized in the form of the native tribes. Now they are kept behind the separation fence that our army guards, but still their terrorists attack us in our cities. Only last week a man from the Nandi tribe, passing for one of our own Ethiopian Jews and dressed as a Hasidic man in the thick black coats so strange here in this hot land, boarded a local bus and proceeded to blow himself up. For such cowardly atrocities we have no choice but to go into their enclaves, behind the fence, to search their houses door to door and line up their elders for inspection even as their youths throw stones at our soldiers. Our prisons overflow with their terrorists and still they would not give up this ridiculous demand for "their" land. We have tried to be reasonable, really we have.

Drive down Lake Victoria today and you will see a peaceful and prosperous land. Our farmers grow pineapples and bananas and pawpaw, our military's planes pass overhead, the jets reflected in the calm surface of the water, filling our hearts with pride. Across in Uganda we must still contend with Idi Amin's despotic regime but we are secure in our homeland. We pull into the hotel and order a McDavid kosher Hot-David frankfurter and eat it in the comfort of our air-conditioned car.

25.
When I was ten or eleven we went to Haifa, the nearby city by the sea. There, on the pedestrian street in the lower Hadar, there used to be a McDavid restaurant. They are all gone now, having been edged out by competition from American fast food chains, though I recently read in the paper that they are set to return. I remember that day for some reason, though the colours have been washed clean in memory's uncertain rains. My father was driving the kibbutz's car. It was humid, Haifa was a strange exotic place for us, filled with city folks and their city ways. The smell of exhaust fumes and women's perfumes such as we did not have on the kibbutz mingled with the smells of food, of fresh jam-filled donuts coated with sugar powder, and fresh bagels with sesame seeds, and falafel frying in hot, industrial oil.

I do not remember what my father's business in town was, but that, when it was concluded, he took me, holding my hand in his, into McDavid. It really did exist, you know, as strange as that sounds. My father bought me the Hot-David frankfurter. It came with pickles and mustard, yellow and green like the fields of the kibbutz. It was the only time I think I ever ate at McDavid.

26.
Enough, enough. Who is this interloper interjecting into our narrative, our narratives? We edit, we mix and remix. Jewish Uganda, with its suicide bombers and military occupation, never happened, but it didn't have to happen, either. All is possible in the seas of chance and probability. We cut and paste and remix and reboot:

27.
Tel Aviv, 2011. Here on the banks of Lake Victoria couples stroll arm in arm on the beach, boys play beach ping pong, girls lie in the sun or sip cool drinks at the waterside bars. Kwasa-kwasa music from the Congo mixes with South African reggae and Malawian pop. Children the colour of olives run and laugh in the surf. Our people have come here unwillingly, persuaded by the Zionist Congress and Herzl's mad dream of a homeland, of statehood. A backwater British colony, it were but us and the local tribes.

But we are Jews, we are used to living on sufferance. At first there was conflict but cooler heads prevailed. We were together the subjects of the British, united in a shared history of suffering. Their boys married into our tribes, their girls took our young men to their families. We did not fight the British. We bided our time until Independence, in the 1960s. Together we formed a country for ourselves, we built plantations, planted fields, fished, returned to the way of our forefathers. Not for us the factories and shining cities of another present. We built no tall houses, no eight-lane roads or mega-malls. We are a backwater, a tributary of history, a hidden cove. We take in history's forgotten refugees.

Come to Tel Aviv and the music welcomes you, the mix and remix of a thousand tunes and styles from across the continent. The drummers gather at dusk on Mungo Park Beach and the sound of their drums unites, suddenly and clearly, and for a moment, standing there on the shore of the lake with the sun setting in the distance, that sound is like the single vast beat of a great, unknowable heart.

A Heap of Broken Images

Sunny Moraine

"Odette nodded at my notebook, where I was writing as she spoke. 'Do the people in America really want to read this? People tell me to write these things down, but it's written inside of me. I almost hope for the day when I can forget.'"
— Philip Gourevitch, *We Wish to Inform You That Tomorrow We Will Be Killed With Our Families*

"Are you going to take a picture?"

I ask it because it seems like a sensible question. The shorter of the two humans has brought his camera with him, and since we entered the houses of the dead he has held it in his hands and a little close to his chest, as though he's afraid that someone might snatch it away from him, or that he might drop it and it might shatter.

I ask it because I am their guide and it is my task to show them what they ask to see, and I am wondering, now, if they really wish to see this.

The shorter man—I have been told that his name is *Jacob* but the syllables feel strange in my mouth and I have to struggle with them a little—looks at me as though he is only just now seeing me. He nods once. He lifts the camera to his face and I hear the soft *whirr* of its processor. And then, as though he performed the act entirely for my benefit, he shows me the image he has captured.

Here: It's not well framed. He clearly gave little thought for the arrangement of it. Half a skull takes up the lower left-hand corner, pushed most of the way under a desk. The fractured curve of a broken spine extends into the middle-foreground, disappearing into a fold of old blue cloth from which ribs protrude. On the right, a severed arm stretches into the frame as if reaching for the skull and the spine. It clearly isn't from the same corpse. It's much too small. Draped and tangled over everything, heavy flowers in brilliant red and pink, green vines, and dried skin of no color whatsoever.

There are other bodies. Look closer and you will see that the floor is nothing but bodies. That you can't see the floor at all. That you cannot, in fact, be absolutely sure that the floor is even there. If you walk into this room, you'll walk on the dead. So we don't invite them to walk inside, and without invitation they never do. We all stand in the doorway and I deliver the information I have to share about this place, and then there is silence.

I feel their discomfort. I was raised in the *jodenja klimenji*—the Way of Welcoming. It is our highest calling to give comfort to a guest, to put them at ease. But it is also our highest calling to give them whatever they ask for, within reason. And if they ask to come here, I cannot do anything for what I know they must feel. I cannot unmurder the murdered. I cannot change who did the murdering. And I cannot tell them how they should feel, a generation after the fact. There are things I wish I could say, things I *would* say if everything were different, but I also cannot change who I am. So we stand in silence, and the dead are also silent, and I wait for one of the living to speak.

The first sun is low and tosses our shadows out in a long diagonal across the room. The second sun is rising behind us. The light is shifting and strange, and it makes it difficult to be sure just how big the room is. How much death it can hold.

The taller one—I think his name is *Aaron*—points to a stack of crates in one corner next to a row of bookshelves. Another corpse is slumped against it, scraps of dried paper skin, the head gone. "Shairoven, what are those?"

"Goods," I say. "Clothes, probably. Foodstuffs. They thought that they could buy their lives from their attackers. You must understand that such things are not strange to us; in our culture there is an idea of a blood price. Life has monetary value."

"Why didn't the colonists take them?"

I shrug—it is a very human gesture but I can't help it. Five full cycles as a *klimenjiani*—what I have heard them call a *tour guide*—and I have adopted many human habits. "There are many things about what was done in those months that we do not understand."

What I do not say is that I suspect that the killing distracted them. It must have been very distracting. It must have been very tiring, also. It's said that all throughout the time of killing, the rank and file were urged on by overseers of death with bullhorns and amplifiers. They were given rhythms by which to work, to make it easier for their bodies to move without the burden of thought.

I have tried to understand this. When I run I think of the beating of my own heart. But then I think of blood and falling bodies and my imagination fails me. How can they be the same?

How could they have done it? Were they blind?

The flowers nod in the breeze that comes in through the open windows. It should not be as lovely as it is—all those long bones. The large, elongated skulls. The vines and the blossoms. Graceful and clean. Even the faded blood on the walls looks like an abstract mural in dark swoops and swirls. I have heard the humans say that our people are beautiful. I wonder if that is a truth that is not always true.

"We should go," I say gently. At my sides, my hands are clenched into fists. I hope they will not see. It would shame me. "You will be late for supper at the hotel."

≈†≈

Much like the killing itself, it remains a puzzle to us, that the humans come to Lejshethra for this. Why they come. Why they want to look. These are not their dead. They pay no respects, they make no offerings. They just stare with their tiny eyes, and I can never say for sure what they're thinking.

They have told us that there are entire pathways of schooling back on Earth that deal with nothing but the killing, that try to pull it apart like a corpse and understand how it happened, why so much murderous hate could arise so suddenly in the human colonists. I have heard that they believe that it was not sudden. That it built over years, that there was tension where my people could perceive none. Two cycles ago when I first heard of this I took it to my body-sire and told her of it, and I think I was lucky to escape the back of her hand.

"Ignore such things, Shairoven," she said to me. She turned back to the *tijath* she was cutting for the meal of second sun. "The humans fixate on what's past, even after blood-price is paid. Mind your manners and ignore their habits. They can't help what they are."

My body-sire's right arm is missing. Her back is a mass of crisscrossing scars. We were told—not by her, for she never speaks of those months—that she survived the massacre of her district by hiding herself under the corpses of her neighbors. There were many who survived that way, but we don't speak much of the ones with visible scars. The blatantly accusing nature of the evidence they carry with them is a form of rudeness that can't be erased or undone.

My body-sire makes her place secure through her denial.

I have never discovered how to tell her that this makes me so *sad-angry-trapped* all at once, that it makes me feel as though I am buried under a pile of corpses and I am being cut with long knives and I do not understand why. We have no word in our language for such an impolite emotion.

≈†≈

I arrive at the hotel after the meal of first sun to collect the humans. They have told me that today they wish to travel to the city center to see the memorial that the human government erected to the dead of the killings—or to the killings themselves, but the difference has never been adequately explained to me, and I am afraid to ask. I am afraid that my people would see it as overtly accusatory, and I am afraid of what the humans might say.

In the groundcar on the way from my home to the hotel, I think about all the questions I would like to ask and never will. *Why do you remember? What do you think? Do you feel guilty? Do you think that you should? Do you hate us now? Will you hurt us again?*

Their leaders said, of course, that they did not hate us and that the killings will never be repeated. But I am not sure I find this convincing. I am full of doubt both impolite and inconvenient, and it pulls at me like a hungry child. Many hungry children. There were camps full of them after the killings, orphans all with no mate-sire or body-sire and often missing siblings. I have seen images, and in those images what stands out most are their enormous eyes. All the confusion of an entire people could be held inside such eyes. *Why?* This is what they would ask the humans I am going to see. In this we are alike.

I would also like to ask whether the humans live with ghosts as we do. I wonder whether it is forbidden for them to acknowledge or speak to the ghosts. I wonder whether they can put the ghosts here aside and leave them behind. In the end most of them return home to Earth; very few humans live here now. They thinned our numbers, but in the end they were the ones who ran.

In the groundcar, the humans and I ride in silence. My head is still buzzing with questions. My mouth is sealed by my raising.

Every time, this is a little more difficult.

"How long have you been a guide?" Jacob asks me eventually, and I am relieved because this is a question that I can answer without offense. I tell him five cycles, and he smiles and pats the knee of his companion.

"We're lucky to get someone so experienced."

I incline my head at the compliment.

"Aaron and I have been studying the massacre since college," Jacob says after another few moments of silence. "We're both writers— did we tell you that? We're doing a series on what it's like for the children of the colonists now, so this is excellent material."

I nod again. "I am glad to be able to help," I say, and inside the eyes of the hungry children are growing and growing and for an instant I am afraid they will swallow me. I am glad that the groundcar is on automatic because I could not see to direct it now. Everything is questions, beating against the inside of me, smothering me like a mound of corpses, and really all the questions are a single question: *Why?*

Why did you kill us? Why do you come here now? Why did you build the monument, why are you writing about it, why are you sitting here and smiling at me like that when my body-sire has lost her arm and my life is all of the ghosts I will never welcome, and instead I welcome you?

We keep the houses of the dead but we would never go there if it weren't for you and every time I am there I feel that I might fall apart into hacked-up pieces and lie there among the dead because I cannot make any of these other pieces fit.

I smile at them, at these writer humans who walk oblivious among the ghosts. It is said among my people that the *jodenja klimenji* is the most demanding of all the disciplines, and the most pure, because it means the utter denial of self. And every moment of it I wonder if I am really strong enough.

And every moment of it I wonder if it is right for me to be so.

❦

The memorial itself is a single black spike one hundred feet high. It impales the sky. Every time I come here, I think, *It looks so angry.* And I am never sure where the anger comes from or where it is going. Perhaps it is my anger that I am feeling. Inside the spike, it is apart from me and safe to face. It stabs and stabs blindly, forever.

The spike is bounded by a circular plaza dotted with stone benches. There are no trees. We three are the only ones there. We stay for a few minutes, and then we return to the hotel in silence.

❦

There is a river that alternately circles around and cuts through our city. Its banks are part of what make this region so excellent for farming, and I understand why this was the initial locus for the human colonization. The river is the center of many things. After second sun, after I have returned to my home and bathed and oiled my skin, I dress in the lighter clothing of repose and walk down the broad path that leads from my street to the river where it touches the edge of my home district. The bank is paved here, lined with flowerbeds and hanging colored lanterns.

It is lovely. It is all that I remember seeing here, but I have been told by humans and by human texts that the paving and the flowerbeds and the lanterns are all recent additions. Before, this was all rich red soil and black rocks, like other points along the river's bank, and then at the time of the killings it was paved with bodies as people tried to flee across it and were cut down or trampled or carried away and drowned.

There was a major sanitation problem in the weeks after the

greatest bloom of killing, which added to the already rising tide of human refugees flooding back to Earth ahead of their fear and their shame. The water was choked with bloated corpses and undrinkable. This is what I have been told, by humans and by those of my own people to whom I know I should not listen. But though they tell the same story, the humans and a few of my people, the telling is so different that I cannot think of it as the same.

It is the river Laijan, which means purveyor of life. I stand at the edge of the paved bank and I look into its depths. In the twilight the water looks like black blood, calm and placid and flowing without a heart to pump it.

Tomorrow is the last day that the humans will be here, and before I said goodbye to them today they asked me for a favor. It is not the first time I have been asked for what they want. But I have always said no, *impossible, it cannot be done, no one will agree to it.*

And I have been lying.

And today I said that I would try.

I do not know if this is dishonor or a fulfilling of my raising. I am pulled between what I have been taught and what I have been taught; again I think I could fall to pieces, and then I think that maybe I have always been in pieces, broken apart from myself, and so there is no more damage to be done.

I look into the flowing black water and I think of empty eyes and outstretched hands reaching up from those depths and beckoning me. There were many bodies that were swept away by the river in the growing-season flood that year and many were never found. They are all still there in the life of the river. There are other people strolling, idling along the bank in the cool of the evening; I could call, *Don't you see them? Don't you hear? How can we deny our own spilled blood, whatever price has been paid?*

My mouth is full of ghosts. I place my hand against it and hold them in until they are silent again, and the ones in the water fall silent as well.

I am in pieces but I am alive. Tell me how this is a reasonable thing.

❧

Before first sun I am awake and back in the streets, leaving my body-sire and my two siblings sleeping at home. They do not know what I intend; if they did they would try to stop me, for this is not shame of any accidental kind but shame that is sought for, and that is the most profound shame of all.

The streets are still mostly deserted but I keep to the shadows, moving as quietly as I can. I live in one of the more affluent districts and I am passing into places that are clearly less so, with waste uncollected by the entranceways and roofs in need of repair. And on, further, into a place of real destitution, where the cracked and dirty street is dotted here and there with people who have no roof at all but sleep surrounded by whatever they can carry with their mangled limbs—in whatever sleep their rage allows them.

This is the district of the self-exiled. They Who Will Not Release Their Grasp. I was taught to pity them and fear them, for they carry the specter of what was done to us in their minds and bodies like a plague and they will not give themselves over to denial as my body-sire has done. They stand and they insist that we look on them, and the pain is too great, and we fear what the humans would do or say, despite the fact that the humans themselves seem to want to see such things.

Sometimes I think our ways have become confused, like tangled limbs that no longer fit the body to which they were attached.

Three cycles ago I came here for the first time because of a request like the one that sends me here now. I turned away then, at the cusp of fulfilling what was asked of me. I could not bear it. I am not sure what has made me decide to try again, but I know that all night I tried to resist it and it would not be held back.

Down a narrow, stinking alley I find the door I am looking for. I lift my head at the same moment that I raise my hand to press the call-bell and I see the sky lightening for first sun, pale pink. I think of blood just under thin skin, warm and alive.

The door opens and the sky seems to fall away again.

She is missing an arm like my body-sire is, but there the resemblance of their scars ends: her face is practically half gone, twisted with scar tissue, hairless and purple and swollen. One of her eyes is not there at all. The scars wind down her long neck and vanish under her worn tunic but I know they continue. She is stooped with pain that never goes away. Her ghosts are vengeful and they tear at everything that comes near, including her.

"Shairoven," she says. She sounds unsurprised to see me. I incline my head; I am not sure how much respect is due to her, and again my heart says one thing while my raising says another. She is lower than a beggar, lower than a criminal, because she has committed the unforgivable sin of inhospitality to those who have, in the end, observed the proper rites and dues, and paid the owed blood price.

And what I cannot tell anyone, not even her, is that my heart tells me that she is braver than anyone I have ever met.

"Jaishevkin," I say. With clear effort, she stands aside from the door and invites me in.

Inside is dim and cramped and smelling strongly of old rotting grass. I can barely see the chair she motions me into. Thin light seeps in through the threadbare curtains that cover her single window. She sinks down onto the cot that serves as her bed and leans over her knees. Whenever she moves I am freshly reminded of how thin she is, as though she is already one of the dried corpses in the houses of the dead, animated by the sheer magnitude of her indignation. Whereas they remain quietly and unobtrusively dead, as is right.

"You have come to ask me to meet them," she says. I am not astonished that she should guess this; there is really no other reason for me to be here. So I nod.

"Before, you ran away." She has only one remaining eye but it is like a knife, cutting away pieces of me and letting them fall to the floor. I cannot move under its edge. "Every time you run away. Will you run now?"

I am not sure how to answer that. The directness, the bluntness—close to brutality. No delicacy in her approach. It has been cut and burned out of her.

"I don't wish to run," I say finally. My hands are turning over and over each other in my lap, as though I am washing them.

"You all run," she says. At last she looks away from me, turning her horribly scarred face to that thin light. "They run too, even if they think they do not. They study and they write and they talk, and they congratulate themselves on their bravery, but they are still running. And they are putting it all into little boxes with clear tops, so they can look at it without feeling any pain or dirtying their hands. They don't *feel*."

She turns back to me and her single eye is blazing. "None of you feel. You have forgotten how. We remember. And we frighten you."

I did not come here for this. I came here to ask her to accompany me back to the hotel, and to offer her payment for her time and her effort. Now I am not sure why I am here at all. I am sitting under a knife; I am drowning in a river of old blood; I am buried under the pieces of myself and I cannot breathe, and I was never even part of this, does she understand that? I bear no scars. *When it happened I was not even born.*

I open my mouth to say *I am sorry that I disturbed you. If you will not come with me I will go now.* And then I think *I am running again,* and *I don't wish to,* and what comes out of my mouth instead is, "Why?"

Jaishevkin looks at me for a long time. I cannot read her face under the scars and this is only part of why I have never felt easy around her.

But her eye is still a heated knife and I am still trapped under its edge.

And, strangely, part of me is content to be so.

"They have very many reasons, don't they?" she says at last. The words are accusing but all the bile has gone out of her voice and now she sounds only sad and very, very tired. I think that I have never been as tired as that. But I am beginning to feel how one becomes so. "They say that it was land restrictions. They say that talks broke down. They say that it was many accumulated *cultural misunderstandings*." And there again is the bile, the bite, just for a moment and gone again, like something emerging briefly from black water before sinking back out of sight. "I have heard them say that it was the delayed mental strain of encountering a new sentient species. I have heard them say that it was simple fear, that they thought that we would attack them and so they struck at us first. I have heard every reason, Shairoven. I have heard them all."

"And which do you believe?" My voice is very soft. Suddenly I feel breathless. I am afraid. I am on the edge of a great unknown expanse. I am spreading my arms because I am just mad enough to think that I might fly.

"I believe all of them," she says. "Or I believe that *they* believe them. And now I think you will ask me what I really believe."

Jaishevkin gets slowly to her feet and makes her way over to the little window, pushing aside the ragged curtains with her remaining hand. In the brightening light of first sun the scars on her face are sharper, darker, but their jagged lines are also smoothed out into something almost beautiful.

I wait. I don't ask.

"I don't know why," she says softly. "I have thought and read and argued and I do not know. There are all the reasons. And then there is what happened. And in between..." She falls silent.

And I am silent. I am trying to understand this. I have taken this—the Not Knowing—for granted, because while I have asked the question I have never seriously pursued an answer. It has never until now occurred to me that perhaps there is no answer, no one answer, that any one person can find.

And now I am wondering about the questions. About the right ones.

"Will it happen again?"

Again, she does not answer at once. Her fingers move across the curtains, dancing in a vague kind of pattern—it seems strangely appropriate that the hand they left her would be entirely unmarked, graceful, lovely.

"That all depends," she says at last, "on how we remember."

I want to ask more, because now I am full of new questions. How we remember? How should we remember? In the human way? In our way? In the houses of the dead or in their studies and writing? In the ghosts that float in the river Laijan and dance on their banks? In the flesh of my body-sire? In that black spike stabbing always up into the sky? In the way we make it so heavy and so big with our careful silence and our smiles and bows? In the way that I fear it might crush us one day, once it is too big and too angry at being ignored?

How do we remember?

But Jaishevkin is already shaking her head. "No more questions." She turns away from the window and she is blanketed in shadows. "I will not meet with your humans."

Everything in me sinks in disappointment. I am confused, I am breathless with fear, and I feel as though everything is slipping away from me and whirling into a mess of color and time, but I had hoped to at least be able to fulfill the *jodenja klimenji* and bring my guests what they want. I was holding to the idea of it like the one solid thing I can see. "I understand, Jaishevkin," I say. "I will—"

"You should meet them instead."

I stare at her. I do not understand this at all. Have I not already met with them? Have I not been meeting with them every day for over a week? Have we not spoken, do they not know my name and the pertinent details of my personal history, have I not given them all the information they require?

"You should meet with them," Jaishevkin says again. "You should meet them as you are. You should let yourself *feel*."

Our farewell is mostly silent. I am so confused as I make my way back through the dirty streets that I barely see them at all and more than once I nearly make a wrong turning. That I should meet with the humans? That I should *meet* them? I think about everything that Jaishevkin said, about what she might have said if she had agreed to meet them after all. About their writing. About how they smile at me.

About how they remember.

And I think, *My body-sire will never be whole again.*

I listen to the soft padding sound of my feet against the pavement and I think about that sound multiplied a hundred-fold, a thousand-fold, as we all ran for the river. For Laijan, for life, with death following behind.

When it happened, I was not yet born. From what I know of human lifespans, neither were Aaron and Jacob. We are looking back behind us at the death that follows us wherever we go, and we have all three been told *here is how you are to look at so much death so that it never catches you and here is what you are never to do. And here is how you should look at the ghosts.*

And here is how you should look at each other.

They smile at me that way because they are trying very hard to not see me at all.

When I am home I am still the only one awake. I bathe myself and dress in my formal *klimenjiani* clothing, light and softly hued. I do not know exactly what I will say or how I will find the words to tell what I feel. I do not know what my body-sire will say when she hears of it, and I do not know if I will be allowed to remain a *klimenjiani*. I do not know what will happen after today. I do not know if my body-sire will ever be whole, or if I will ever be whole, or if any of us will. I do not know what Aaron and Jacob will say to me. I do not know if the death that follows us will catch us someday, or if Laijan will carry life, or if the ghosts that surround us will ever truly be seen.

But I am going to meet the humans.

Fleet

Sandra McDonald

When I officially became a girl, I took the new name of Isa. At the time I was nine years old. In the Umatac village records I'm still a male named Magahet Joseph Howard USN. It's good luck to be given the name of an ancestor from Before Silence. My brother calls me Shithead, because he's my brother. But most people call me Bridge, because the governors gave me that. Someone in every village is appointed to stand with one dusty foot in the past and the other planted in the Great Future, ready to take action when ships appear on the blue horizon.

Sounds important. Don't be fooled. We're not some backwards cargo cult, building mock radio towers in the magical hope of luring back civilization. Civilization will come again regardless. We're sure of it.

It's hot today, late afternoon. I'm sitting on the beach and thinking hard about taking a nap. A dozen yards offshore, blue waves roll around Fouha Rock, where the gods created mankind. No kidding: it's a giant limestone phallus jutting out of the sea.

"What are you staring at, Shithead?" my brother Rai shouts when the canoes return.

"Your tiny shriveled-up balls," I yell back.

The men laugh. Among them is my husband Pulan Robert, who comes to me at night with reverence and good humor. He has a second wife, Kami Brittany, who bears him our children and hopes that one day I'll be gored to death by a boonie pig. She can't say that too loudly, though, for fear I'll call down upon her a vengeful taotaomo'na. Those are the spirits that slink through the nunu trees under moonlight, and moan during storms as if in great pain, and brush their invisible cold hands over your nape when you least expect it.

She's right to worry. I know the names of seven thousand taotaomo'na. Seven thousand ancestors who perished here in the After Silence. There's a man in Yigo who knows twelve thousand. The oldest woman on the island lives in Dededo, and she knows fifteen thousand. The governors gave them to her, just like they gave them to me, through white caps clamped to our skulls.

I try not to think about the white caps too much.

The men beach the canoes and haul out their catches. Pulan Robert smiles at me and waves over to where Kami waits with our youngest daughter bouncing on her hip. A moment later his smile dims. Our teenage boy with

"I'm going t

tuba by the ruins

Merizo's alw

Husto, though, a

and this makes tl

to piss. A woma

drags in the dirt.

"You're the

Her name is

While working

shifting, stinkin

breathing bad a

merciful, but N

cared for her un

"I'm Isa," I

"I 'ound the

I shake my

She waves

Fleet. She

though, there's

imagination of

"I don't see

"'ailor," sh

"Show me.

Chickens s

and bushes pe

hut without do

looking closely

his eyes half-li

sharp curved k

"The 'eet,'

The rips in

in over the ree

side of a boat.

"Good day

He strugg

arm. He starts

English or Ch

But I kn

languages bef

Russian.

---

visitors have arrived. Four men, tall and lean, with walking sticks wrapped in copper wire and the green ribbons of Agat village.

Rai stops beside me and frowns. "They're late."

"They're on time."

"Late," he insists. "They'll slow us down tomorrow."

"Two days to get there," I tell him. "Then you'll see Angelina again."

At sunset our entire village dines on roasted fruit bats, fresh rabbit fish, breadfruit, cakes, and tuba. The musicians play nose flutes and drums for the children dancing around the bonfire. Three of the men from Agat know of me, but the fourth keeps sliding glances my way. Beneath my blouse, my bra is stuffed with soft grass. I wear a wig of long hair, dark and straight.

"Babae?" he asks his companions in Tagalog. Many Filipinos clustered in Agat in the After Silence.

"Oo," his friends say.

He wants to know if I'm a girl. Yes, they say. But he looks at me doubtfully. Wondering what's under my skirt, maybe wondering if he can put his hands under there to squeeze and rub.

Pulan Robert puts his arm around my shoulder. He smells like salt and fish and Kami.

"You should stay here," he says that night, in our bed, as we stare up at the tin and thatch ceiling. Kami's hut is bigger, but mine is closer to the cooling ocean breeze. Mosquitoes nibble on our arms.

"I have to go. Someone has to remember the dead," I remind him.

"I'll come along and keep you company."

"Rai is coming."

"Rai is too impatient. He won't pay attention."

I kiss his nose. "Rai will always pay attention to me."

Rai's impatient because it's been six months since he's held his wife in his arms. In the morning, he's awake before anyone else. At breakfast, somber Irao speaks quietly to his crying children. The fourth from our village is Husto, who has spent the last week pleading to our little governor that he should be excused from this duty. She stands firm. The lottery is fair and the gods have picked him to take his turn digging. I wonder if we're going to have to physically lift Husto in the air and carry him away, but finally he pries himself away from his weeping mother.

"Travel safely," Pulan Robert says, with a final warm kiss.

"I will," I promise.

The men from Agat lead the way down the road. We follow, and only Husto looks back.

Despite t
could drive a
of Cocos La
Point. The sh
international
war—you co
rubble, and b
up north wor
tried rowing
shredded ou
walking stic
outside the v

The coa
more of the
worked on
gutted and s
by earthqua
skeletons of
honeymoon

Imagine
fucking or h
in the midd
the next, a
computers.
and electric
the skies ab
moon and
what the N
close to the

I rub m

Our first s
the Lady.
and the Sp
chiefs. Wh
my cock.
anyways,

After
few famil
year and c
ownership
religion.

My throat goes tight.

To Nena, I say, "He comes from Yona. They speak strange up there. Nothing more than that."

Her expression falls. "Not 'eet?"

"Not Fleet, no," I say confidently. "When the Fleet returns, an armada of ships will sail into the bay bearing food and wine. They'll set off fireworks and play the United States anthem. This is just a lost fisherman who needs our help. Return to the beach and find my brother Rai. He's the tallest, the most handsome. Bring him here. But don't let anyone else see you. They'll claim the reward his village has for him."

A new light gleams in her eyes at the mention of reward, and she hurries off.

If Nena had bothered to examine the Russian's clothes, she would have seen that even stiff with sea salt, the fabric is newer and finer than anything we can weave or dig up here. He's wearing lightweight boots with fresh rubber soles. For a white man he's pale—a sailor who doesn't see much sun. Maybe he came from a submarine. The governors showed us pictures of those.

"Who are you?" I ask in Russian.

His rambling stops. A hairy brown spider crawls down his leg. He doesn't brush it off.

"Did you come alone? Can I call someone for help?"

"Sergei," he murmurs.

Maybe that's his name, maybe someone else's. Before I can ask his head slumps over and the knife tumbles from his lax fingers. I see dark blood on the back of his skull. There's a swelling there, a stone-like bump. No other major injuries on him, no jewelry or electronics, only the knife and its leather sheath strapped under his left trouser leg.

He may not have much time left, or he could recover enough to cause serious damage.

As always, I am sworn to uphold Rule Number One.

I squeeze his nose shut and clap my hand over his mouth.

Life is a stubborn habit to break. It's a sacred thing, to watch the spirit struggle to take flight. You can see it in the flopping fish pulled from the sea, or in the panicking pig as the knife pierces its throat. The Russian makes muffled sounds and jerks his head, but has no strength to fight me off. I pray to the gods and governors for him. No one here will mourn his death with a nine-day feast. But most living things deserve kindness in their last moments, to hear words ushering them to arms of their ancestors.

When she returns with Rai, Nena's eyes turn accusatory.

visitors have arrived. Four men, tall and lean, with walking sticks wrapped in copper wire and the green ribbons of Agat village.

Rai stops beside me and frowns. "They're late."

"They're on time."

"Late," he insists. "They'll slow us down tomorrow."

"Two days to get there," I tell him. "Then you'll see Angelina again."

At sunset our entire village dines on roasted fruit bats, fresh rabbit fish, breadfruit, cakes, and tuba. The musicians play nose flutes and drums for the children dancing around the bonfire. Three of the men from Agat know of me, but the fourth keeps sliding glances my way. Beneath my blouse, my bra is stuffed with soft grass. I wear a wig of long hair, dark and straight.

"Babae?" he asks his companions in Tagalog. Many Filipinos clustered in Agat in the After Silence.

"Oo," his friends say.

He wants to know if I'm a girl. Yes, they say. But he looks at me doubtfully. Wondering what's under my skirt, maybe wondering if he can put his hands under there to squeeze and rub.

Pulan Robert puts his arm around my shoulder. He smells like salt and fish and Kami.

"You should stay here," he says that night, in our bed, as we stare up at the tin and thatch ceiling. Kami's hut is bigger, but mine is closer to the cooling ocean breeze. Mosquitoes nibble on our arms.

"I have to go. Someone has to remember the dead," I remind him.

"I'll come along and keep you company."

"Rai is coming."

"Rai is too impatient. He won't pay attention."

I kiss his nose. "Rai will always pay attention to me."

Rai's impatient because it's been six months since he's held his wife in his arms. In the morning, he's awake before anyone else. At breakfast, somber Irao speaks quietly to his crying children. The fourth from our village is Husto, who has spent the last week pleading to our little governor that he should be excused from this duty. She stands firm. The lottery is fair and the gods have picked him to take his turn digging. I wonder if we're going to have to physically lift Husto in the air and carry him away, but finally he pries himself away from his weeping mother.

"Travel safely," Pulan Robert says, with a final warm kiss.

"I will," I promise.

The men from Agat lead the way down the road. We follow, and only Husto looks back.

Despite the solemn occasion, I like these trips. Before Silence, you could drive all over Guahan on asphalt roads, from the turquoise waters of Cocos Lagoon all the way north to the limestone cliffs at Ritidian Point. The shrine for the Japanese soldiers who killed themselves, the international airport for big jets, the army tanks abandoned after the war—you could visit them all in just one day. Now the roads are all rubble, and bandits control the bridges, and some of the white villages up north won't let you pass over their lands without payment. Rai and I tried rowing around the island once when we were young. We nearly shredded ourselves on the reefs. Ours is the age of footpaths and walking sticks, and many people die without ever having stepped outside the villages they were born in.

The coastal route to Layon is pretty enough, but I'd like to see more of the old military bases. My namesake Joseph Howard USN worked on one of those. The concrete shells of the buildings are all gutted and stripped out, the roofs blown away by typhoons or leveled by earthquakes. Those ruins are less sad, somehow, than the iron skeletons of hotel high-rises in Hagatna, the resorts where the tourists honeymooned and gambled away their fortunes until the Night of Fire.

Imagine it: two hundred thousand people drinking or dreaming or fucking or hunched over military equipment in the middle of the night, in the middle of the endless ocean, and in the gap from one minute to the next, all the technology died. No telephones, radios, satellites, computers. All the power stations erupted into fire. All the transformers and electrical wires sizzled and fried themselves into charred metal. In the skies above, enormous waves of green light shimmered against the moon and stars. The governors gave me just enough science to know what the Northern Lights are, and why they should never be seen this close to the equator.

I rub my head, remember the tight white caps, and keep walking.

❧

Our first step is Fort Nuestra, high on the bluff, to make our offers to the Lady. She's not the oldest of our gods, but she's the one Magellan and the Spanish gave to us while they burned our huts and killed our chiefs. When I was very small, I would pray to the Lady to take away my cock. She never did. I don't hold it against her, though, not much anyways, because Pulan Robert likes it well enough in the dark.

After praying and leaving gifts we continue on to Merizo. Only a few families are left to greet us. Merizo went to war with Inarajan last year and came out on the poorer end. The fight was supposedly over the ownership of a prized carabao, but was probably about skin color or religion. For now Merizo only has one worker to send to the landfill, a teenage boy with a topknot dangling from his otherwise bare skull.

"I'm going to dig up a radio and battery," he tells me as we drink tuba by the ruins of a church. "I'm going to call Jesus Christ."

Merizo's always been known for this kind of talk. I don't mind it. Husto, though, announces that Jesus Christ died on the Night of Fire, and this makes the boy's parents angry. While they argue, I walk away to piss. A woman with limestone white hair follows me. Her left leg drags in the dirt.

"You're the 'idge," she says, the words slurred.

Her name is Nena and she should be dead now, or so the story goes. While working at the landfill she was accidentally buried by the shifting, stinking debris. By the time they pulled her out, she'd been breathing bad air for too long. A quick death might have been more merciful, but Nena's father carried his only child back to Merizo and cared for her until he died in the war.

"I'm Isa," I tell her, pulling down my skirt.

"I 'ound the 'eet," she says.

I shake my head, not understanding.

She waves her good hand toward the ocean. "The 'eet."

Fleet. She found the Fleet. She wouldn't be the first. Usually, though, there's a lot of tuba involved, or smoked weeds, or the fanciful imagination of children.

"I don't see any ships, Nena."

"'ailor," she says, and gestures toward the jungle.

"Show me."

Chickens scatter before our feet on a narrow path. From the vines and bushes peek out old cement houses on cracked foundations. One hut without doors or a roof is so overgrown you'd miss it if you weren't looking closely. Inside sits a white man, his face ghastly with pain and his eyes half-lidded. He smells like shit and urine. In his right hand is a sharp curved knife.

"The 'eet," Nena repeats.

The rips in his clothing and long scrapes on his arms say he washed in over the reef, but any fool fisherman from the north can fall over the side of a boat. I kneel in the doorway.

"Good day, sir," I say. "Can you tell me your name? Your village?"

He struggles to focus. Twitches the knife, as if trying to raise his arm. He starts to ramble—short, disconnected words, none of them in English or Chamorro or Tagalog.

But I know these words. The governors gave me nations and languages before they gave me names to carry. This man is speaking Russian.

My throat goes tight.

To Nena, I say, "He comes from Yona. They speak strange up there. Nothing more than that."

Her expression falls. "Not 'eet?"

"Not Fleet, no," I say confidently. "When the Fleet returns, an armada of ships will sail into the bay bearing food and wine. They'll set off fireworks and play the United States anthem. This is just a lost fisherman who needs our help. Return to the beach and find my brother Rai. He's the tallest, the most handsome. Bring him here. But don't let anyone else see you. They'll claim the reward his village has for him."

A new light gleams in her eyes at the mention of reward, and she hurries off.

If Nena had bothered to examine the Russian's clothes, she would have seen that even stiff with sea salt, the fabric is newer and finer than anything we can weave or dig up here. He's wearing lightweight boots with fresh rubber soles. For a white man he's pale—a sailor who doesn't see much sun. Maybe he came from a submarine. The governors showed us pictures of those.

"Who are you?" I ask in Russian.

His rambling stops. A hairy brown spider crawls down his leg. He doesn't brush it off.

"Did you come alone? Can I call someone for help?"

"Sergei," he murmurs.

Maybe that's his name, maybe someone else's. Before I can ask his head slumps over and the knife tumbles from his lax fingers. I see dark blood on the back of his skull. There's a swelling there, a stone-like bump. No other major injuries on him, no jewelry or electronics, only the knife and its leather sheath strapped under his left trouser leg.

He may not have much time left, or he could recover enough to cause serious damage.

As always, I am sworn to uphold Rule Number One.

I squeeze his nose shut and clap my hand over his mouth.

❧

Life is a stubborn habit to break. It's a sacred thing, to watch the spirit struggle to take flight. You can see it in the flopping fish pulled from the sea, or in the panicking pig as the knife pierces its throat. The Russian makes muffled sounds and jerks his head, but has no strength to fight me off. I pray to the gods and governors for him. No one here will mourn his death with a nine-day feast. But most living things deserve kindness in their last moments, to hear words ushering them to arms of their ancestors.

When she returns with Rai, Nena's eyes turn accusatory.

"He passed quietly, without pain," I say. "His people from Yona will want to come and retrieve his bones. Rai, bury him in a shallow grave. But don't tell anyone, or let them help, or they'll want the reward, too."

Rai balks. "What reward?"

I squeeze his arm. "The people of Yona will be grateful to know what happened to him."

He opens his mouth, maybe to say the people of Yona are nothing but swindlers and drunkards. My fingers dig deeper into his skin. He's not an idiot, my brother, so he goes silent. Nena, bent over the naked corpse, sniffs in grief.

"'is clothes," she says.

"I took them for his people," I tell her. "His last words were to thank you, Nena. His spirit rests in peace because of your kindness. He asked that you seclude yourself and say rosaries for him. If you don't, his taotaomo'na will be very angry. Will you do it?"

She nods emphatically. "Yes."

Back at the church, the others want to know where Rai is. "Too much feasting last night," I lie, and they sympathize. Everyone here has suffered from the squats before.

Husto gestures to the folded fern leaves in my arms. "What's that?"

"A gift for the taotaomo'na," I warn him. "Don't touch."

We bid farewell to Merizo and detour into the valley to visit both Tinta and Faha Caves. I worry that Nena won't do as told. Or that Rai will discover something incriminating that I left behind. But the caves require my full concentration. Back in World War II, the Japanese soldiers spent years raping the women, killing old and young alike, forcing people from their homes to concentration camps. Here, as the end of the war drew near, they herded villagers into caves and tossed grenades in after them. Other victims were tied up and beheaded and left in the dirt.

I don't have their names—no Bridge does—but we know that the Japanese brutality made the people of Merizo rise up in rebellion. We honor them, too, in this sacred place heavy with memory.

"You tell the story well," Irao comments, afterward.

"I wish I didn't have to tell it at all," I reply.

After the ceremonies we trek back to the coast, where dark gray clouds are rolling in from the south. We make it to Achang Bay before the rain starts. The only shelter is an old fueling station with two walls and a sand floor. Irao and Husto sit to one side of me, and on the other sits the man from Agat who doesn't believe I'm a woman.

"The gods don't want us to go to Layon," Husto says as water pelts down.

"You whine like a child," Irao tells him.

The man from Agat looks like he's thinking of putting his hand on my thigh. I slide my fingers along the sheath of my knife, and he decides to stare at the rain instead.

By dusk the weather is clear but it's too late to continue on. The men look for wood dry enough to burn while I worry about Rai. It doesn't take that long to dig a shallow grave, and the detour to Tinta and Faha cost us time.

Irao knows me well. "He'll be along soon."

"Hmm," I say.

Eventually the men build a fire, and we eat supper quietly, and afterward they smoke and drink more tuba. Rai does not come. We all stretch out under the dark, starry sky and rising full moon. I'm halfway through the first thousand names in my head when from the jungle arises a long, low, awful moan of pain. Someone—or something—in agony, in torment.

We all sit up in fear.

"It's a pig," says one of the men from Amat.

"It's Anufat," says Husto, naming the ugliest and meanest of the taotaomo'na. Anufat has fangs and claws, and sometimes not even a head.

Irao tosses sand at Husto. "Stop telling stories."

"He wants his gift," Husto insists, pointing to the fern leaves I'd forbidden anyone to touch. "You said it was for him."

"It's for another," I protest.

The moan again: drawn out agony that makes my stomach flutter. Not Rai, I tell myself. But that fear grabs me and doesn't let go, and after the third terrible time, I stand up.

"I'll come with you," Irao offers.

"No. I'll go alone." I pick up the folded leaves. "Stoke the fire and stay here."

By the time I reach the edge of the jungle the fire is bright again, the men nothing but silhouettes. A narrow path, mostly overgrown, curves from behind the fueling station into the nunu trees. Brown snakes curl away from my bare feet. The knife in my hand won't do anything against a spirit, but I have salt, too, and words, and if I have to run I can run, too, faster than anyone can imagine.

The steady sea breeze shifts the trees and leaves, makes shadows flicker, tricks my eyes with movement—and then a hand clamps down over my mouth, yanks me backward. The dead man's clothes and knife spill from their leafy envelope and scatter on the ground. My knife gets lost in the bushes. Someone speaks low against my ear, a command of some kind. I stop struggling.

"Who are you?" I ask in Russian, muffled, garbled.

He repeats his command. Be quiet, he's saying. He pulls me backward through brush into a small clearing where Rai is curled up on the ground, his hands and ankles bound, his mouth gagged.

"I'm a friend," I insist, the words mostly unintelligble. "Friend."

His free hand gropes my hips and ass. Looking for a weapon. He finds my cock instead and makes a startled noise. A moment later he yanks me down to the ground against Rai and lays a sharp blade against my exposed throat. My skin stings. Rai grunts. The moonlight illuminates the stranger's pale face but I can't see his eyes, or what emotion might be in them.

"Who are you?" he demands in Russian.

"Isa."

He yanks at my wig, rips at my skirt. My cock hangs out, long and soft. He slaps at it and says, "Not a woman."

If I had my knife, I'd cut his hand off. Instead I keep my chin up and stare straight at him. "Sergei?"

He hesitates. The slightest flick of his wrist and he can end my life. I'm breathing fast and my insides are watery. Some things you can't control.

"That's the last thing he said," I tell him. "Sergei."

Another long moment. Then, "How did he die?"

"From his head injury. He said you might come, that you'd tell us everything. Not that you'd attack and try to kill us."

The Russian sits back on his haunches. Rai grunts against his gag. Carefully I put my hand on his leg. He can't understand what we're saying. He thinks that we're only a few moments from death, and I wouldn't call him wrong.

"You're Sergei?" I repeat.

"Yes. He was Vasilly."

"You're from Russia?"

"There's no Russia." His voice is flat.

"You're the first visitors from the outside world in a hundred years," I say, and the thrill of it runs through me. No other Bridge has ever found a man from away. The governors will be happy with me. Maybe I can finagle a reward; fewer workers to the dump each season, perhaps, or some other special favor.

Sergei points his finger and says, "Don't move."

He retreats to search through Vasilly's scattered clothing and boots. In the darkness I tug on Rai's knots, but my fingers are trembling and the cords are wound too well.

Sergei returns with Vasilly's knife. He unscrews the base of the hollow grip. Inside are blue fireflies. Electric lights. I haven't seen those in a long time. The weapon is some kind of tracking or communication device, designed for stealth. He slides out a narrow part and wedges free a luminescent strip. Quick, efficient moves.

"We've hoped for your return," I say, trying to sound awed. "Prayed for it."

Sergei pockets the strip. "Forget prayers. We're only here for information."

"Honored visitor, our governors would be happy to share anything we know."

He snorts, though I'm the one who should laugh. Information. Fishing reports, maybe? Average daily rainfall? No man treks across the Pacific, dares to swim between the reefs, and subsequently avoids the local population without good reason.

"How is it that you speak Russian?" he asks.

I duck my head. "There was a man, many years ago. He washed ashore the way your friend did. He recovered and lived in the jungle by himself. I would visit him, bring him companionship, and he taught me to speak it."

He looks at my cock and shakes his head. Imaging perversion, maybe. Defending his imaginary countryman from the likes of me. The truth is much worse, of course. Those white caps, burning hot. My hair never grew back.

"Our governors would greet you with open arms," I insist. "They've kept all the records from the Before time. They know everything about the island and what was here when the world went silent."

Behind me, Rai struggles quietly against his bonds.

"What governors?" Sergei asks. "Where?"

"I'll take you," I tell him.

🙰🕆🙰

Sergei wants to leave Rai behind. I can't risk it. Despite Rai's many fine qualities, he's terrible at keeping secrets. Sooner or later he'll tell Irao and Husto what he's seen. They'll tell people at the landfill. Those people will go back to their villages and spread word. And the governors will most definitely not be pleased.

So instead I convince Sergei that the governors despise me and consider me crazy, an insult to their masculinity. They'll only allow us near their village if a local man guides us. Sergei looks doubtful, but it's not hard for him to believe that here I'm an abomination.

Eventually he unties Rai and lets him stand. I try to soothe over their unfortunate introduction to one another.

"He's Fleet," Rai says, both angry and amazed.

"No, not Fleet," I tell him. "Just a fisherman lost in a storm. He come from Hawaii."

Of course, we haven't had contact with Hawaii since Before Silence. Any stray fisherman would have to survive four thousand miles of open sea to reach our shore. But no one ever taught Rai geography.

Still, he's skeptical. "If he's a fisherman, why did he want to kill us?"

"He thought we killed his brother. He was afraid."

Sergei watches us. He can't understand a word of Chamorro, or maybe he's just pretending not to. Perhaps they don't have white caps where he comes from.

"Hawaii," Rai muses. "We could go there. We could trade, maybe, and no one would have to dig at the landfill anymore. My children, your children—Isa, this could change everything for them."

"The governors will decide," I say. "I have to take him there."

Rai hesitates. He's my big brother. He used to fight bullies for me when we were dusty children. He cried the day our uncles took me away to Talofofo. He came to walk me home when they were finished burning knowledge into my head. But the mother of his children is waiting for him at Layon.

"I'll take him by myself," I tell him. "Go get Angelina."

He frowns. "No. I'll come."

"You don't have to—"

"I'll come," he says curtly.

We circle through the jungle to avoid Irao, Husto and the men from Agat. For hours we walk along the old highway. No sentries or dog raise an alarm as we ghost through Inarajan. I wish we had water. Sergei's careful to walk behind us, never letting Rai or me out of his sight.

"Is there an army?" Sergei asks.

"Not anymore," I tell him. "Most of the military evacuated or died off After Silence."

"What about an army of your own people?"

I don't think that he wants an entire history of the militia here, how the local men trained under the Spanish and fought the Japanese and eventually became the Guam National Guard.

"There's no need. We only fight each other once in awhile. Do they have armies where you come from?"

"No," he says, but I think he's lying.

We trudge on. Boonie pigs trample away in the bushes when our feet come too close. To stay awake, I recite the second thousand of the names in my head. In my fatigue, some syllables slip out.

"What are you saying?" Sergei asks tightly.

"I'm praying," I tell him. "For your friend. You were very close?"

He grunts.

"He said your name before he died. He sounded... fond."

"He was only a man from my—" Sergei says, and stops. From his ship? From his base? Maybe from his bed.

Carefully I say, "If there are others of your people nearby, they are welcome as well."

Nothing. I glance back. Sergei has stopped to stare at a faint orange glow in the hills. Rai glances, too, but only for a moment. Those are the lights of Layon. The last gift of the old world. There aren't many options for garbage on an island like this. You have to pile it somewhere, otherwise you dump it into the ocean—all those car batteries and paint cans, light bulbs and lead pipes, the plastic wrap from food, the dirty diapers and soiled cat litter, generations of toxic messes.

"What's up there?" Sergei asks.

"An old landfill. They burn off the gases so they can dig."

He swats at a bug on his neck. "What are they digging for?"

I shrug. "Anything useful."

The sky is pink-gold by the time we reach the old satellite tracking station above Inarajan. It's just a bunch of concrete buildings now, long abandoned, but Sergei pokes around in interest.

"What was this place?" he asks.

"Something called NASA," I tell him. "People used to visit the moon and this place helped them not get lost."

"A tracking station."

"Do people still live up there? On the moon?"

He kicks at an old fencepost. "If there are, they don't answer when we call them."

For the first time I really think about the world Sergei comes from. Out there they've had the raw materials, factory resources, and technical know-how to manufacture new transformers and power stations. By now they've rebuilt the radio stations, the telephone systems, and maybe even the internet. They probably have medicines like aspirin and insulin, and no one dies of illnesses like appendicitis or childbirth.

All of these things would make life on Guahan easier.

But at a cost. Magellan taught us that.

"Do you trust me?" I ask Rai once we're walking again.

"What's kind of stupid question is that?" he asks, brushing thick green leaves from the path.

Sergei says, "Stop talking."

"You must be completely honest with anything the governors ask you," I tell him. And then, to Sergei, in Russian, "I'm sorry. I asked my brother not to let them beat me when we reach our leaders. I shame them, the men."

Sergei says, "If they beat you, why do you dress that way?"

He reminds me of the villagers when I was still Magahet Joseph Howard USN. Dress like a boy. Act like a boy. Can you teach a stone to act like a tree, or a bird to act like a dolphin? The governors said many long-ago ancestors were proud to be Fa'afafine, in the manner of male and female alike. Their approval made the criticism go silent, or at least less vocal.

"I follow my heart," I tell Sergei. "As all men and women should. Don't your people do that?"

Sergei coughs. "Perhaps."

"Vasilly was more than your friend, wasn't he?" And some of this is just guessing, but a name murmured in longing is hard to forget.

His face turns hard. "It doesn't matter. He's gone now."

Several minutes later we reach the outskirts of Talofofo Park. The parking lot has long returned to vegetation, and the gondolas disassembled or left to rust. Here the governors live in the old history museum, flanked by ramshackle huts and old latte stones and the fresh waters of the Ugum River. It's all small, unimpressive, nothing to look at twice. A sentry yawns when he sees us.

"Who comes?" he asks.

"Rai of Umatuc," Rai says. "And my sister the Bridge."

The sentry yawns again and scratches his ass. "What business?"

"This man comes from away," I say.

Sergei nudges me nervously. "Tell your governors to come out here."

"The governors are old men who believe in tradition," I reply. "They'll give you all the old records here, but we have to do things their way."

He continues to look skittish. But the sentry shrugs as if unimpressed with our visitor and pushes open the museum door. Inside all is dim and empty. I remember being nine years old and standing here with the children of other villages, waiting for our education from the wise governors. We all thought we'd been picked for a special destiny.

There's no such thing as destiny. Only inevitability.

The sentry takes us into a courtyard with woven mats circled around a cooking fire. "Wait here."

Sergei shuffles his feet, undecided, but I plop down and Rai follows.

An old man in a threadbare shirt shuffles from the house a few minutes later. "Isa," he says, a toothless smile on his face. He shakes Rai's hand, nods respectfully at Sergei. Behind him, a hunched servant brings out tea. The old man, Kepuha, sits with a creaking of his knees.

I introduce Sergei in Russian and explain that Kepuha, too, knew the mythical old stowaway, learned this strange foreign language.

"We must celebrate your arrival," Kepuha says, all kindness. "Such a momentous day."

"They say you can help me with information, sir," Sergei says.

Kepuha nods. "Yes, much information. All the old missiles. All those other terrible weapons. It'll be a relief to be rid of them."

Sergei relaxes. He's close, now, to what he came for.

Rai can't follow their words, but he knows some kind of agreement is being discussed. "Honored uncle, will they trade with us?"

"A good question to ask," Kepuha says.

We all drink our cool, sweetened tea. More servants bring toasted bread, boiled eggs, and strips of bacon. Kepuha turns to Sergei and talks more about weapons. On the roof of the museum, another sentry appears. Some young men carry large baskets through the far end of the courtyard. The skin on my neck prickles.

"Honored Kepuha, my brother and I have family business in Layon," I say in Chamorro. "We should depart."

Kepuha waves his gnarled hand. "There's time to rest. You must be exhausted."

Even as I watch, Rai's eyes slide shut. He leans sideways and sprawls into the dust. Sergei realizes at the same time I do that our food is drugged. He leaps up, tries to dart away, but gets no further than a few feet before a guard knocks him down and kicks him in the ribs.

"My brother—" I say, slurred. "He didn't—"

"Sleep," Kepuha says. "You did well, Bridge."

My ears fill with a rushing noise and the sluggish crawl of my own heart. A sweet cool river, just like the river Ugum, carries me away to darkness.

⭐

The next time I see Sergei, he's screaming. The soldiers have him naked and strapped to a table, a white cap affixed to his head. I know what it's like to writhe as knowledge is forced into neural connections. Like lightning striking the brain, over and over. But Sergei's pain is worse because they're not putting data into his brain. They're yanking it out.

The back of my throat burns with bile.

Colonel Kepuha of the Guahan Militia stands beside me, watching through the mirrored window. Electric lights illuminate the rooms down here under the museum. Fresh, cool air circulates from pumps. The entire base runs off the power from recycled material dug out of the Layon landfill. Trash converted to fuel. One of the last great technological achievements of the old world. After Silence, our ancestors couldn't fix the whole island. But they could fix this place.

Sergei screams again.

"Is this... necessary?" I ask.

"He wouldn't answer questions about his homeland," Kepuha says. "But we'll find out."

Take a hump of land in the middle of the Pacific Ocean. Build a fort on it. Build another. Keep building, decade after decade, ports and airfields and depots of concrete and steel. Swap ownership during wartime. Swap it back. Add secret research labs dedicated to memory research. The future looks unlimited. But then civilization collapses, all of it, swallowed up by solar megaflares, and that hump of land has to fend for itself.

"You did well, bringing him here," Kepuha says. "We'll dig up the body of the one you killed and find out what we can from it."

With effort, I keep my voice steady. "Who says I killed him?"

He turns to me. "Of course you did. You learned your lessons well."

One foot rooted in the past. One planted in the future. The job of a Bridge isn't to greet the Fleet, but to stop it.

"What of my brother, sir?" I ask. "He thinks the strangers were fisherman from Hawaii. I'll make him swear not to tell, and if he does, no one will believe him anyway."

Kepuha smiles indulgently and starts walking down the hall. "Your brother is a good man?"

I follow. "Yes. Very good and honorable."

"Even honorable men can have loose tongues."

"You can trust him as much as you trust me," I promise.

We've reached another window and another memory room. The table inside is empty.

"When you finished your training as a child, how many names did you leave with?" Kepuha asks casually.

I rub the goose bumps on my arms. "Seven thousand."

"You left with one thousand," he says. "We give you another thousand more every time you bring us someone from Fleet. A reward for good service. A way to fill the gaps."

"But that's not—" I gulp against a new surge of bile. "That's not possible. I'd remember."

The doors in the room open and two guards drag Rai inside. He fights them, my brother does, but they're much stronger. They strap him down and reach for a cap.

Colonel Kepuha says, "No, you won't remember. You never do."

Remembering Turinam

N.A. Ratnayake

Outside, the sun was setting. Salai's journey had started in the cold peaks of the Dorhal Mountains, at the Temple of Heremi, built where the River Khem found its source. He had descended with the Khem to the west, into the secluded valley-basin sandwiched between the curve of the Dorhal range and the Western Sea. Salai had grown nervous as he approached the the Rytari checkpoint at the bottom of the mountain pass. Brown-skinned Turians like Salai were easy to spot among the Rytari and were often stopped. But the soldiers had noted Salai's simple robe, the orange sash at his waist, and the single small pack on his back, and waved him on without so much as a word.

Salai had left the Khem the previous day and tracked north of the river, down from the irrigated, tea-growing communes of the foothills into the lower, rolling hills of farmland that made up the northern part of the valley. It was late summer. The grass was dry and a deep reddish brown, replaced in patches by swaths of yellow and green where Turians grew acres of corn, squash, lentils, and beans.

After three days on foot, the end of Salai's journey was at last in sight. His pack was lighter than when he had started, since he had been slowly eating the food carefully packed within and drinking measured amounts of water. He took a careful sip to wet his dry mouth and throat and looked to the south.

Salai could see the main town of Turinam straddling the Khem in the middle of the valley. Turinam had served as the independent center of Turian commerce, culture, and government in the valley for generations. Now it flew a Rytari flag and served as the regional capitol for the Lord Governor, who reported directly to the Rytari Senate.

On the far side of the town, Salai could see the new Rytari settlements, as easy to spot against the backdrop of Turinam as his own skin was to the Rytari. Built haphazardly, with an eye towards haste, the structures paid no heed to Turian custom or the traditions that had kept the land and people in a sustainable cycle for generations. This river valley being the latest addition to a vast empire, there was plenty of land to be had—or reallocated.

Rytari kept moving in. Every month, a transport airship arrived in Turinam from the Rytari-conquered city-state of Aish, on the other side of the Dorhal Mountains. Each landing would bring more settlers, escorted by soldiers and carrying new machinery. The airship would stay a week, then depart with Turian grains, beans, lentils and tea, as well as fish from the village of Korasca, where the Khem met the Western Sea.

The new settlers had an insatiable need for fields to be leveled, domiciles to be built, and machine shops to be outfitted to repair their technology. Last month the Governor had ordered the construction of a new railway from Turinam to Aish, planning to bore straight through the Dorhal range. Most Turians were skeptical that anyone could accomplish this, even the Rytari with their machines. But it meant jobs, and the settlers kept moving in.

At the top of the hill, surrounded by fallow fields and ill-used, simple equipment, Salai paused to remember a part of his childhood. Though it had been almost fifteen years since he had been to this place, and he was now a young man instead of a boy, it still caused a familiar twinge of home. He approached and entered the small farmhouse without knocking. A woman dressed in a healer's robe looked up from the wood stove in the corner. A brown, fired-clay pot simmered with a substance to which Salai attributed the pungent odor of the room. The woman looked Salai up and down and, recognizing the sash tied at Salai's waist, raised her eyebrows.

"Auyashti, brother. You are in the Heremitian Anushasan, by your sash." She looked somewhat older than he. Her face, while still smooth, bore the signs of having seen long hours of work for a long time.

"Auyashti, sister. You must be Jaeda of the Altharian Anushasan?" She nodded, but said nothing. Salai continued, "I received your letter, but it was difficult to leave Heremi until three days ago. I am here now, and I hope I am not too late."

Jaeda's expression was difficult to read. She gestured to the door leading out of the kitchen into a small room beyond and turned back to her pungent stew—a professional at work, who saw little benefit to small talk. Salai watched her for a few moments and then stepped through the door to which she had pointed.

❧

The room was dim, being lit only by a candle burning on the writing table set against the far wall, where a window looked out at the Dorhal Mountains fading into the last deep purple throes of dusk. A shelf on the side wall was triple-stacked with books, and a wooden bed frame held up a pallet against the near wall. On the pallet, Salai could make out the crumpled figure of an old man. The old man's breathing was slow and deliberate—occasionally an unnerving rattle betrayed how laboriously the air filled and exited the lungs.

"Jaeda?" the old man asked. His voice was faint, but it did not waver. "No more of the samahin. I would rather have a hastier death than any life lengthened by this taste in my mouth." The old man's words were appropriately clipped and cadenced, his sentences adhering to flawless Rytari spoken grammar. Each syllable was distinct, cold, and efficient—interlocking with its partners like the metal links in a chain stretched taut.

The younger pulled back his hood and spoke—though in a different tongue. Salai's voice rose and fell, lilting and flowing like a stream through a forest on a summer day. The old man started at the sound of this language, and was silent for several moments after the younger man stopped speaking.

"Salai," he finally said.

"Grandfather."

"I do not know from whence you learned these words, and I do not want to know. My life is near an end, and you would be wise to take care of yours."

Salai spoke again, new beautiful syllables weaving in with the old.

The old man's response startled Salai with its forcefulness. "Stop," Grandfather snapped, which reduced him to a fit of coughing for a few minutes. "Salai. I am overjoyed to hear your voice. But if you still love me at all, do not speak Turian to me. I will not speak to you if you say another word in Turian. They will kill you."

Salai said nothing for a moment and waited in the room. The old man didn't move. Salai opened his mouth to speak again, and his next words were in Rytari—though his sentences were less structured than Grandfather's.

"There are no soldiers here. The new settlements are across the river. The Rytari will not hear us. Those words I spoke... I do not know Turian. I was only quoting what I memorized from a book I found at Heremi."

"Not among those left in the library, I presume?"

"No. I was put in charge of restoring the shelves in the lower chamber of the library. When I tore out one of the shelves, I found the book. It is old, and in pieces. The cover is gone, so I don't know the title. It had both Turian and Rytari writing."

"I recognize the words. It is the work of Azdara, a Heremitian philosopher. How did you know how to sing the Turian glyphs?"

"You taught me, Grandfather."

Grandfather said nothing, but tried to sit up slowly. Salai saw him struggling and moved closer to help him lift his body a little higher into a new position. When he was stable, Salai moved to the writing table and sat down in the chair. He turned it around to look at Grandfather, who spoke. "I do not recall ever doing such a thing in your early schooling. I could not have. Your generation is forbidden from even hearing Turian, let alone learning it. It is a capital offense."

"It was not in my formal schooling. You sang me a song about the Turian alphabet when I was a child." Grandfather paused, and Salai could see him straining his memory. A slow realization broke on his face and then a look of puzzled wonder.

"Salai," he said, "That was over twenty years ago. You were no more than two years old."

"I know. But I remember. I have used my required study of meditative practices to focus on the unearthing of memories."

There was a light tap at the door. Salai glanced at the door, then at the bed. Grandfather nodded and raised his voice. "Come in, Jaeda." The added energy of his speech caused more coughing. Jaeda entered and placed a steaming bowl of the pungent stew and a cup of tea on the side table next to the bed. Grandfather reached for the tea first and sipped it, soothing the cough in his throat.

Jaeda turned to Salai. "I doubt you want the samahin, since you are in good health. There are rice, beans, and lentils in your grandfather's pantry, fresh produce on the table, and I have brought in more water. As you are not ill, you are welcome to cook them yourself." She then turned her head to address them both. "I bid you good night, brothers."

"Good night, sister," both men responded in unison. Jaeda left, and Grandfather began eating. Salai watched and waited. He wasn't hungry.

"So," said Grandfather between bites. "You are now a Heremitian scholar. What do you study, Salai?"

"You should know, Grandfather. You were at Heremi, before you left."

Grandfather stopped eating briefly and looked up, a strange expression on his face. "It is true that I was at Heremi. You were not even born—times have changed. With what does the anushasan occupy itself these days, now that the temple is run by a Rytari chancellor?"

Salai continued. "I don't think much has changed. We study the same long tradition of subjects that have been contemplated at Heremi for centuries."

Grandfather countered gruffly. "Ah, I see. So, languages? You study the languages of those states not yet absorbed into the Republic, so as to enable the Rytari to trade with and spy on them. And of course you study the Rytari language itself. History? No doubt solely the history of the Rytar Republic, and its version of the story of all other peoples. And translation? No doubt you translate Rytari books into other languages for dissemination."

Salai tensed at the tone in Grandfather's voice. "And we apply the laws of mathematics and physics to design new machines or improve existing ones."

"And in so doing you become a part of their machine. Your studies are not pure."

As he resumed eating, Grandfather muttered something that sounded suspiciously like a curse from the tone and inflection. Salai paused and breathed, reminding himself of the benefits of a calm mind.

"What do you mean pure, Grandfather?"

"Theoretical. Abstract. Without an immediate application, and no obvious concrete return."

Salai glanced down at the old man incredulously, looking to see if it were possible that his grandfather could be joking. It was hard to read faces in the candlelight. "But to what end, Grandfather? What did the Heremitians do with that knowledge, if it had no application?"

Grandfather snorted angrily. "Even if there were no Rytari flag flying over Heremi, your words would stamp that temple as an arm of the Rytari state just as clearly. For generations, the Heremitian Anushasan were the keepers of what our Turian culture considered to be the highest questions: the exploration of identity—the unending search for who we are and the nature of our place in the web of existence."

"But Grandfather, what is that worth?"

"Here you are beside my deathbed, seeking answers to something unresolved inside. Perhaps I should be asking that question of you."

The two men were silent. Salai didn't know what to say, and retreated from the debate to think. Outside, dusk had faded into night. Salai listened for Jaeda in the other room, but the house had gone quiet.

"It's hasn't been half an hour, Grandfather, and we are back to our endless semantics," Salai said. "I came for you. And I came for... knowledge. Ever since I found that book... I want to know about the fall of Turinam. And I want to hear the story in Turian."

"No," Grandfather said. "Clearly you have studied the history in Rytari. There is no point in going back to old wounds. It would be inefficient. And why in Turian? You said yourself that you do not even know the language."

"I have trained my memory, Grandfather. I will remember it until I can write it down. And then I will keep it until I can translate it. You are one of the last of our people who remembers that day, who can tell it from how our people saw it. Tell me of the people who were there, which ones you loved and why. Tell me of your friends who died and of the part of who we are that died with them."

Salai felt uncomfortable making such a plea—emotions always

made him feel as if he were not in control. But he saw that he had made an impression on Grandfather's thinking, and that gears were turning in the old head, so he waited.

"It is hard," Grandfather finally said slowly. "I have not talked or thought about that day in decades, except in my nightmares. And I am ashamed to say that after all these years of being denied my own language, even in my own home, I find it easier to think in Rytari. Huh! Here is a dying man, Salai, who cannot think in his own native tongue."

Grandfather simply breathed for a few minutes, and Salai didn't say anything. Their eyes met, and two hardened visages for a moment let go of their stubbornness. It was Grandfather who broke his gaze first as he began, in a voice that was soft and strong and sad.

"For days we had been watching the siege of Aish, on the eastern side of the Dorhal Mountains. We saw Rytar's legions of armored soldiers, some on foot and some riding mechanical beasts, and in the distance their artillery lining the horizon. Aish fought bravely, but they fell like corn stalks before the scythe against... against the mautkatai."

The inflection and tone of the word made Salai shiver in the warm night. "What are the... those things?"

"Mautkatai are a horrid form of mechanized infantry, Salai—brainless machines that are sent in waves before the living Rytari soldiers in order to soften the enemy. They are as big as a man, and, how shall I say it, unwind when released."

"Perhaps a heavy clockwork spring mechanism inside."

"If you say so. I watched from the mountains through the telescopes at Heremi as the mautkatai flew forward and spun, with a dozen arms each holding a blade. The defenders' ranks broke, whole swaths reduced to piles of screaming meat. I could not watch it long, but the Rytari soldiers had an easy time mopping up the remainder with their skirmishers and projectile infantry."

Salai tried in vain to suppress the slight nausea he felt at the description of the killing machines. "Rytari troops are everywhere today. Why have I not seen these mautkatai?"

"That was our word for them. I do not even know what the Rytari word is. I have not seen them in decades, not since the invasion. Perhaps when the Rytari discovered our countermeasures, they were deprecated and replaced with something even more efficient at killing, machines too expensive to waste on display for the utterly conquered people that we are. Or perhaps even the Rytari do not like seeing them; they are not a cruel people, after all—merely ambitious."

"So what did our people do after seeing the slaughter? Surely it was clear that the Rytari would come for Turinam next? We are the next and last point west on the map."

"The conquest of Aish relied on ground forces, and we knew that the peaks of the Dorhal would give us an advantage. The passes are narrow, and the roads are hardly adequate for facilitating the march of large armies. And it was winter—we felt confident that the snows that were just beginning would buy us time to construct defenses. So we began. Scouts kept an eye on the Rytari armies massing at makeshift forts in the eastern foothills, while we trained with rocks, slings, bows, and spears. The Rytari artillery occasionally fired on the mountains, but the projectiles rarely came close to us. We learned how to ambush in the passes. We carefully set up large boulders, placed to crush advancing lines of troops who would have no way to escape from the path. Piles of stones were staggered in clearings to act as fouls for the mautkatai, which, though deadly, were after all were incapable of guiding themselves around an obstacle."

"I am impressed at your tactics, Grandfather."

"So were we. Ah, we were so impressed with ourselves, and—may our elders forgive us—we actually wished for battle. We, a peaceful people, when faced with death looked forward to killing." Here Grandfather shook his head in disgust. "But our hubris showed its worth. Our preparations were for nothing. After weeks of these drills and shoring up of defenses, they came."

"The written history records a glorious charge up the mountain by Rytari infantry, generals bravely in the fore."

"The written history is wrong. In the earliest hours of the morning, while it was still dark after one of the midwinter storms had passed, a scout cried out. We ran out from the encampment and looked up. Above us, emerging from the night fog like ghostly leviathans in the great deep of the sky, were the agents of our downfall."

"Airships! They used airships?"

"It was the first time we had seen such things. They had not used them on Aish, perhaps knowing that they could keep such vehicles in reserve. Our puny projectiles, struggling against the height of the Rytari craft, only bounced off of the armored hulls. But the airship assault was deadly for us. Some dropped mautkatai among us, others dropped fire. And not a one stopped to tarry with the mountain defenders; all sailed leisurely and imperviously over our lines, our boulders, our carefully laid defenses."

"They went straight for Turinam. And no defenders were in the city?"

Grandfather nodded bitterly. "We hadn't thought to station anyone back in the valley in reserve; it seemed preposterous to have defenses in the valley behind us. If the enemy infantry could break through in the passes of the Dorhal, we knew that we stood no chance on open ground. We had never even considered air power. The airships rappelled down thousands of soldiers directly into Turinam. They took the Council Chambers, the marketplace, the main bridges, and the fishery docks in Korasca in a matter of hours. Any who resisted were slaughtered outright. The airships returned for us, and we had little choice but to surrender. Rytar took Turinam and the valley without so much as a single certain Republic casualty."

Salai's lip curled. "I can't believe it. That such a learned culture could fall so easily to such an ignorant oppressor. Why did we not start studying the arts of war when Rytar was on the horizon for decades? What were you and your anushasan wasting your time on when war was coming?"

Grandfather furrowed his brow and coughed, but continued. "We are not a violent people, Salai. When we took up arms, we were destroyed utterly by those who had studied nothing but war and exploitative machinery for generations. And all for what? Our land is fertile, but merely one dot on a map of a thousand cities that live under a Rytari flag. We have no wealth that the Rytari would recognize as such. Our wealth lies in knowledge, but it is not even of the sort that they value; it is theoretical, meditative, contemplative. They stole hundreds of volumes of our more advanced mathematics and physics, with which they now use the likes of you, Salai, to improve their machines of profit and conquest. But they have no use for it otherwise. We are a conquered people because of a principle, nothing more. The principle that the Rytari should control all of this continent from sea to sea, simply because it sounded like a grand idea and meant more land. Every scholar of history and language who chose to defend Heremi was rounded up and executed."

"Except for you and a handful of others. How did you escape death Grandfather?"

This time Grandfather was silent for a long time. "Here is my last confession, Salai. And I can only hope that my shame can be forgiven by our elders and your generation. You seem to know that I was in the Heremitian Anushasan before the fall of Turinam. Do you know why I never returned after?"

Salai frowned. "I always thought that you left to teach Rytari language in the new schools. That's what you did for the last few decades, right? I've never known you to be anything else but a teacher of Rytari literature and grammar. I thought you wanted to."

"I had to say so every day of my life. In time I came to believe it.

You see Salai, the Rytari are a practical people. They would not throw away a linguist by killing me if they could derive some use from me. In exchange for my life I became a tool of their occupation, a deculturalizer of my own people. I taught the language of our oppressor, and in so doing replaced our natural mode of structuring thought and knowledge with a foreigner's."

"And the other Heremitians? Were they not linguists and mathematicians as well?"

"They refused. And they were killed. Heremi banished me, but could not publicize why. Do you see? I am the lone traitor, living a lie because I was a coward. And I have paid for it in my private moments. Now nearly all books in Turian have been destroyed. You, my grandson, study your own history in the Rytari language, the language of the people who destroyed your history. Do you see? We do not have a history anymore. This is what it means to be a footnote to someone else's story."

"I... I don't understand Grandfather. Why was our culture and language targeted? There are so many other conquered peoples whose languages are not even questioned, whose traditions are not outlawed in the slightest under Rytari law. Why Turinam?"

"Think about it, Salai. Our anushasan were for communal benefit, like Jaeda's healing knowledge from the Altharian Anushasan, and for the study of higher thought at the temple at Heremi. What is the single biggest threat to a nation that thrives on war and competition? Ideas. The idea that people can live successfully in cooperation for mutual sustainability. The idea that the pursuit of higher knowledge for its own sake is valuable for the soul. The idea that there is another way. The Rytari fear this, because it undermines everything their society is built on. So our culture was destroyed."

Here the old man restarted his coughing fit, this time hacking. Salai blinked back tears and rushed to hold a cloth to Grandfather's mouth, catching the blood that dripped from his lips. When the fit subsided, Salai spoke again, quietly. "I am sorry to cause you pain Grandfather. You should not be speaking so much now."

Grandfather was curled into a crumpled heap, Salai's hand on his head. "No, I must. Now I see how little time I have to say these things." He gripped his grandson's arm, and with great effort, continued. "Salai. The language we speak affects how we think. Language shapes how we view the world. Without our language we do not have our whole culture. Without our culture we are not a people. I am complicit in a form of genocide of my own people."

Salai fought against the bile rising in his throat. "I will kill the

Rytari, and drive them out."

"No! When we took up arms, we were destroyed utterly. You are foolish, as we were, if you think you can stand up to Rytar with force."

"They are passive now, not expecting a resurgence."

Grandfather gripped the younger man's arm harder, and tears filled his eyes. "Salai! Turinam was not a battle but a massacre. We turned our backs on everything our elders had taught us about the fruits of violence being illusory and temporary at best. Do not make the same mistake I did."

Salai flared in anger and desperation. "But then how shall we resist? Or are you saying that I should simply accept our fate? That I should stand by and allow my people's history to be raped, as you did?"

Grandfather's hand dropped from Salai's and the younger man felt a rush of hot blood pounding in his ears. He swallowed hard and struggled to clear the anger from his mind. As he felt himself start to drown in anger, he grasped at the lifelines dangling from his meditative practice. His heart slowly stopped pounding. When he came back to his senses he was confused by a shuddering noise from beside him. Salai looked down to see Grandfather sobbing and coughing. Cheeks burning now with shame instead of anger, Salai gently put his hand on Grandfather's shoulder.

"I am sorry Grandfather. I am sorry. Forgive me." He let Grandfather just breathe for awhile. When Salai spoke again it was with deliberate calm. "I don't know what I should do, Grandfather. What should I do?"

There was a long silence before Grandfather responded, his breathing now very ragged. His words were strained.

"Learn," Grandfather said. "Learn Turian, our language and culture, and spread your learning. Give us a language again. Undo what I have spent the last half of my life doing."

"Where do I start?"

Grandfather gestured weakly to the bookshelf. "Behind there. A journal I wrote after our defeat—I only hope it has stood the wear of years. I had planned to leave it there to decay after my death, but now... I think you should take it. It is some of my old work, what I could remember, handwritten side by side in Turian and Rytari."

"You never told me the story of the fall of Turinam in our language."

"It is written there too, in both languages. If you remember the song I sang for you as a child, that is well. Then you can tell the story on your own. Maybe what you do with my work will one day make up for my cowardice. Goodbye, Salai."

"Grandfather, I—"

"Stop. Thank you for coming to me. You have my love."

After that, Grandfather never spoke again. He lived for some time longer, into the still hours before dawn, but Salai never knew whether it was minutes or hours or days. He simply knelt and wept and when he was done weeping he sang the song that Grandfather had sung for him decades ago, the lullaby in Turian from his childhood.

❦

In the morning, Salai awoke to find he had fallen asleep while knelt in meditation by the bedside, his whole body slumped forward, face mashed into the pallet. His knees and back ached. Grandfather's cold form lay on the bed, eyes closed. With pained slowness, Salai raised himself by pushing down on the bed frame with his arms, leveraging his stiff body up on to the pallet to sit. He muttered softly, massaging life back into his legs.

He heard soft noises from the kitchen and continued rubbing painfully. When his legs felt ready to support him, Salai left the bedroom and walked into the kitchen. The sun had not yet risen, and the pale, pre-dawn morning was cool and dry.

"Auyashti, brother," said Jaeda. She was seated quietly at the table. Salai paused. Jaeda pushed a steaming earthenware mug on the table towards him.

"Auyashti, sister," said Salai, who moved to sit down at the table. Salai's tired fingers slipped, and he dropped the mug, spilling some hot water on his hand. He spat out a curse and reached for a cloth with which to mop up the spilled tea. Jaeda touched his hand.

Salai looked up at the healer in surprise, but she was not looking at him. Her gaze was fixed on the hand that had been holding the mug. "The burn is only minor," she said. "Would you like a salve for it anyway?" Salai considered more the feel of her hand than the pain in his own, and he was tempted to answer her in the affirmative simply to retain her proximity.

"No," he said finally. "But thank you." He withdrew his hand and sipped from the remaining tea in the mug. It was spicy with a hint of sweetness, but dark and strong to the core. Turinam tea. "You must have paid a lot for this. My grandfather likes the best."

Jaeda's look softened, and she looked down. "The Lord Governor was healed of a serious illness last year. In gratitude he decreed that we Altharians may purchase domestic tea at cost for the comfort of the ill. It seems a small comfort when thousands of our own people can no longer afford the daily joy of their own traditional drink, which they still must grow for others. But it is something."

Salai nodded and sipped quietly. His gut felt turbulent. Jaeda was looking at him closely. She started to say something, caught herself, and then started again. "I am sorry for your loss today. But know it was good for him to see you before he died. He asked after you often."

"I wish I had come sooner." As he said it, the wall in his chest holding back the tears broke, and Salai cried. Jaeda did not move to comfort him, but sat quietly and let him weep. After awhile, Salai's tears slowed.

"Brother Salai," said Jaeda as the room slipped back into quiet, "I heard you last night... you sang in a beautiful language."

"Forget it."

"I think... No, I know it is Turian. I had a sudden memory from when I was a small child. A lullaby or a child's playful tune. A memory I had forgotten. It's funny how song can pull us back to emotions long buried."

Jaeda put her hand on his again, and Salai looked at her. Though her features were relatively plain by Turinam standards, Jaeda did have an air of unassuming strength and intelligent kindness from which Salai felt the prickles of early attraction. He frowned and buried the thought. Now was not the time for such feelings. He spoke of Grandfather instead.

"He was one of the last who remembered our history before the oppressor."

"Teach me."

"Teach you what?"

"Turian."

"I don't know Turian. We will have to learn it together. And it is forbidden. Risking my own life is one choice—"

"—And risking mine is another. It's my choice, not yours."

Salai looked hard at her. "Why do you want this?"

"I am Turian too. I too long for something within me, as if something inside were taken from me—even though I may have never had it. It's like a painting that has been torn to pieces, and we are trying to pick them up from the floor. If enough of us carry enough pieces, maybe someday we will be able to put them back together. This is how we can fight."

Salai nodded and managed a weak smile. "If ideas are our weapons, then maybe our only shield can be memories—the knowledge of who we are."

She smiled too, for the first time since he had met her. They sipped their tea, her hand on his. Outside, the sun was rising.

I Stole the D.C.'s Eyeglass

Sofia Samatar

Dakpa I keep my sister, *kpoyo* I lose my sister.
Dakpa I keep my sister, *kpoyo* I lose my sister.
The termites listen. Their hearing embraces all sound, even the smallest. They hear the future. They chew the present away as the dark devours the moon.

I don't mind if you want to consult the termites first, old man. Ask them: *Should I help this hard-eyed child?*

I'll wait.

❦

You probably think I'm funny, with my skinny body, my big ankle-bones, the spots on my legs where bites have festered and left sores. Sickly, you'll sigh, and weak. You'll think of my sister Minisare who could carry a young tree across her back. Tall and lively she was, and when the chance came to work at the D.C.'s house, when a relative of my mother's who cooked there said, *Send one of your girls*, it was Minisare my mother wanted to send, not me. But Minisare refused. Let the white man clean his own dirt, she said.

That's how I came to work at the D.C.'s house, to wear a cotton dress and collect chits my mother could spend at the company store. I carried water to the house, so you see I'm strong even though I'm little. I swept his room. He keeps his wife and children in there, framed and pegged to the wall.

❦

When Ture went to the sky he stole a thunderbolt, and when I went to the D.C.'s house I stole an eyeglass.

It was lying on the table in his bedroom, a flat disc like a stone from the river. He'd forgotten to take it with him to the Site. I squinted through it, then dropped it into the pocket of my dress, chain and all. Afterwards, I told the head cook I'd broken it.

The cook slapped me hard, but I didn't care. I took the eyeglass home, and that night, secret by the fire, I gave it to my sister. It shone in her hand like a snail-track. It was beautiful like her, and strange like her, and she gripped it and kissed me so hard I winced. We could hear my father groaning from his bed: my mother was laying hot stones along his back to ease the pain. The pain of working since dawn at the Site, digging for the D.C. I wasn't like him, I thought; I was a thief. Reckless and clever as Ture.

156

❦

Ture climbed to the sky on a spiderweb. When he got there, the clouds were locked. "Hey!" he shouted, pounding on their shining undersides. Rain fell hard, but the clouds didn't open. Ture began to sing, and his magical barkcloth hummed along with him in the rain.

Door in the clouds, open-o
See the fresh meat I'm bringing-o
Sweet as the oil of termites-o
Cooked by my wife Nanzagbe-o!

Then the clouds opened, and that's how Ture got in and stole the thunderbolt, bringing fire back to earth after all the coals had gone out. In our time, although you should always try to keep your own embers alight, you can be sure of finding a coal at a neighbor's house to start your fire. My mother used to send me out with the coal-pot if our fire died, and I'd sing at the edge of a neighbor's place: "Door in the clouds, open-o!" Minisare taught me that there were other ways. "Here!" she whispered, commanding. "Watch!" She held the eyeglass on a stick.

I squatted beside her. The world was full of Sunday-morning quiet, the diggers sleeping, voices coming faint from the church. Sweat dripped down my neck. Minisare glared with terrible concentration at the pile of dry grass she'd made on the ground.

The eyeglass glittered, fixed in the twisted wood.

Sun filled the forest. I yawned.

Then something tickled my nose: the smell of burning.

"See!" Minisare breathed.

I stared. A thread of smoke uncurled in the air, and a tiny flame cracked its knuckles in the grass.

❦

Sorcery, then.

For a long time I waited for something to happen: for the D.C. to shrivel and fade, for the Site to collapse, for the diggers to stop their pounding. But it seems the eyeglass was only a minor magic, for nothing stopped, as you know, you can hear the roar of the diggers even here. That endless roar, and the thunder of flying-machines rolling overhead, manned by slave-soldiers from a foreign land. People say the noise chased the game from the forest, once, but then the animals got used to it. We're used to it, too. Show me a child who can't read lips.

Nothing changed at all—except my sister.

At first, it seemed only a stranger form of her usual stubbornness. She wouldn't go to the farm. When I went home at night, I heard my mother complaining: "Why did I marry from the west? This is their blood showing, this worthless girl!"

She said this because my father's people came from the western forest: my grandfather had gotten trapped on our side during the Breaking of the Clans. When I got close to the fire I saw her slapping her palms together as if in grief, and Minisare plaiting a mat.

Minisare plaited with tense, quick movements. She'd split the reeds into narrow strands. Firelight streaked them. "You'll ruin your eyes," I said.

She only jerked the reeds harder.

"Her eyes!" my mother said. "If that's all she ruins, I'll consider it a blessing. What she needs is a husband—one with hard hands."

The words chilled me, and later I told Minisare: "You should help our mother on the farm."

"I can't," she said.

"Why not?"

"I have to do something else."

"Something else? What else?"

The darkness was soft, complete, I couldn't see her at all.

"Out in the forest," she said. "I'll show you."

❦

On Sunday, when I'd washed the dress and spread it out to dry, I followed my sister deep into the forest. Walking before me along the path she was still my own Minisare, cool, long-striding, pushing the grass and branches aside with the ease of a swimmer. Several of the neighbors' children trailed us, chattering in high voices. We entered a sunny space where the growth had been cleared as if for a farm. A jumble of objects littered the short grass: pots, blankets, barkcloth, cooking-stones. It was like a house shaken inside-out.

She turned to us, the little children and me. "Now," she smiled, pointing. "You fetch grass. You find me some nice long, hollow canes. The rest of you run to the charcoal-burners and beg whatever you can. Pai-te, stay with me. I want you to check my stitches."

Her eyes were red. She hadn't washed her face. Her hair needed rebraiding. But her energy was the same as ever, her laugh as the children scattered, her taut jaw as we leaned together over the patchwork she wanted me to see, a swollen thing like a dead calf.

"What do you think?" she asked. "You're good at stitching—will these hold?"

"What *is* this thing?"

"I'll put oil on it afterward, of course, to keep off the rain. I think the oil will help the stitches too, it'll keep the air from getting through."

"Minisare." I put my hand on her arm. "Tell me. What is it?"

She looked at me. And I saw for the first time what my mother saw, what other people saw when they whispered about my sister: the chameleon-eye. One of her eyes was a spirit-eye, flecked with cloud, the whole forest trapped in it. Ghosts hung in the trees.

I only saw it for a moment.

"I can't tell you yet," she said.

"You said you'd tell me."

She shook her head. "I said I'd show you."

I looked at the stitches. She'd put pieces of leather and barkcloth together, goat-hair blankets, near-transparent bits of bladder.

There were also scraps of cotton. "Where did you get these?" I demanded.

Her face went stubborn, closed. "Just tell me about the stitches."

I sighed. "They're fine."

"Thank you."

She stood up, the chain I'd given her swinging at her skirt. In place of the eyeglass it held an ugly iron spike.

❦

Minisare speaks of iron.

She weeps for the lost arts. There were smiths among us, once. They made leaping knives, the sight of which killed hope. The women plucked gold from the rivers and the smiths fashioned it into bangles, hot metal dashing into the mold like a young snake. Now smithwork is against the law, like carving, like drum-talk, like kingship, like the intricate and half-remembered varieties of marriage. You can find old pieces of iron in the forest, native iron it's called, black lumps like tree-gum chewed up and spat in the weeds.

❦

Minisare talked all the time when she was at home, sometimes so fast she stuttered. She spoke of going to visit our father's people on the other side of the line.

"You'll never get there," I said. "They'll put you in prison."

She laughed and cuffed my shoulder, throwing me off balance: her arms were heavier than she knew. Heavy with muscle, and ornaments too: wires strung with chunks of iron, battered metal cuffs, strings dangling bags full of something that clacked whenever she moved. She wore iron sticks in her hair and she kept a coil of string there for emergencies and her face was strong and preoccupied and filthy. But she could still sing in a voice as gentle and blue as the mushroom season:

House of Gbudwe, house of my grandfathers,
Strangers are eating oil there.

And sometimes, though less often now, she looked at me and smiled. "Little one," she'd say, and stroke my cheek with a bruised fingernail.

My mother's rages brought the neighbors running. "Look at you!" she screamed. "A brute, a beggar, a sick dog covered in filth from the white man's rubbish pits."

She ran at Minisare, one hand still clutching a lighted tobacco twist, a whorl of dried stuff like a smoky flower. She tried to pull off Minisare's strange ornaments, and Minisare let her try. After a while my mother gave up and sat down on the ground. Minisare walked away toward her place in the forest, leaving deep footprints. When she came back she wore a burn down the length of her arm.

"You have to stop," I said. But she couldn't stop. Even at night she couldn't rest: she worked on her mat because her fingers would not lie still. I found her plaiting by moonlight and she turned her head to look at me, the souls of the dead awake in her spirit-eye. Sometimes I couldn't find her at all: she was prowling at the Site, risking the guards, or sneaking off to see the old witch-woman of the lake. She begged me to come with her. The witch was teaching her the old drum-language, she said. She seized my hand and tapped out a crazy rhythm.

"No!"

I snatched my hand away.

Minisare stared, gaunt in the firelight, her beauty in chains.

"But it's important," she whispered. She took my hand.

My eyes grew hotter and hotter, until the tears came. She didn't notice. She kept on tapping, insistent, my palm the drum's belly, my fingers its liver and heart.

❦

Do you know what the world looks like through the D.C.'s eyeglass?

I do. It's a blurred place; you can't tell the real things from the shadows.

People call you the Old Man of the Wood. You were a carver, once, but life in the mines made you bitter, and now you live alone. Still, I know you've heard of Minisare. Stories like hers travel everywhere, noisy and eager as the drone of the diggers. Stories like hers fall over the world like rain. Minisare, the girl who cooked iron. The girl who could carry a young tree. Big stories, and all of them true. But the small stories are also true. There's the story of how I went to the Site every day to deliver the D.C.'s lunch. The story of how he gave me a chit as a tip, and I grasped that soft scrap of paper and shouted out as the cook had taught me: *"Thank you Commissioner Sir!"* The story of how he seized me in the bedroom one cold morning, his enormous thumbs making my hipbones crack.

This story is also true. My head struck the wall, knocking down two frames. The D.C.'s wife stared up from one of them, pale, trussed in cotton up to her chin. The D.C. muttered. He didn't touch me twice. I twisted and scrambled, I dashed from the room on all fours. Out on the road, I tore off the cotton dress.

I ran. I ran through the cutting grass without feeling anything. When I jumped in the river all the tiny cuts on my legs sang out in pain. I sank to the bottom, through water brown and clotted like a huge fungus. Then I kicked my way to the surface and came out gasping.

House of Gbudwe, house of my grandfathers, strangers are eating oil there. That's a true story, too. What comes up from under the ground of the Site, but oil? Stones, you say; but the D.C. wants them, the D.C. eats them like groundnuts. They are as delicious as oil in the world beyond the glass.

The D.C. eats children. I learned this for myself.

Here is a truth for you: I stole the D.C.'s eyeglass, but the D.C. stole my sister. When I came up from under the river I ran sobbing into the forest, fleeing toward Minisare, craving her strength. The branches of her clearing rang with sound. Children bounced up and down on the bags she'd sewn, each blast of air adding heat to the fire. My sister stood beyond the flames, blurred by the heat as if by tears, and her arm bulged black as she struck a piece of iron.

"Minisare!" I cried.

She did not answer me. A leather mask hid her face, a visor pulled over her eyes like a heavy scab.

"Minisare!"

I ran to her, and then I saw what she had made, out there in the forest. I saw the iron. I saw the beast.

The creature moved. It shook. Its bowels rumbled. It had no eyes. Its whole body bristled with claws of every size. They were made of old knives, hoes, ragged sheets of iron, sharpened sticks. Its bloated hind parts breathed an obscene white wind.

"Minisare," I breathed. And my sister shook her head. She shook her head at me. She motioned me away with one iron-ringed arm. She had no time to spare. The beast absorbed all of her attention: this beast that stank of smoke, of the D.C., of the Site. My hand tingled, as if she were drumming on it, and I thought of the way she tapped without listening to my words, without seeing my tears. I knew then that her strength was no longer for me, but for something else. She had gone through the glass and left me here, on the other side.

☙❧

That night Ture came to me in a dream.

He was strutting around the Site with his belly stuck out. His elephant-skin bag hung heavy on his shoulder. I crawled on the ground, hiding under a banana-leaf, and whispered: "Ture!"

"Oho!" he grinned. "Pai-te, are you there?"

"Ture, it isn't safe here!" I whispered, shrinking under the leaf in terror as machines buzzed overhead. "The D.C. will find you and put you in prison!"

His smile was so wide it cracked his face like an egg. "Ha! Ha!" he roared, slapping his skinny thighs.

Just then a little dog trotted by, almost under his feet, and he stumbled over it. The dog gave a yelp of pain.

Ture's eyes widened. "Ah!" he said, delighted. "Music!" He took his feathered hat out of his elephant-skin bag and put it on his head. Then he began to leap and trip over the dog, always finding his footing at the last moment, and when the dog cried out he sang with it in a high voice:

I am he who looks up
I look down, all men die.
Ture has stumbled-o,
Ture is dancing!

As Ture danced, the D.C. strode toward us, his eyeglass tight in his eye, and a fire came out of it and scorched the earth all around him. I screamed to warn Ture, but Ture only laughed more uproariously than ever and cried: "Do you think I'm afraid of my friend the D.C.? I've taught him all he knows!" And he sang:

House of Gbudwe, house of my grandfathers,
Strangers are eating oil there.

Then he stopped dancing and looked at me sadly. The D.C. stood beside him. And Minisare in her rough jewelry came and stood on the other side, and all three looked down at me with eyes like salt.

"Once," said Ture, "you fought with your sister. You were very young, and you bit her finger. Is that blood in you still, or have you spat it out?"

"I don't know," I sobbed.

Ture beamed. "Music!" he cried, adjusting the set of his hat. And then he kicked sand in my eyes and woke me up.

☙❧

The next Sunday evening I took my mother's digging stick and went behind the house to the termite mound. I broke off two branches, one from the *dakpa* tree, the other from the *kpoyo* tree. I dug two holes in the mound with the digging stick and put one branch in each. The sky was pale red, the ants drowsy in the cold grass.

"*Dakpa*," I said. "*Dakpa* I keep my sister. If I keep my sister, eat *dakpa*. *Kpoyo* I lose my sister. If I lose my sister, eat *kpoyo*."

I went to help my mother with the evening meal. Children laughed somewhere, at someone else's place, and the piping sound came toward us in broken pieces. A sound like a whistle to call the birds. In the morning, when it was just daylight, I woke up and crept out to the termite mound. The termites had been listening to the future, and they had eaten some of both branches. I took the two branches out and measured them on the ground. I thought the *dakpa* branch was shorter. I still think the *dakpa* branch was shorter. I woke my mother and told her: "Minisare must be married."

≈⁑≋

We came for her two weeks later.

My mother had agreed at once that we must find Minisare a husband. "Haven't I been saying so?" she cried. My father was uncertain: he worried that her madness was too well known, and no one would take her. "That's why we must do it now," I countered, "before it gets worse." He hung his head, then shrugged, and that day he began to look for a groom. And he found one: the man who now strode beside my mother, snapping off twigs when they touched him. A noisy crowd followed: relatives, neighbors, friends and trading partners, and then the hangers-on looking for Sunday excitement and hoping to smell food.

I knew, you see, that she would not hear me if I went alone.

My mother gasped and clutched my arm as we entered the clearing. "Don't be afraid," I told her, tense as wood. The groom looked startled, the strange scene piercing the layers of drunkenness he wore like a cloak. Minisare's fire was ashes today, the stones of her forge a ruin. Only her familiar, the clawed beast, gave off heat. Minisare was flinging charcoal into its anus. The children helping her cheered and skittered toward the crowd when they saw their elders.

"Look!" crowed a little boy. "Look what we made!"

The noise of the crowd swelled to a groan. My father stepped forward, his face gray. His crooked back gleamed with sweat. "Minisare," he said sternly. "Minisare, come with us. We have brought you a husband."

A foolish plan. I see this now. But I believed the termites, who had eaten *dakpa*, who had said I would keep my sister.

Minisare pushed up her leather visor and flashed her spirit-eye. Then she tore the beast's skin wide, stepped into its body and closed the skin up again.

People were running, screaming.

"Why didn't you tell me?" my mother sobbed. "It's too late, it's too late now to save her."

She shrank to the ground. Minisare's groom shambled away in panic, crashing into trees, fleeing his demon-bride. And I stood lost, the air thickening around me, until my father seized my arm.

"They've gone to fetch the soldiers," he panted.

When I didn't move, he slapped me. "*Run*, Pai-te."

When I still didn't move, he ran away without me. The children had scaled the trees, their cries snagged in the branches.

Everywhere people were crashing away through the undergrowth, and the shadows of the great flying-machines closed over us, and all the trees rattled their arms, and the side of Minisare's monster split like a wound, and Minisare leaned out and shouted: "Pai-te, run! They're going to start firing!"

She saw that I wasn't moving. She put a leg out of the monster's side.

Death striped the forest, clots of molten blood.

When her foot touched the ground, something leapt up in my throat.

"No!" I shouted, waving frantically. "No! Just go! I'm all right!"

My pulse beat under my jaw, so strong it almost made me sob, a voice singing: *Door in the clouds, open-o!* I knew that voice: it was Minisare's blood talking to me, the blood I had swallowed long ago and forgotten.

"Go!" I shouted.

By this time, there was too much noise for her to hear me. But she understood. Show me a child who can't read lips.

She looked at me from her creature's side, her eyes human now, lonely and radiant. Then she closed the skin, and the beast spun its claws and sank into the ground.

⚕

Dakpa I keep my sister, *kpoyo* I lose my sister.

That is how heroes are made. At night mothers say: "I'll tell you of Minisare, who stole a lamp from heaven." They whisper into their husbands' hair: "Wait until Minisare returns." They say she's gone underground, across the lines, to unite the clans. They say she's stamping the dust somewhere, her iron anklets jangling, her face masked, and everywhere she steps a puff of smoke flies up. Each smoke-cloud puts out teeth. Someday the mines will collapse, and Minisare will burst from the ruins with an army of iron dogs.

And that is also how villains are made. I sat quiet under my mother's shouts as she ordered me to go back to the D.C.'s house. When she ran out of breath I curled up on my mat, Minisare's unfinished mat. I stroked the strands of unwoven straw as my mother mourned by the fire. "Minisare was like me," she often tells me now: "You are your father's child." I don't mind these words. I know that grief is all my mother has in the place where Minisare used to be, and that all the love she had for Minisare must now be lavished on this grief which she carries about like a stillborn child. Also, she's telling the truth about my sister for the first time. The neighbors comfort her while she weeps and tells the truth. Minisare was everything, everything worth having on this earth: defiance, honor, dawn, tomorrow. She was the rain.

And Ture, traitor, thief, where is he? He's hiding behind this story, trying to coax it toward him. He wants to make it his own. Or no, he's not here, he went out of the tale at the same moment as my sister, the moment our history became too small to tempt him. For Ture has no interest in the small. He stumbles over them, sings along with their cries and then moves on. Some people say that he's living with the D.C., that the two of them drink from the same bottle, that the D.C. hides him and uses his power. This may be true. Foolish, clever Ture has always delighted in fire, in iron, in risk, in grand schemes leading to glory or despair. His language is song, not story. He is dancing in the mines and among the flying-machines. He will not remember me.

But I stole the D.C.'s eyeglass. I have that. Wherever my sister is, she's warm, she has light to keep demons and leopards away, she's not afraid. And I'll do more. I have done more. I went to the witch-woman of the lake and squirmed under the thatch of her sinking roof and asked her to teach me drum. The darkness smelled of snails and her hand was as stiff and rough as a hunk of dried fish when I tapped out the rhythm Minisare taught me. A gurgle came out of the gloom: the witch-woman was laughing. She knotted her fingers in my hair and pulled me to her and told me secrets.

I dream of learning more, of teaching others. I dream of *you*, old man. They say you made drums in secret, in the old days. I dream you'll make me a drum. I dream of a clearing on a dark night, and the drum-voice spreading out, crossing the line between the clans.

Ask the termites. They never lie. Come, give me your hand, and I'll prove it to you. I'll pass you the words my sister drummed into my hand. *Forgive me*, the drum-beats say. Do you feel it? That's a true story, too, a small story that's slowly growing bigger: I keep my sister.

Wait while I play you the rest of her message, a gift without weight or outline, invisible until you make it happen, like fire.

Pai-te, it says. Yes, it says my name, my actual name.

Watch your step, it says. *I'm coming back for you.*

Vector

Benjanun Sriduangkaew

You. Are.

(A weapon. A virus. A commandment from God.)

The stage is your skull, the script someone else's, and they are about to win.

Here's a wall. You are the battering ram against an amassed weight of a million shrines nestled in the crook of ancient trees, in the corners between skyscrapers, the solidity of Chaomae Guanim and Phramae Thoranee: for this is your land and yours is a land of many faiths.

The viral chorus is vicious and through you it is a tidal wave breaking upon the shore of your history, of a country shaped like an axe. Flash-narratives howl through your lips, biblical verses and names, stories of killing and fire. You understand none of it, but the virus needs a host—a mind that touches and is touched by Krungthep's subconscious grid—and so you've been chosen, with a bit of chloroform to your face and a counterfeit ambulance where you lay able to see but not to think. Neon glare in your eyes and men wearing surgical masks. Farang men with their cadaver skin and their eyes blue-gray-green.

Fear, panic. You try to remember them, but they've frayed into abstractions under the shadows of anesthetics.

The chips urge you forward and you heave against a network with mantras and prayers for bone, dreams and desires for muscle. These are what protect Krungthep and these are what they want you to destroy, with their falsity of Yesu, with visions of stained glass and cathedrals, and alien insertion of tasteless wafers into pale thin mouths. Find the cracks. Fill them up with false data, false dreams. Yours is a land that does not open its arms to churches; yours is a land that once escaped Farangset and Angrit flags through the cleverness of its kings. About time they fix that.

This is how to rewrite a country's past, and when a past is gone it is easy to replace the present with convenience. Belief moves will, and will moves nations. No screens needed, no competition with other channels. Poured straight into the intent grid this stabs the subconscious, direct as a syringe to the vein.

Holes in your skin oozing pus. Blood in your mouth lining teeth and bruised gums. No pain anywhere, because your nervous system has been deliberately broken and put back together wrong. You try to think of something other than this, other than the ports they've made in your arms and between your vertebrae, other than the cold metal jacked into you to dictate your heart and measure your synapses.

You dream of ghost dances and processions to pray for rain, a black cat yowling in a wicker cage slung between villagers' shoulders. You dream of leaving offerings, fruits and sweets and glasses of cream soda to divinities you can understand.

❦

There was a war between China and America, and it left the world a series of deserts, the sky a pane of broken glass.

Krungthep has clawed out survival from the aftermath's bedrock under the engines which process intent into power, and power into a shelter that makes Krungthep possible. It is expanded and strengthened year by year; it can be turned, with the right adjustment, into a weapon. From shield to sword. From sword to gun. The woman who created this system died young to a sniper. She's celebrated now, her name a byword for martyrdom and progress. No daughter of Prathet Thai, and few sons either, have done more.

Second phase of infection. It returns you to a time where you wear a body in place of plastic, in place of the coffin in which you've been interred. In this present there are no temples or mosques in the city, by the rivers or punctuating the soi. Only churches with their naked Yesu, their clothed altars that mean nothing to you, their abjection before a fancy whose appeal you cannot understand.

In the streets billboards and signs shine neon Angrit, foreign brands, foreign elegance. No Thai anywhere, for why should a language exist that's spoken by less than a hundred million, next to one spoken worldwide? Where's the efficiency in so many letters in the alphabet, and vowels and consonants? Twenty-six is all anyone needs. The chips bombard you with linguistic algorithms and statistics. In a world of Angrit, Thai is unnecessary.

Listen. Your sister's speaking faultless Angrit in the style of foreign news anchors. The cousin from overseas won't have to pinch his face and look away and sigh at everyone's pronunciations, everyone's misspellings. No more shame. Everyone will be perfectly equal, rid of that embarrassing accent. Forget the tongue you've spoken since birth. Childish toys are to be put away; sick things are to be put down. (Observe those phrasal verbs, the ambiguities. The qualities of *away* and *down* can both mean death.)

The logic of this does not slot quite right but soon enough the thinking part of you is thrust back to a corner, smaller than you, than half a raindrop. You try to hold onto it but it slips and drips. It is gone, it is vapor, it was never there.

You stagger out of a classroom taught by a woman with ashy hair and painted pebbles for eyes. That school's all air-conditioned rooms and corridors polished to a shine, populated tidily by children of the rich and powerful. Yellow-headed classmates with their loudness and their big bodies close in on you. (This is not the sort of school your parents could afford.) You look for, and cannot find, dark hair. Reflections of you dwindle, so small you can thread yourself through a needle's eye.

Was the city of your birth ever so crowded with people who looked like that?

Yes, it was. This is how things have always been, and it follows this is how things will be. This is logical, this is sensible. This is peace and progress.

Out through the school gate, part of a crowd pouring out, you hope for familiar smells of roast pork and sticky rice, for colors you recognize: an old tree with a pink sash around it to mark the spirit residing within. Tiny plates of food at the base of a utility pole, to curry favor with any small god that might live in the wires or the concrete. It does no harm to put such things out. But they are superstitions and the farangs passing by smirk. A tourist, more freckles than skin, pauses to blink at it; her spectacles give off a flicker. Photo snapped and uploading, to be laughed at and rendered into a joke. Who believes in divinities so diminutive? Yesu-Lord is large and he lives everywhere, not just in a pole or a tree. Or his ghost does. Or his father. One of them or possibly all. Nano-missionaries have been drilling you with parables and sermons but they don't take. It is not a strength of will or integrity of self that protects you but sheer confusion.

Outside you can feel tubes in your lungs sucking and working to keep you from drowning in your own fluids. Despite the nutritional drip-feeds, hunger burns a black cinder-path through your stomach.

❧❦❧

Words beat strident against your shell. (Cell. Angrit, full of similar words.) They're discussing the danger of storing so much information in one place, eggs in one basket. But they haven't so many baskets left and must make do, and after all they're in no danger. Who will dare, except China, from whom they have hidden with perfect care? Who has the power to strike, except China, whom they will defeat and take back what's theirs?

A memory blankets you, duvet-thick against a day too warm.

Mother has remarried and the half-and-half sibling she puts on your lap has huge Barbie eyes (did you ever play with Barbies with their blue eyes, their blonde hair?). Her new husband is much older than she is and feverishly happy that she's given him such a beautiful baby, and everyone agrees it is beautiful. Half-and-half always are, with that kind of nose and that kind of hair, shampoo-ad perfect from infancy. The weight of the new sibling—surprising heft, surprising mass—presses down and you cannot stand up. You fight to breathe; you avoid inhaling your stepfather's cologne, which nauseates and fails to hide the stink of his armpits.

Mother's happiness is glass. There is cash for your grandmother's hospitalization now, the cardiac treatments that insurance doesn't stretch far enough to cover. You think you've failed. Sixteen and not making the money that would have mooted the marriage. Some of your aunts cringe and judge, but those are the ones who never did anything for Grandmother. Younger-Sister Gung, ten, makes faces at the new husband's back.

Neither of you calls him father, not in any language.

Cut, call the chips. Camera panning elsewhere.

In a Jatujak barber's you are with your farang friends who wear crosses gleaming silver on identical columnal throats. They are each garlanded with identical blonde hair. They don't need a stylist. A look and a laugh, that's all they require to make you ugly and hard. Wonderful waists, wonderful legs. An instinctive grace from a lifetime of certainty that they are exquisite. Among them you fade. Among them you lose dimension until you're paper.

A cross is just two lines of unequal lengths intersecting: what is that next to Phra Puttachao, who has a human face, perpetually at peace? You touch your own neck and find there is a cross there too, where the loinclothed god-son-prophet bows his suffering head. Under your finger it seems to turn fleshy and your nail comes away tipped crimson.

You are—

You look at the daub of red until it dries to brown crust. You find an Internet café and take a seat. Around you: sultry air thickened by fish sauce, sweet chili dip, and deep-fried fish cakes.

No one here wears a cross. No one here has sun-spotted cheeks. The ceiling fans whirr against dust, hair, dog fur. An auntie laughs into her headset, talking to a child studying abroad. Two students argue about test results over shaved ice drenched in condensed milk and red syrup.

The computer you've picked boots up crankily. A CRT flickering with artifacts, mouse and keyboard caked in food-smears. In the entire café this is the sole tribute to archaism, decades out of step next to sleek machines with screens half as thick as your thumb.

Spam strains the seams of your inbox. Clicking through you delete and delete, catching junk-fragments of sentences like poetry with its pancreas hanging out, its diaphragm wrapped around a sleeve. A few messages you print out on dot-matrix paper, crackling fragility and ink barely visible. Fold. Roll into a tube. Twist.

Tug that into your collar, where it'll rest against your pulse.

The weeks are rubber bands, pulled twang-taut then loosened by a hand caring nothing for clocks and calendars. You relive job interviews and rush hours that are indeterminable. You recede to history lectures that pass by in eye-blinks. You're now working at an advertising firm under a white boss, who wears t-shirts and jeans to work even though everyone else is in business casual, who puts his feet on the table even though he knows it offends.

His secretary is his girlfriend and she hates you. Thai girls are out to steal her man, she thinks, and when she looks at you the spots in her cheeks brighten—like rashes, like chickenpox—and she keeps postponing the pay raise that should've been yours six months ago. You've attempted to explain she has nothing to fear but it is no good. The gulf between Thai and farang is too large for the common quality of *woman* to bridge.

When she hears about this your fiancée laughs and laughs. She wears a man's shirt and belted trousers, she has cropped hair and a voice rich for singing, all her earcuffs are avian and all her rings reptilian. You wouldn't trade her for the entire world.

Two years together and she leaves you for a man, having let her hair grow out and having put on a skirt. You find yourself a boyfriend. It's just as well, for under the grace of Christ certain acts are forbidden; under his grace certain acts will send you to burn.

It is getting hard to tell what happened and what didn't. You want to make it real, that coil of paper. It is not. Nothing is.

❧❦☙

News is supposed to report truth.

On TV the prime minister is shaking hands with a blue-eyed man, who is President of the United States. His wife is First Lady, which drives you to question why the man is not First Lord. A rousing speech concerning an alliance against China, a partnership of equals, a fight against nonspecific tyranny. Tonight everyone will dream of this broadcast, struck and inspired by its righteousness. This is how to overwrite the intent grid. A disease, and you the vector.

Your heart feels absent, as though it has been exhumed and made to beat behind someone else's sternum. Sternum. Were you in med school or is that just mathayom-thon biology?

There's a showing of *Anna and The King* after work and the theater is packed, a reminder that these days the palace is a relic and mortuary; the last queen was exiled when the Americans brought you absolute democracy and rewrote the constitution, which is good, which is right. Monarchy was holding your country back, as were the shrines which have been replaced by churches. The new prime minister is America-approved, and that's best of all.

On the wall the film plays out, fast-forwarding in spasms, slowing down to linger on certain shots: contrast the demure farang lady and the faintly repulsive monarch. Characters meant to be Thai speak your language terribly. You find this odd, then you don't.

Beside you someone reaches over and clasps your wrist. A tiny owl glitters at her earlobe, a miniature crocodile at her thumb. You remember with a jolt buying her both. You remember wearing accessories that match, and holding onto each other in a theme park crowd.

When the movie finishes you leave together. In the parking lot, under a scorching sun, you ask, "Who are you?"

She nudges an abandoned trolley full of dirty plastic bags. It rolls down the ramp, where it judders against an empty stroller. Crash. "What do you mean?"

"Aom wouldn't do that." You are amazed you can speak with your own voice. The chips must be busy. Or maybe they are done with you, now that you've paved a way into the engines for them, now that you drift in your tank broken and limp.

The one who wears your fiancée like a badly fitted suit becomes your mother at sixty-five, twice divorced and haggard at the edges. "There's not much time."

You look at her. The hum of the nano-missionaries, which has become white noise, rumbles. Passages from the bible concerning sinners and punishment, a salt pillar looking back. "There isn't any time left. It's already finished. It's done."

"Not yet." This time it is your sister. Gung at six months along, gravid and radiant. She tilts her head and smiles, leans into you and whispers a trojan into your ear.

❧

You are—
I am.

❧

Alertness snapping in her with such force that it bows her spine. A visceral waking that returns flesh to the bones of her ghost, mind to the husk of her corpse.

173

Corpse is what she is. The first she does is accept that; the second is to remember that Aom didn't leave her, not for anyone. In the absence of everything else, in the presence of amniotic fluids and electric currents in her jugular, selfishness is her final bastion.

The abduction wasn't accident. It was sacrifice. An easy step to take when all with meaning has already been lost. Easy to be a patriot, that way, if it can be called patriotism when what she does is courting survival.

Between excited chatter over the concluding phase, they put her under, casual as drowning a small animal. But the trojan compartmentalizes and this time she flows with it, a swimmer with rather than against, in control. She splits: the shadow-theater puppet in its two dimensions, and a ghost hovering at its shoulder to watch and edit decisions. The remote protocols they've installed with needles and scalpels have quieted to an ignorable buzz.

You—

I am, I am, I am. Outside she must have lost motor control. In here she flexes and tenses and knows her strength, honed and muscular. This is where she needs to be. They have protections, but those are useless when she's already inside.

It is too late to fix the distortions they've inflicted on Krungthep; afterwards someone else will do that, tending each node one by one in the tunnels, under the safety she has purchased with everything.

She tries not to resent, tries not to regret.

The machines they've linked to her are the bare essentials, equipment to monitor vital signs, a server on which the control protocols are hosted. It is the latter that she will attack.

Poured into her with the sanctity of an incantation, the trojan has been precisely crafted. Without a vector it would have been useless. With her in place, anything is possible.

She flips a port open, and waits.

⚕

Five, eight, some age in the between. You've given yourself an electric shock courtesy of a finger too curious, a power outlet too close to the ground. Wail in your mother's arm; let the tears flow. She smells expensive. You stop when you see that Mother is a woman with light brown hair, pointed nose, and pale eyes. Modernly dressed, hair parted just so, Hollywood tidy. She moves cinematically, poised for cameras.

The virus-dreams have reached childhood.

Sunday and they dress you for church, in ribbons and little-girl frock, all pastels. Temples are flattened to grainy pictures and stained postcards trampled underfoot, peeking out over the fraying edges of carpeting, hiding under calendars that tell the year in *Anno Domini*. Five hundred and forty-three behind the real one.

Among the pews you huddle as the man in black gives sermon, his voice the beehive chorus of the nano-missionaries. You squeeze your hand into the child's fingers and pinch her cross until it bleeds onto the marble, spotting her tiny footsteps red. When no one is looking you break the cross into two, then four. When no one is looking you use a little marker to scribble Thai onto signs when you can, even if it doesn't take on surface that's gloss and metal, even if the marker is too faint. You wear the tip to a dry nub even so.

Under the not-mother's absent gaze you cut a green mango to slices, mix your own chili salt, and eat it in place of pudding and peanut-butter sandwich. These gestures do nothing. You know that. But it comforts you to spend these grains of freedom you've sieved like gold out of the muck, and you miss the taste nearly as strongly as you miss the dead.

The end is soon. It'll be the end for you, too.

❧ ❦ ☙

Security tautens and loosens in these last days according to the pitch of collective nerves. She ascertains that she's in a ruined hospital in Palangkaraya, basement level, far from home. It chills her until she remembers the distance is irrelevant, that come success or failure she will never leave this place. What remains of her will not survive being disconnected from the tank.

All is anatta. Sangkarn is transient. She needs to let go. Panic rises anyway, even though she's so detached from flesh that she should be beyond this choking terror, above this mindless fear of the grave.

Eavesdropping on them calms her in stages. The farangs are happy to be done, happy to—soon—be home. The shattered city unsettles them and, fingers tight over their crosses, they joke about Indonesian boogeymen, le-ak flitting at night with entrails streaming like tassels on a kite. They discuss taking Jakarta, one more strategic gain against China. China, China. The word preoccupies them the way oxygen preoccupies lungs; the rest is peripheral, mattering insofar as to how it might provide advantage in the coming war. There will be one. They intend to press the issue. They will regain their pride.

She unpacks the trojan as they watch the cinematography they've made of her life, the disease they've made of her puppet-self.

❧ ❦ ☙

I am.

A leap from the precipice of metal and flesh, a weightless

somersault in free fall and you're inside. Impactless you land on your feet. Ghosts don't make splashes and you orient without having to try. This is what happens when they hold the door wide and invite you in.

There are nodes where they've latched parasitic to Krungthep's dream-grid and you know every one, for each link was made through your brain. You carry a schematic on your forearms, on the inside of your elbows, the way patients carry injection scars.

In churches you turn altar cloths from cream to red, the color of blood and nation. In Baiyoke Tower, you change the locks on doors and wedge elevators open. You pull keys out of your mouth and leave them in particular cars, and in schools you replace the language of textbooks. At construction sites you push with a fingertip and scaffolds crumble, wreathing you in cement dust. You visit certain embassies and edit the flags and emblems, minute tricks. Symbols are all there is to the mesh.

While your puppet-self fulfills her part you wander Krungthep one last time, exerting the sinews of memory. A chedi's curve, the green spikes of a durian at market, half of Pridi Panomyong's face from the monument at your campus. The pieces of city their programs have rubbed out.

The launch wrenches at you, for you are everything—disease and vector—and it almost sweeps you away, shattering you in pieces and distributing them across the grid: that will complete the infection, finalize the murder.

Traffic has always been potentially two-way. They had to leave it so to operate and manipulate you. Now you tear that path into a wound, and what flies free is not their erasing of Krungthep, their unraveling of the dream-grid. It is their future laid bare. A hemorrhage of classified data and logistics, maps of where they're strong and where they're weak—the weapons they have, the weapons they don't have; what survives of their country and what does not. There will be no war for them to win.

They shut everything down: too late. That opening was all anyone needed, and at the other end there are waiting hands on machines which reel in and gather the data you've unspooled. Data that can be used to keep Krungthep alive. Data that can be sold, for that's the game everyone must play, now.

You imagine farang men yanking out cords, slamming down on circuit breakers with fists suddenly sweat-wet. You imagine them howling, animal panic.

The casket opens; the liquids buoying you pour out in a briny flood and the puppet of your skin sags on knees that no longer work. They tear it out, to end your dreams of home and bring you death.

There is light, and you laugh.

Forests of the Night

Gabriel Murray

"I've always thought there was something quintessentially Oriental," said the Captain's friend Burroughs, "about the tiger. Don't you think, Captain?"

The Captain loved to hunt, so when Burroughs had come to him that morning, claiming that his tenant's sheep were being taken by a beast, he saddled up and took out the dogs without being asked twice. He didn't ask me along; he didn't have to. I was the one doing the saddling.

I wondered if Mr Burroughs remembered that I was present. Maybe he did and maybe he didn't. He only seemed to ever ascribe to me a very select quality of presence, whether or not I was actually there at the time, and it didn't involve considering his words by how I might take them. *Mr Burroughs doesn't mean ill*, the Captain had explained to me once with a clap on the shoulder and a flash of toothy white. *He's a bit of a berk, though, and you should know that. Good to know which of one's friends are berks.* The Captain regarded many of his friends with a certain fond contempt; I came to understand that this was a matter of course when it came to having friends from public school.

Today the Captain was indulging Burroughs less than usual. The dogs had promptly set to howling, so he was distracted. "I suppose it comes from the Orient, yes," he said with a shrug that indicated he wasn't paying attention, "in that limestone doesn't pop out of the ground here either, so you could call it quintessentially Kentish if you liked."

I hid my amusement at the conversation by leaning down to pat my favourite wolfhound on the head. The Captain had stern words on the matter of giving the hunting dogs attention when they were failing— spoiling a lesser creature just confuses it, he said—but he wasn't looking.

Burroughs wasn't finished, though: "So much beauty—yet really just a big brute, a big dumb brute. And beautiful and wild and incomprehensible. But deadly, if you forge in without knowing what you're after. Very Oriental, I find. I saw a man-eater in a cage in Ceylon, but all I wanted to do was reach out and touch it."

"It's a cat," said the Captain, glancing up at both of us. He'd dismounted to see if anything had startled the dogs, to terrify them so. He was perfectly without motion when he stood still, possessed of not a single nervous habit. His thumb was hooked into his belt and his jodhpurs were still pressed. "Beautiful, perhaps, but it's a bloody great cat. And I am nearly one hundred percent certain that no travelling circuses have come through Yorkshire of late, and that none of our neighbours are madmen with penchants for zoo-keeping, so I don't honestly know what you're on about, Burroughs. We're looking for a hungry wolf. Maybe rabid, so I think we should keep the dogs at home. Perhaps that's what they're smelling, do you think, Jack?"

"They've a nose for sickness, sir," I answered neutrally and straightened up in the saddle.

"Perhaps. I saw a paw-print," said Burroughs with the airy stubbornness of an aristocrat.

The Captain smiled without sincerity, as if to say, there's Burroughs being daft again. But he was a gentleman, as he was teaching me to be, so he nodded. "I'm sure you did. I'll keep looking," he said, mounting again and bringing his horse about. "Jack, let's take the dogs home."

I nodded my assent and clapped my hands for their attention, but I was uneasy. Burroughs was a berk, you'd get no argument from me there. There was, however, at least one thing in the world upon which Mr Burroughs and I agreed: in the blood and wool and loamy heath we'd seen the impression of a great cat's paw. But the Captain was a man of Reason, and reasonable men did not see what plainly couldn't be there.

Leave off, Burroughs, I could've told him. *You won't convince him that way*. But Burroughs never would have listened to me anyway.

We rode home.

My mother let me go right away when the Captain came back for me in Kuala Lumpur, which I can't help but resent slightly. It wasn't as though I hated the idea of going with him, either. She may not know it, but I understand her there. No one met Captain Lyons and didn't want to go with him.

When I met him the first time I was struck by how quiet he could be, how self-assured. I knew British men as red-faced braggarts, often with wandering hands, and had never formed a favourable impression. Jonathan Lyons, by contrast, was tall and copper-haired and aquiline, with touches of silver at his temples. My mother and he regarded one another for some time at the door, and then he doffed his hat and she invited him in.

Still, I might have appreciated some weeping and wailing. But my mother hadn't been raised to weep or wail and neither had I. "This is the boy?" was the Captain's question.

"Yes," she said with her hand on my back. "Named after his

father."

I certainly wasn't, but I was now, I supposed. I stood up straight and prepared for hawkish scrutiny, but instead I was regarded by those steady copper eyes without tension. It was strangely discomforting. I had the impression he blinked as a courtesy. "I'll call him Jack," he said. "Does he have his letters? And some schooling?"

"Of course," she said coolly. "We do have schools here."

He walked a half-circle around me for more inspection, then stepped back, visibly relieved. Perhaps he hoped to ascertain that I was really his son. He had nothing to worry about there. From the moment he stepped through the door I knew that he was my missing piece, the stranger I didn't recognize in my face when I looked in the mirror. "I can't acknowledge him," he said. "He'll have to call me Captain Lyons."

She bristled. "Then why—"

"I will send him to university," he said, crossing his arms. "He'll want for nothing that a common English boy with sponsorship would have. But he will have to be my valet until then. There is no other option."

When we parted he kissed my mother on the cheek. "*Selamat tinggal*," he said in very precise Malay.

The irony was that I'd far more preparation to go to university than to be a valet, and maybe he knew that, too. I should have been angry. I was sort of angry later, once I thought about it. It didn't matter. I was too taken with him and his bearing, the way he spoke and the copper in his hair. He was so poised, so indifferent, that little glimpses of his approval were like flashes of gold. Already I wanted him to like me.

❧

One disembowelled sheep was a waste of wool, but not really the Captain's concern. Two were gruesome, but still a favour he was doing for an old mate. A horse, however—

"You see it! You see! Its neck is broken," Burroughs nearly howled in the late morning when the Captain answered the summons with me in tow again, "and teeth wouldn't snap it so clean, something *smacked* it, Lyons, with its paw. A wolf doesn't hunt like that, it goes for the jugular. This is a cat. Do you really think a lone wolf could kill a horse? One of *my* thoroughbreds?"

I was groggy and wanted to leave. I didn't care about Burroughs' livestock or his madcap theories on what was killing them. His talk of the Orient had driven me to uncomfortable dreams, where I loped around the Captain's Yorkshire estate on four massive feet and thought idly about getting something to eat. It was Hell on my sleep and made me nervous of how useful I was being at any given moment. I really hated Burroughs then, I didn't want him to utter another word about *the Orient* and remind the Captain about me, not when things were going so well between us.

"I know what your theory is, Burroughs," said the Captain with a weary brush of his fingers across his forehead.

"You've come recently from the Orient—" Burroughs glanced at me; I shrank. "Do you think perhaps—"

"*Burroughs*," the Captain said sharply. "I'll tell you if I find anything."

The dogs were still inconsolable. They were useless for proper hunting, too: the Captain and I had taken them for a boar hunt at another school friend's well-stocked estate, but when I brought them in they barked at each other and the air and then bolted in the thick of it, spooking the Captain's horse. He was thrown, but he landed on his feet with his lance in his hand and he waited for the pig to charge him.

I didn't even have time to be afraid for him. He was like how I imagined Lord Wellington from the Waterloo histories; he just pulled the lance out of the pig when it stopped thrashing and said, "My handkerchief, Jack."

His friends were crowing about "Lord!" and "now *that* is a hunter!" but I worried for the dogs. This was the sort of uselessness that couldn't be sanctioned in hounds.

"I will have to think about putting them down," muttered the Captain, much more ruffled by the dogs' behaviour than by his close scrape with the boar's tusks. That didn't seem to concern him at all. And why would it? There was a Cape buffalo's skin in his game room, elephants' tusks too. "No, I'll speak to the veterinarian first. Perhaps they *are* sick."

❦

My marksmanship didn't exist before the Captain took it upon himself to create it on his shooting range behind the rosebushes. He had no interest in grooming me for military service—either I'd feel the call to it or I wouldn't, was what he said—but found it a crucial skill for any young man to possess.

Was it so wrong to be happy?

"Cradle the stock against your shoulder like so," he told me, "and be sure it's solidly placed, or when it punches back it will hurt you. Rifles are loud. Don't let the noise startle you into losing your grip on the gun."

Even so, it was louder than I expected. I punched holes through two targets and the blast punched holes in my ears, or so I felt for minutes afterwards. The Captain was delighted, though, and clapped his hands.

Later, he introduced me to moving targets: "Aim just in front of the bird. It's not going to stay in place." And: "Never rush your shot. It doesn't matter if a wild boar's charging you directly or if George's dragon is—it'll gore you all the faster if you miss."

He smiled after the lessons. He was pleased: largely with himself, like he'd just taught me a new trick. "A quick lad," he said. "We'll make a hunter of you yet."

☙❦❧

I lived downstairs, one storey below the grand ballroom, though as far as I knew the Captain didn't dance. There I slept on a feather mattress and dreamed a memory from not so long ago.

I was practising with the rifle after the Captain's lessons, loading, aiming, and firing at the targets behind the rosebushes. I could see the frustration on my own face when the barrel jammed, the vindictive triumph in my eyes when I shot a squirrel that'd been irritating me with its chatter. I smiled at my own impatience.

I watched myself through the eyes of an observer who circled me lazily from a distance, but not a vast one.

I woke up and went to check the lock on my bedroom door. In the morning I was woken again by a long, twisting, miserable sound that I couldn't quite place.

Once I saw a Chinese funeral march in Kuala Lumpur, all in white. The family hadn't been wealthy and couldn't pay for a large well-ordered procession. So they dragged together all their white and they made up for it with their wretched howls: howls which frightened my mother's cat, which my cousins took to calling "ghoul noises," which even my mother deemed an unconscionable nuisance after a certain point. The hounds were making this noise.

The door to the kennel was torn off its hinges. The bitch must have put up the greater fight. Her hide had been torn up in great rents but she hadn't been devoured. The stud's abdomen was all but gone, one of his legs too. Another dog was missing his forepaws and sprawled with his head at an odd angle. The others were flecked with red to greater or lesser degree and howling, but alive.

I found myself stepping over their remains, nearly slipping on the blood. I scratched one of the other dogs absently and was disturbed by the tranquil pace of my heart.

The Captain wasn't faring so well. He'd wrapped himself in what looked like two dressing-gowns over his clothing. The sound had rendered him wan and ill. The Yorkshireman groundskeeper was worse, though: he'd blanched bone white and had already been sick on the kennel floor, by the look of it.

Captain Lyons said, simply, "I'll put together a hunt."

The room smelled like the dogs' blood. I knelt next to the bitch. "Sir," I called. "Look."

He looked. So did the groundskeeper, still mottled and silent in the corner.

I motioned to the deep, dark scores in her side, made with an impossibly long sweep.

꿹♊꿷

The Captain recovered his spirits in time for the next day's hunt. He was shaven tidy again and his copper moustache twitched over his mouth like a curry-brush. I imagined him intrepid with a machete, plumbing King Solomon's mines.

I didn't want to go with him. My dream was too much with me, loping around me in a lazy circle, watching me shoot even now. I remembered the scores on the dogs' bodies. But after breakfast I encountered the Captain on the grounds and he hailed me, distracted: "Ah, there you are, lad. Come along and saddle Cleto, all the men are going to need their guns."

It was a kindness, I reminded myself. I knew how much I stuck out in the hunting party, like a sallow little thumb. The hounds whined in disharmony, always one too high or too low to ignore. On a normal hunt it would've been irritating, but the noise was just about the only thing keeping me from falling off my horse. I hadn't slept well at all. Every time I'd woken in the night, I found my dreams slinking away from me on soft-padded feet.

I put a hand on the stock of one of the Captain's rifles. The mist penetrated my shabby jacket and clammied up my skin as we rode onward over the moor, mindful of our footing on the heather.

"Oi, Lyons!" Our neighbour Mr Gaffney pulled up his horse short in front of the Captain impudently, forcing him to do the same. "What's the matter with your hounds? The cat got in the kennel, didn't it? Where's their trail?"

"There isn't one," I answered, preoccupied with Cleto. "The tiger lost them in the rain and it hasn't come back. It should be wounded."

Gaffney raised his eyebrows at my speaking up. The groundskeeper was more concerned with the content. "Tiger?" he repeated and the Captain settled his butterscotch eyes on me too.

I was aware again of sticking out. A rich gentleman, a working fellow, and an Army Captain were still three Yorkshiremen when it came down to it. Contrast me, the boy here on a kindness.

I swallowed. "There's no cat so large," I said: truthfully, too, though that was not how I knew. "I mean, it couldn't be anything else, sir, however ridiculous it sounds. And I'm sure it does."

"A tiger," Gaffney repeated, more amused than bemused. He was a sportsman and to him this was sport. The Captain looked at him through half-lidded eyes, but Gaffney was too blooded himself to mind an Army Captain's opinion, so went on, "What a bedevilled idea. It'd be a stranger to these parts, to be certain."

Like me, I thought.

❦

The cat followed me every night now. His stripes rippled like a hypnotic illusion when I closed my eyes, sometimes to find myself wearing them. I don't know when I started thinking of it as a "he," but it might have been when I found myself sitting up in bed and the tiger sitting up in the doorway watching me. Its eyes were dilated black in the near-darkness. Its tail flicked back and forth behind it like an angry snake.

"You killed the dogs," I said.

He smiled. How can a tiger smile? But he did, and I knew that he was, too.

"You couldn't have been hungry," I said, angry. "There are sheep here for miles. But you killed the dogs."

"I was tired of their noise," he purred, curling his tail around his great brutish feet. "I don't lie. Men lie to make themselves feel better about the things they do. Tigers destroy what ails them. And they feast."

I understood him so well and saw him so clearly outlined in the doorway that I was sure I was not dreaming. But he didn't kill me; he turned and padded off into the hall and I woke up in the morning with the door as closed and latched as I'd left it.

❦

The next week I was awoken by a furious knocking and the butler's voice. I knew what he was after before I opened my eyes, because I'd seen it happen.

"The master's putting together a hunt, boy," he said. "Go, go— quickly now!"

My tiger was no longer merely wild, but a man-eater. Mr Burroughs had been found dead on the stones of the open gallery in his manor house where he liked to smoke. I knew because I'd been there and seen him surprised, then running briefly because cats like to play, then bleeding. He was fairly wretched to the last of it. I watched him die with disappointment and contempt.

I washed up in the basin. I looked in the mirror and wondered why my eyes weren't slitted in the light.

Mr Burroughs, pitiful irritating Mr Burroughs with his endless talk of the Orient. Had he really touched a man-eater? He had now. I hated the Orient, hated Malaya, hated myself and everything I brought here; I wished desperately to turn myself in, but for what? They'd put me in a sanitarium and then nothing could help me.

I answered the Captain's summons instead. I felt like I was walking to the gallows. He, by contrast, was taut and alive; he'd recovered his spirits since the deaths of his dogs, and far from destroyed, he was flushed and lively and glowing with anticipation. He wasn't fond of Burroughs, I knew, so I supposed he planned to save his condolences for the widow. His anger about the man's death seemed to be fixed to a very sharp point, aimed directly at the cat. A tiger's skin was one of those missing from his game room wall.

It occurred to me that he finally believed in the beast. Of course it was immature of me to resent that he hadn't just taken my word. But I did, so really, neither of us was thinking about poor old Burroughs at all.

I didn't hate Burroughs. Neither did the Captain. But I had to admit that I didn't miss him.

It was strange to feel like the murderer of a man you literally could not have murdered. It was even stranger to cease caring about it for the time being. I found myself saddling up all the men, who were all ignoring me, including the Captain—valets became invisible at times like this—and our cocksure neighbour Sebastian Gaffney nearly cuffed me at one point, but I avoided his ire and we were off with the dogs. Riding with them was exhilarating; I wondered what I would do if I encountered the tiger. Would it recognize me? Was I mad?

No one there had tracked a tiger before, but the Captain discussed some common-sense strategy with the other men: "shoot for the head no matter what," one of them was saying, "it may kill some of the dogs first but let the dogs distract it, and then we'll drag the damned thing in and see who the Devil we have to blame for its being here—"

But I had walked with the tiger in his vanishing stripes and I was unsure of our prospects. Before we reached the ridge above Burroughs' house, the dogs were giving the howl they did when they lost a trail and the tracks were gone.

"Damn you, Lyons," Gaffney snapped, bringing his mount around, "Tomorrow I'm calling the Mayor and he's going to send for a game hunter."

Cleto was nervous, I could feel her shifting. I put my hand in her mane and looked to the Captain, but the Captain didn't have any answers and I realized I was going to have to decide what to do.

❦

That night I didn't dream, not even passingly. The tiger let me be. The moonlight did not, though; it was particularly bright around the hour of two-o'clock and I still woke. I wondered who the tiger was going to kill next. My door was still latched, of course, but that didn't mean anything and was small comfort to my nerves: he'd come in and out with impunity, like he was invisible to everyone but me.

I stared at my face in the mirror and I was finally certain of it.

I sat with my head in my hands for quite a time. And then I dressed and belted my rifle to my back and pulled on my boots and set off on foot into the mist and heather.

On the grounds of the Gaffney estate, in the garden where Mr Gaffney would go for his walks and entertain his arrogant perspectives on politics and modern man out loud to his guests, I found what I expected to find. I was less frightened than I imagined I would be, because it was difficult to be frightened at the sight of your constant companion, whom you saw night after night and day after day. He visited me in my bedroom, after all. He knew me better than anyone else here.

Gaffney had been dead for some time, because the Captain had already consumed most of him by the time he looked up at me. I advanced over the stones of the path, but when our eyes met I couldn't go further. Absurdly, I felt ashamed.

There was blood all down his face and chest. He looked superbly poised. He arched his fine eyebrows at me.

"Are you really a tiger?" I asked with a measure of disbelief.

"It's something you could call me. Once I was a wolf," he said with a shrug. "But I went to Malaya and I have been a tiger ever since."

I said nothing.

"We are beautiful creatures," he said, baring his teeth to smile. They were flat and human. "Poor Burroughs wasn't wrong. And we are wild. And men cannot comprehend us. But Burroughs insulted me." He closed his mouth and annoyance clouded his handsome features, the lines between his butterscotch eyes. "I am English," he said with coldness and pride.

He had no care for his fine hunting clothes, not his jacket or his jodhpurs, and they were all splattered with Sebastian Gaffney's blood. Gaffney was beginning to stiffen. I didn't care to look down at him again, but the smell of his entrails was drying out. Some of the gore was starting to make the Captain's arms sticky, though. He wrinkled his nose in distaste and licked the back of his hand fastidiously.

"Are you going to kill me?" I asked.

The Captain looked up. His tongue was red again. "I sired you," he said. "When I came to see you I wondered if you'd be another wretched little Malay, simpering along like the others." He smiled and his voice softened and came out a purr. "But no, you were a tiger."

He crouched down over the corpse again and tore out more of Gaffney's guts. I saw a man; I saw a cat, hunched over its kill, the speech was all the same to me. "Shed that skin, Jonathan," he said, "and I will teach you how to feast."

I could feel the crawl of my hairless skin, cold and vulnerable. I could feel the weakness of my muscles: a man's muscles. I could feel the man's weapon on my back, which was dead weight on a cat's impatience. Captain Lyons had taught me how to use that weapon, a crucial skill for any young man to possess. The gun wasn't important to him, though. He could shoot a gun if he liked, or slide adeptly off the back of a panicking horse and skewer a pig with a lance. What mattered was that I could hunt.

"You're mistaken, Father," I said as I slung the rifle off my back.

My father looked up at me.

I cradled the stock against my shoulder. "That isn't my name," I said and waited for the pig to charge me.

What Really Happened in Ficandula

Rochita Loenen-Ruiz

When the young ones ask me where their father is, I have no words to give them. What do I tell the children when we are gathered around the fire at night?

❦

Through the porthole, Gemma could see the green curve that was New Cordillera.

Six hundred and twenty leaps from their first jump spot—a convoluted journey made to throw off any possible pursuers.

Gemma took a deep breath and smoothed out the pages of the journal she was reading.

"So you won't forget," her grandmother had said. "I know you have heard us tell it over and over again, and perhaps you don't wish to read of it as well. But there is no one else to whom I can trust this record of what our tribe has endured."

In the end, she had taken it with her. It was not a large book and, like those who were on the ship with her, she had taken only bare necessities and small mementos of the life she'd left behind.

New life was what waited for them on New Cordillera. A new land given to them by the great god Kabunyan—a country shaped in the image of the one they'd left behind. Green and rich with promise—a world beyond the reach of the Once-masters. A place nurtured by the goddess who had placed them in the wombs of their birth-mothers.

"Go," her mother had said when Gemma told her of the invitation she'd received. "I am too old to break with this old Earth, but you are young. You must not think of what you are leaving behind, Gemma."

"All the young ones are going," Gemma's grandmother said. "As one of the eldest, the burden of history will be on your shoulders."

"I don't see why," Gemma said. "We're going to build a new life. Why do we need to take the memory of bitter things with us?"

Her grandmother sighed.

"Do you only choose to see the benevolence of the Once-masters?" she said. "Do you wish to forget that their kindness is locked up, as is the heart of the god whom they keep behind the white doors of their steepled houses?"

Gemma did not reply. She knew very well what her grandmother spoke of. Had she not known it herself that first day at school when she stood up and gave more correct answers than the children of the Once-masters?

"You are clever for a little sister," they had said to her afterwards. "But cleverness will never hide the fact that you came from Ficandula."

❧ ⚜ ☙

They came to our village carrying weapons like none we had seen before. Their leader was a man they called "Captain".

"Captain," they said. "This and this and that and that."

They pointed with their fingers at the boys who were sharpening their arrows in preparation for the big hunt.

We smiled and offered them our hands. We tried to tell them we were their friends.

Our chief's eldest son was there. He was the tallest among the boys, but he was shorter even than the shortest of the men in Captain's company.

"Line them up," Captain said.

And he started counting the boys.

They stood straight with their chins held high, shoulders held back. Oh, we were so very proud of them.

❧ ⚜ ☙

Gemma had always been the fastest in the races they held at the village. When the school announced that there would a be a grand race at the end of the school year, she had raised her hand and begged to join the runners on the list.

There had been some murmuring among the teachers, but Gemma's class adviser said there was no reason why one from Ficandula could not join the race.

Perhaps it was because she had come to school much later than the others, but she didn't understand the cautionary words her village mates spoke to her when they heard of her participation in the race.

"You give us pride," they said. "But you must be careful not to win."

"I will win," she said. "You will see it, big sisters. I will win and Ficandula will bring home the winner's flag."

There had been fear as well as hope in the eyes of the elder girls, but she had thought it was nothing more than a fear that she would lose.

At the starting line, the children of the Once-masters stared at her bare feet with contempt.

"You cannot win," they said.

She had simply raised her chin and smiled as she walked to the start block.

❧ ⚜ ☙

"What is it?" Apo Unying asked.

"Maybe it is a test," Manang Lunag said.

It was getting late in the morning and the boys were starting to get restless, but they did not move because Captain said they must stand still in that long line.

Soon, Captain's companions came peering through the doors of our huts.

"Where are they?" they asked. "The fathers? Old man, Lakay? Where is Lakay?"

They pulled the grandfathers from their hammocks and harangued them.

"Where are the men?"

"They are preparing the hunt," Manang Bagwis said. Manang was one of the Aunties and she spoke the words of the white ones as well as your father did.

"They have gone up ahead," Manang Bagwis continued. "But they will return."

"We will wait," Captain said.

He walked the line. The Apos were made to stand beside the boys.

"But grandfather is old," Manang Bagwis said. "Surely, you will allow him the courtesy of resting. He has earned his rest, for he hunted well enough for the tribe when he was young."

Captain stared down at Manang Bagwis. His white face was splotched with red, and his big nose seemed to grow bigger still.

"Silence," he thundered. "This woman. So noisy. Like a Parakeet."

Manang Bagwis retreated.

Captain stared around at all of us. His big eyes bulging, a horrendous, inhospitable blue that seemed to grow until it filled the sky.

We trembled at his look. Perhaps he was indeed kindred to the gods we had heard of. Perhaps he was descended from the foreign gods we did not know.

We waited and we waited and we waited.

The men would come when the young boys did not appear. They should have been in Tuguinay where their fathers were waiting for them. Instead, they were here—sweating in the hot sun—standing straight as they could with their chins held high.

❦

Even as she broke through the ribbon, Gemma could hear a murmur rising from the grandstand. She raised her hands in victory, but no one came to greet her. She stared in bewilderment as the students crowded around the boy who had come in behind her.

"I was first," she shouted as they hoisted the boy on their shoulders and flung the colors of the school around his shoulders.

"You ran in bare feet," a white-haired man said to her. He looked her up and down through his gold-rimmed spectacles and sniffed. "I wonder what the Governor must be thinking to allow savages like you among our children."

She stared at her bare feet. She always ran fastest this way. The leather shoes the school required felt like bricks around her feet. She walked to the sidelines where the girls of her village were watching.

"It's all right," they said. "You ran well."

Their arms embraced her, and their voices whispered love in the tongue the school forbade them to speak.

"Come," her adviser said. "You must put on your shoes. You were disqualified, but you did well. Don't tell anyone, but I am proudest of you."

In spite of her teacher's kind words, Gemma could only see that her teacher's skin was the color of cream speckled with red—the same as the boy with flame-colored hair who stuck out his tongue at her and carelessly waved the winner's flag above his head.

❧❦❧

The men came in at noon. There was your father, Wigan. Slow and patient and wise, that was your father. There was Namolngo. He was my younger brother. He was fond of laughing and he loved to drink rice wine. There was old Cayabyab. He should not have been in the hunt, but he was the best when it came to tracking wild boar. There was the father of the beautiful twins—he was also your uncle. The uncle of Paola, Paola's father, the fathers of your cousins, and there were my cousins and the big cousins of your baby cousins.

They were all there because it was the time of that hunt when the young ones join the ranks of men. They were laughing as they came up and your uncle was making a joke about young sons who refuse to grow into men.

They did not mind Captain and his men at first. After all, these white ones tramped about the mountains every now and then. They liked to make funny noises and they pretended to understand our language. They tried to make us wear their clothes, and they gave us funny-tasting food.

They bumbled about like giant children. They knew nothing about the world and they did not understand the ways of the gods. They were very foolish, and among ourselves we called them the Giant Orangutang.

"Oh, they are here again," your father said. "These giant Orangutang who have nothing to do but walk and walk all day,

swinging their long hairy arms and their long hairy selves, smelling of meat and sour sweat."

"They have lined up the boys," Manang Bagwis said. "And they made even the oldest Apo stand in the heat of the sun. They have no respect."

"That is because their bodies are so large they have no brains," Papa Manyok said.

We all laughed and our tension eased.

The fathers were here, the men were here.

"Make them go, Wigan," Manang Bagwis said. "Send them away. They are scaring the children, and they stink so much we cannot eat."

"I will speak with them," your father said.

He was a very wise man, your father. He spoke the words of the white ones and was not quick to anger as some men are.

❦

She learned to keep to the background as her elder sisters did. She obeyed the rules. She learned to smile with her lips, and not to laugh out loud. She never ran a race at school again.

"Gemma," her cousin's voice brought her out of her memories.

"I'll be right there," she said. She folded the journal into the blanket her mother had woven for her. Through the porthole, she had a clear view of mountain tops and green fields.

"We are waiting for you in the great hall," her cousin said. "We'll be landing soon."

"How many more hours?" Gemma asked.

She tucked the blanket and the journal into her carry-all.

"Hours?" her cousin's voice was breathless with laughter. "More like minutes."

❦

There are no more men in Ficandula and there never will be. It is a rule the white ones have made. They took the baby boys away after the men disappeared.

"They will be fostered well," they said. "Boys need fathers and there are none in this village."

Even though we pleaded with them, they never brought back our boys. Perhaps they thought the absence of men would mean the death of all Ficandula. They forget the gods who love us, for how else do you think you and your sisters and your younger cousins came to be?

The white ones have built their places in these mountains, and they think that makes them one of us.

How funny they are to think that way. They tell us we cannot talk to our gods because our gods are deaf and dumb. They tell us our gods have no eyes to see and no wisdom to impart.

They sit inside their square houses, they paint their houses white. White, white, all white. Just like their skins.

They have no respect for the dwelling places of the spirits, nor do they honor the resting place of the dead. Let them trespass at will, because the spirits wreak their vengeance for us, my child. There is nothing their science can do to disprove that.

❧ ❦ ❧

Ampual came to them in the place called the Sole of Maknungan. Gemma recognized him from the images the blind carver called Silwan had made of him. The god of the fourth Skyworld had long black hair braided through with threads of many colors. His skin was smooth and dark as the bark of the kamagong and he wore a belt made from the spine of the giant alligator called Timpalak.

He was beautiful to look at, lovelier than the white ones who strutted about in suits that made them look as if they were ready to be stuffed into a burial urn.

"So you are the children of my sibling's thought," he said.

And he laughed loud and long before he embraced them one by one.

"What do you mean?" Gemma's cousin asked. "And why have you summoned us to meet you here?"

"Today, I am only a messenger who serves the purpose of my sibling," he said. "But if you are brave enough to board my ship, I will take you to that place prepared for you."

"Is this sibling greater than you are?" Gemma asked.

He leaned towards her, his nose almost touching hers and then he smiled.

"Sometimes she is my sister, and sometimes she is my brother. When she is giving new life, I call her elder sister. At other times, she is something else. It is a power granted to very few, for not all gods may change according to their will. Is that enough for you, inquisitive child?"

Gemma flushed under his look and he threw his braids over his shoulder and winked in the way girls did when they wished to kiss and to embrace.

"It will be different where I am supposed to take you," he said. "It is my elder sister's place, and she has never been one to abide by rules created by the minds of mortal men. If you choose to journey with me,

I will return to this place when the light of the Skyworld falls on Ficandula."

❦

When Captain saw your father, he spat on the ground. He opened his mouth very wide and started shouting loud words.

I will not repeat them because they are blasphemous words that only an ignorant Orangutang would speak. Captain would soon pay for his blasphemy, but he did not know it just yet.

He blew on a whistle and his men came running and they pulled all the men to where the boys and the Apos were lined-up.

Your father tried to reason with Captain, but Captain was caught up in madness. Perhaps he had been bitten by a wild dog. He was salivating at the mouth, and you know it is never wise to cross the mad dog when it is on a rampage.

Your father was reasoning, still. His voice rose above the noise of the men as he tried to tame the madness in the heart of Captain's voice.

Captain stopped shouting. He clenched his fist and closed his eyes, and then he opened his eyes again and his fist shot out.

We all fell silent.

Truly, this was madness, and we didn't know any more what to do.

"Line up! Line up!" Captain shouted.

And his men pulled all of the fathers and the uncles and the cousins until they were standing three rows deep with their sons behind them.

He barked an order to one of the men and they went to where the horses and their cart were standing. They pulled the cart until it was in the center of the village. Flies were buzzing in the back of the cart, and there was dried blood. I thought they must have butchered a carabao or maybe a pig, or maybe they had gone hunting.

"This," Captain shouted. "This!"

His madness was on him again. And he threw back the sacks that hid what was in the back of the cart.

❦

Perhaps it was true what Ampual said. Perhaps the one called Maknongan looked down from the Skyworld and saw the sufferings of those who dwelt in Ficandula. By the time Gemma completed the required schooling, there were rumors of new mandates being handed down from the offices led by the Once-Masters.

Ficandula was a disgrace, one of the reports read. A village filled with rebellious and insurgent women. A hotbed of unrest, and no one knew what vipers were coddled there. The women must have loose morals, for even in the absence of men, there were always young children about—young girls with skin the color of earth, and eyes as dark as the night. Some pamphlets spoke of them as subversives, and it took Gemma the longest time to understand that they were writing of her and her cousins and the elder sisters who walked barefooted and bareheaded in Ficandula.

"They are not content to have taken our boys," Gemma's aunt complained. "Now, there are rumors that during the next visitation we will lose our girls."

"So it has come to this," Gemma's grandmother said. "They truly mean to erase the memory of us from the face of the Earth."

And so it was that when Ampual returned they were waiting for him. As many as had strength in their bones, for there was no telling what use the Once-Masters would have for the young when they got their hands on them, and there was no knowing what evils awaited the older ones as well.

"I hear they are very kind," cousin Zurina said.

"Kind?" Ilyana's voice was filled with contempt. "I have heard their kindness is such that they willingly gift women with big bellies even if the women do not ask for it."

"What's so bad about that?" Zurina asked. "After all, we would never have been if our mothers did not bear us?"

"But we were given as gifts to our mothers," Gemma said. "We were answers to the prayers they offered at the altar of the goddess Ubing."

"It is she, is it not," Ilyana said. "It is she who summons us through Ampual."

❧❦❧

We knew at once that it was the work of the gods. The heads of these men were on the cart beside their bodies. Their eyes were closed, as if they were sleeping, and we thought the gods must have been merciful to them because sometimes a man's head will be chopped off when he is awake and there is a look of terror on it. These men looked as if they were at peace.

We nodded our heads and said our commiserations to Captain. It was not his fault that the gods had slain these men.

Where were they found? What had they done that the gods should be so angered as to take their heads?

"Ficandula," Captain shouted.

And he made gestures with his hands.

"This village is closest to Ficandula. There is no one else. Tell me who did it and I will spare you."

Our men looked at each other. They stared at the bodies in the cart and they looked at Captain, not understanding what it was that he wanted.

The gods had killed those men. This is what they said to Captain.

❦

"I wove a blanket for you," her mother said. "And in your carry-all, you will find the colors of our tribe and the symbols that belong only to Ficandula."

"You will not change your mind," Gemma said.

"I cannot," her mother said. "Your grandmother is on her deathbed, and I cannot leave her."

Her mother's arms enclosed her for one final embrace, and their tears mingled as they pressed their cheeks to one another.

"I will keep your memory alive," Gemma said. "And I will keep the histories fresh in the minds of my tribe sisters."

❦

You would think an intelligent man would understand. How hard is it to comprehend the ways of the gods. They slept in the longhouse of the god of war, and for their trespass, he took their heads.

"A lie," the Captain said. "A lie. A lie. A lie."

He made a gesture with his hands and his men crowded us into carts and told us to leave. All of us women with our little girls and with our babies.

"Where are we to go?" Manang Bagwis asked.

"Go," one of the men said. "Just go away."

"What about our men? Our sons? Our fathers?"

The man who looked younger than any of the others stared at us with miserable eyes. His eyes were a fallow brown, and there was sadness in it and hopelessness and despair.

"Just go," he said.

❦

Their voices echoed within the belly of the ship as one by one they recited the names of the men who had been taken from their tribe. Fathers and sons, uncles and brothers, and more recently, the names of the boys who had been taken away.

Gemma recited along with them, and to the names of the men, they added the names of their mothers and their grandmothers.

"These names, we will always remember," they said. "Because of them, we can dream and look towards a different future."

And it seemed to Gemma that the ship shivered as they made this oath.

❦✝❧

When we returned to our village, there was a sea of blood. We looked and we looked but we did not find any of the men. We called and we shouted, but nobody answered.

You would think the blood would smell. That is what we thought as well. That night we did not sleep in the village, but we went into the forest and slept there as our forefathers did before us.

In the forest, a dream came to all of us. In this dream, your father was standing with his cousins and his brothers. He was standing with all the uncles and all the other men of our tribe. Around their necks were the teeth of the great boar and they carried bright shields and machetes in their hands.

"We have gone to hunt," they said. "We will take the heads of the Orangutang and offer them up to the gods. You will see what you will see."

And we heard the sound of the gongs and the echo of their voices as they wandered away from us towards Ficandula.

❦✝❧

"My sister waits," Ampual said.

From the portholes, they could see green stretched out below them.

"I have other journeys to make," Ampual said. "There are other children who must be visited."

"Will they come to New Cordillera as well?" Gemma asked.

"There are other places on this world that will be home to others just like you," Ampual said. "Only time will tell if your paths will cross with the paths of those others who are the thought of my other siblings."

"Will we see you again?" It was Gemma's cousin who asked.

Ampual smiled.

"Perhaps you will see me, perhaps you will not. But if you build a house for Ampual of the fourth Skyworld, I will come and rest my head there when my travels allow."

As he spoke the walls of the ship turned transparent, and they could see out into the rich green of the world that lay beyond. Below them was green valley. A sparkling river run through it and circling the valley were mountain terraces all planted with young rice.

"Welcome to your home," Ampual said. "Welcome to New Cordillera."

His words fell into the wind, and then the ship was gone and they were standing at the edge of a mountain, the breeze blowing through their hair, tears standing in their eyes, and there walking towards them was a woman with eyes that shone like stars in the night sky and arms stretched out in welcome.

"My children," she cried. "As I desired, Ampual has brought you to me."

☙❦❧

There are sounds that haunt our dreams even now. They are like to the sounds we sometimes hear in the mountains when it is very late at night. There are those who would send the Once-masters away, and we have seen those marked as the beloved of our gods as they run and hide from the hand of those who now rule over us.

We have no men or boys to send out for the great hunt. But we remember everything.

Here is your father's belt. Here is your father's blanket. Here are the skulls of the ones he hunted.

This is how a warrior carries his spear, and this is how he bears his shield. We have woven charms into the sheath of your machete. We have baptized your armbands with our tears.

We will beat the gongs and we will offer up our prayers. Hunt well, young ones. We will wait for you on the road to Ficandula.

☙❦❧

Skulls line the entrance to New Cordillera. On Gemma's fiftieth birthday, the white ones came through the portal above their new home.

When they landed, the women lured them into the village. They feted them with rice wine, with songs and with dances. Then, when the men fell asleep, the women took up their machetes.

Upon Ampual's visit, he found the longhouse the women had built for him. Its walls were decorated with the bones of their enemies, and its floors were lined with skins—dried and stitched together.

"You have taught them well," he said to his sibling.

"Not I," Ubing replied. "History has taught them all they ever need to know."

☙❦❧

Author's note. This story is loosely inspired by a little known incident in Hungduan (Ifugao) during the early part of the American occupation of the Philippines. Two archeologists who had violated a sacred granary were beheaded by tribesmen, and the Americans inflicted reprisals upon the men of the village.

Afterword

Ekaterina Sedia

From the Colonized Mind to a New Frontier

The book you have just finished reading is remarkable—and when I was in your shoes, as I was when I just finished reading it, it left me a bit whiplashed. The stories were diverse, sure, and yet I was stunned by the remarkable thematic coherence that runs through this collection: certain images and ideas kept popping up over and again, telling us that the state of post-colonialism comes with its own set of markers and phenomena. Regardless of the culture that has experienced colonization, its aftereffects and post-concerns are quite similar.

Instead of analyzing individual stories, I decided to tackle the emergent themes—the book is certainly larger than a simple assemblage of individual stories, and I'd like to approach it as an entity in itself rather than dissecting it into parts; after all, more than one story in this collection warns us against this reductionist impulse. Instead, I will treat it as holistically as I can, since many of the themes seem to flow from one story to the next, and to develop almost independently of the writers' will—and this, I believe, is a sign of truly talented editors, who have selected the stories and positioned them to assure both thematic unity and clarity of purpose.

The main and most obvious theme that becomes apparent early on is the push-pull of the contradictory demands of assimilation versus appropriation—that is, as the colonizing culture attempts to assimilate the colonized into its imperial (or colonial) hive-mind, it is also eager to appropriate the trappings of the culture it has taken over, thus leaving the colonized twice bereaved—robbed of what was theirs, and the stolen cultural treasures replaced by the dominant faux-narrative.

Meanwhile, the trappings of the colonized are left empty, divorced from their cultural meaning and memory—mere trophies in the hands of the colonizers. This twin cultural assassination is apparent in many of the stories, and mirrors closely the real-world narratives.

This insight is something that I feel is uniquely endemic to this particular book, or to this particular kind of story. Too often, the colonizers perceive assimilation as voluntary, and appropriation as paying their respect to other cultures, rarely realizing the true nature of the destruction that they are causing. However, these writers see clearly the harm being done. There is a mournful thread running through, based on the realization that the colonized often irrevocably lose their own voices, and even when they do create their own stories, it is done in the language of the outsiders. This narrative transplant, when the colonized people tell their story in the language and story structure of the conquerors, is a simultaneously fascinating and heartbreaking phenomenon.

This is the terrible duality of the colonized mind, which often comes to accept the outsiders' values as its own. This is not a free choice but a necessity—understanding the language of the dominant group is a matter of survival. (It is of course no mere coincidence that these stories are written in English.) Through needing to understand the dominant mindset, the oppressed are forced into accepting it, and this is the burden of post-colonialism: while the literal and the military shackles have been shed, the colonized mindset remains, and colonization finds its logical extension in cultural colonialism—and again, it is no coincidence that Hollywood, films and books feature so commonly in these stories.

These stories so persistently pushed upon us through every worldwide media outlet are not ours, these writers seem to say, but we will take them and make them our own. The difficulty, of course, is that taking something back and being taken over by it are not easily distinguished. Sometimes rebellion and consent may look remarkably similar. Sometimes we rebel by writing our own narratives, but end up complicit when those narratives are subsumed by the dominant culture and its language, awash in its story structures and values.

These values are so pervasive that the world we live today is constructed along the axes of the Western (or colonizing) thought: the constant Aristotelian dichotomies bisect our discourse and thoughts in every direction. Emotion and reason, art and science, male and female—all of these sharp dualities are not necessarily endemic to any given culture, but more often then not are introduced there by Western colonization.

Interestingly, this is another common thread: whether we look at the stories set in the colonized lands or in the West, science is often pitted in direct opposition to a holistic view of the world. By extension, science is often presented as a tool of the colonizers. Western reductionism, the need to dissect and disassemble and take apart, to study the details in order to comprehend the whole, is the very nature of the scientific method, and has transcended its applications, being often applied to entire peoples and cultures and souls. We see it in the reductionism of literary analysis, the reductionism of anthropology, and of cultural history. We see echoes of this idea in many of the stories; some even take the dissecting tools and (in some cases, literally) turn them against the conquerors.

It's a notion many of the writers explore—the weapons of the colonizers taken up by the oppressed in act of liberation. Yet, one cannot help but remember the immortal Audre Lorde's quote about the master's tools that cannot dismantle the master's house, and the sense of loss and uncertainty lingers in these stories, as we are left to wonder—along with the writers—about the price paid for knowledge, as well as the adequacy of a blow that is a mere reflection of the attack.

The solution offered by several of the stories seems to be found in the integration: the tools of the colonizers are flawed, and they have to be modified, infused with cultural memory and meaning, in order to serve the oppressed. Because the very nature of post-colonialism includes the impossibility of being entirely rid of it, the best we can hope for is to comprehend the past, recognize the ongoing colonization of the mind and of internal landscapes, and to resist it as best we can.

Resistance, then: several of the stories talk about its nature, and the emerging consensus appears to be that resistance is often indeed futile; but the futility of it is not a good enough reason to stop trying. The very nature of the colonizing influence is that it is elusive and shifting, often changing its appearance or mode, and thus is extremely difficult to confront. The quest for recognition of it is never-ending, and resistance takes as many forms as the influence itself—from warfare to art. Here again we see Hollywood emerging as the cultural constant, as the colonizing influence so significant that it doesn't need to hide—or that, by its very nature, is forced to take on many forms.

This shifting nature imitates the shifting internal boundaries as well, something that the stories in this anthology touch upon over and over again: sometimes the shift is occurring internally and sometimes externally, when the very buildings and external landscapes become mutable, deviating from known history and the memory of those living in the stories, becoming reflections of the changes taking place in the colonized psyche.

And this brings us to the final theme: transience. During colonial history, the boundaries between nations were constantly changing. As new colonies were acquired and relinquished, the conquerors redrew the internal boundaries between the conquered peoples in order to negotiate with each other, resulting not only in arbitrary divisions between nations, but also in the inherently transient nature of colonial history. The changing borders mimicked the cultural erasure and retellings, and became lines drawn in the sand, erased and drawn again. As were the colonial histories—histories retold by the conquerors, histories designed to cast the colonizers in the best possible light and to erase as much of the cultural memory of the colonized as possible.

This shortness of colonial memory is meditated upon in some of the stories as well—due to the transient nature of any specific legacy, coupled with the lasting impression of colonization itself, this transience is often remarked upon, and the loss of cultural memory in this context dovetails nicely with the theme of the intentional erasure of the colonized memory and history.

It is interesting, then, to see the role the US plays in many of the stories: the American narrative presents the country as a colony that has fought for its liberation, but in reality of course it was already settled by the colonizers, and its separation from British rule was hardly an act of anticolonial rebellion. The genocide of the native populations in the US are barely considered in the dominant narrative, and slavery has been consistently downplayed or justified. From that position, the US has risen to be the dominant colonization power today—be it through direct occupation of foreign territories, or the occupation of minds by the Hollywood machine. At the same time, the US is still often an aspirational goal for those who seek to leave their home countries for a variety of reasons, and the theme of immigration—and its disappointments—is also present in this book.

We find ourselves rebelling against the lies and the dominant narratives fed into our collective psyche, *Clockwork Orange*-style, by Hollywood's dream factory—a truly terrifying notion, if you think about it for a bit. We find ourselves looking for ways to escape, but realizing, time and time again, that the post-colonial world is still rife with colonial injustice and oppression. And yet, slowly, slowly, we are finding voices to tell our stories, to reclaim what has been lost of history. These broken, half-forgotten histories and dreams will never be restored to their original form, and part of living in the post-colonial world is making peace with that. Because we can still create the future, and try to hope that it will be treated better than our past. The writers in this book are taking a step in that direction—because the frontier that they see is one not in space but in time, a time when all voices are heard and all stories are listened to, when no history is erased, no matter how small or inconvenient. We see a different frontier—and I hope that this book let you glimpse it as well.

Contributors

Djibril al-Ayad is the *nom de guerre* of a historian, futurist, writer and editor of *The Future Fire*, magazine of social-political speculative fiction. His interests span science, religion and magic; education and public engagement; diversity, inclusivity and political awareness in the arts.

❦

Aliette de Bodard is a half-French, half-Vietnamese who lives in a Parisian flat with more computers than warm bodies. When not busy working as a Computer Engineer, she writes speculative fiction: her Aztec noir trilogy *Obsidian and Blood* is published by Angry Robot, and her short fiction has been published in markets like *Clarkesworld*, *Interzone* and *The Year's Best Science Fiction*, garnering her a British Science Fiction Association Award, and Hugo and Nebula nominations. She blogs and geeks on food over at aliettedebodard.com.

❦

Joyce Chng was born in Singapore but is a global citizen; she writes mainly science fiction (SFF) and YA fiction. Her stories can be found in *The Apex Book of World SF II* and *Weird Noir*. Her novels are published by Lyrical Press. Her website is A Wolf's Tale: awolfstale.wordpress.com.

❦

Fabio Fernandes is an SF writer living in São Paulo, Brazil. He has several stories published in online venues like *Everyday Weirdness*, *The Nautilus Engine*, *StarShipSofa*, *Semaphore Magazine*, *Dr. Hurley's Snake-Oil Cure*, and *Kaleidotrope Magazine*, and in anthologies like Ann and Jeff VanderMeer's *Steampunk II: Steampunk Reloaded* and *The Apex World Book of SF*, Vol. 2 (ed. by Lavie Tidhar). Two-time recipient of the Argos SF Award (Brazil), Fernandes co-edited with Jacques Barcia in 2008 the bilingual online magazine *Terra Incognita*, and has translated into Brazilian Portuguese several SF works, such as *Neuromancer*, *Foundation*, *Snow Crash*, *Boneshaker*, and *The Steampunk Bible*.

❦

Ernest Hogan is descended from a curandero who once treated Pancho Villa. He is no relation to Ernest Hogan, the Father of Ragtime. Despite his Irish name (and ancestors) he is a born-in-East-L.A. Chicano. He coined the term "recomboculture", and wrote the novels *Cortez on Jupiter*, *High Aztech*, and *Smoking Mirror Blues*. He's all about impurity. You can read about it in his blog, mondoernesto.com, and his Chicanonautica column at labloga.blogspot.com.

☙❦❧

Rahul Kanakia is a science-fiction writer who has sold stories to *Clarkesworld*, *the Intergalactic Medicine Show*, *Apex, Nature*, and *Lady Churchill's Rosebud Wristlet*. He currently lives in Baltimore, where he is enrolled in the Master of the Fine Arts program in creative writing at Johns Hopkins University. He graduated from Stanford in 2008 with a B.A. in Economics and he used to work as an international development consultant. If you want to know more about him then please visit his blog at blotter-paper.com or follow him on Twitter at twitter.com/rahkan.

☙❦❧

Rochita Loenen-Ruiz is a Filipino writer living in the Netherlands. A graduate of the Clarion West Writer's Workshop, she was the recipient of the Octavia Butler Scholarship in 2009. Her fiction has been published abroad as well as in her home country, the Philippines. Recent publication credits include *Bloodchildren: Stories from the Octavia Butler Scholars*, *Weird Fiction Review*, *The Apex Book of World SF 2* and *Philippine Genre Stories*. Her non-fiction has appeared in *The Future Fire*, *Weird Fiction Review* and the Filipino publication, *Our Own Voice*. She is a regular columnist for *Strange Horizons*. Find her online at: rcloenenruiz.com.

☙❦❧

Sandra McDonald's first collection of fiction was a Booklist Editor's Choice, an American Library Association Over the Rainbow Book and winner of a Lambda Literary Award. Four of her stories have been noted by the James A. Tiptree Award Honor List for exploring gender stereotypes. She is the published author of several novels and more than sixty short stories for adults and teens, including the *Fisher Key Adventures* (written as Sam Cameron). She holds an M.F.A. in Creative Writing from the University of Southern Maine and teaches college in Florida.

☙❦❧

Sunny Moraine is a humanoid creature of average height, luminosity and inertial mass. They're also a doctoral student in sociology and a writer-like object who focuses primarily on various flavors of speculative fiction, usually with a decidedly queer bent, some of which has appeared in places like *Clarkesworld, Shimmer, Strange Horizons,* and *Apex Magazine.* Their first novel *Line and Orbit,* co-written with Lisa Soem, is available from Samhain Publishing. They spend most of their days using writing to distract from academics, except for the occasions when the two collide.

❦

Carmen Moran grew up in East Germany, where the combined forces of her family and pre-reunification lack of TV introduced her to crafts and poetry from an early age. Following her move to Edinburgh, Scotland in 2000, she started taking life drawing and illustration classes, and was soon found making random attempts at world domination through the production of illustrations for various publications, and the creation of an army of Minimonsters. Since then, she has helped to set up Craft Reactor Edinburgh, and when she is not trying to scare small children, she can often be found at craft fairs, flogging the produce of Carmenland to the general public.

❦

Silvia Moreno-Garcia is Mexican by birth, Canadian by inclination, and lives in beautiful British Columbia with her family and two cats. Her short stories have appeared in places such as *The Book of Cthulhu* and *Imaginarium 2012: The Best Canadian Speculative Writing.* She has edited or co-edited the anthologies *Fungi, Future Lovecraft* and the upcoming *Dead North.* She owns and operates Innsmouth Free Press, a micro-press dedicated to the Weird and horrific. Her first collection, *Shedding Her Own Skin,* is out in 2013. She is working on a novel about a garbage collector who meets a drug-dealing vampire in Mexico City. Maybe it'll be publishable one day.

❦

Gabriel Murray, contrary to the implications of his fiction, is in fact quite fond of cats. He is a graduate of the 2007 Clarion Writing Workshop and a member of the Outer Alliance. He reads submissions and reviews movies and books for *Strange Horizons* and has had work published or forthcoming in *Daily Science Fiction* and *Ideomancer.* He has studied, among other things, Victorian poetry, anti-intellectualism in mad scientist narratives, Latin, law, and vampire cinema, but prefers postcolonialism and bubble tea.

❦

Shweta Narayan was born in India and has lived in Malaysia, Saudi Arabia, the Netherlands, Scotland, and California. She was the Octavia Butler Memorial Scholarship recipient at Clarion 2007. The clockwork bird showed up one day and hasn't left yet; other stories about her have appeared in Shimmer's *Clockwork Jungle* issue (reprinted in *Steampunk II: Steampunk Reloaded* and *The Mammoth Book of Steampunk*), *Realms of Fantasy*, *Clockwork Phoenix* 3, and *Steam Powered: Lesbian Steampunk Stories*. Shweta's other fiction and poetry have recently appeared in places like *Strange Horizons*, *Goblin Fruit*, *The Apex Book of World SF 2*, and the 2012 Nebula Showcase Anthology.

☙❦❧

Dinesh Rao, originally from India, trained as an ecologist and specializes in the behaviour of spiders. His short stories have appeared in the *World SF Blog* and the *Indian Journal of Science Fiction Studies*. He now lives in a small coffee town in Mexico with his wife and daughter. His blog is at pointsofdeparture.wordpress.com.

☙❦❧

N.A. Ratnayake is a science teacher, writer, and stubborn idealist living in Boston. He is an aerospace engineer by training and an omnivorous reader. Though presently a New Englander, he was born and raised in the American West. The mountains, rains, coasts, and deserts of the West have been the backdrop for a rich interplay of conquest, struggle, identity, and hope—themes which often emerge in Ratnayake's stories. "Remembering Turinam" is his first professional publication. He tweets at twitter.com/quantumcowboy.

☙❦❧

Sofia Samatar is the author of the novel *A Stranger in Olondria* (Small Beer Press, 2013). Her short fiction and poetry have appeared in several places, including *Strange Horizons*, *Clarkesworld Magazine*, *Stone Telling*, and *Goblin Fruit*. She is Nonfiction and Poetry Editor for *Interfictions: A Journal of Interstitial Arts*, and blogs at sofiasamatar.blogspot.com.

☙❦❧

Ekaterina Sedia resides in the Pinelands of New Jersey. Her critically-acclaimed and award-nominated novels, *The Secret History of Moscow*, *The Alchemy of Stone*, *The House of Discarded Dreams* and *Heart of Iron*, were published by Prime Books. Her short stories have sold to *Analog*, *Baen's Universe*, *Subterranean* and *Clarkesworld*, as well as numerous anthologies, including *Haunted Legends* and *Magic in the Mirrorstone*. She is also the editor of the anthologies *Paper Cities* (World Fantasy Award winner), *Running with the Pack*, and *Bewere the Night*, as well as *Bloody Fabulous* and *Wilful Impropriety*. Her short-story collection, *Moscow But Dreaming*, was released by Prime Books in December 2012. Visit her at www.ekaterinasedia.com.

≈†≋

Benjanun Sriduangkaew spends her free time on words, amateur photography, and the pursuit of colorful, unusual makeup. She has a love for cities, airports, and bees. Her fiction can be found in *GigaNotoSaurus* and *Beneath Ceaseless Skies* as well as the anthologies *Clockwork Phoenix* 4 and *The End of the Road*.

≈†≋

Lavie Tidhar is the World Fantasy Award-winning author of *Osama*, of *The Bookman Histories* trilogy and many other works. He won the British Fantasy Award for Best Novella, for *Gorel & The Pot-Bellied God*, and was nominated variously for BSFA, Campbell, Sturgeon and Sidewise awards. He grew up on a kibbutz in Israel and in South Africa but currently resides in London.

≈†≋

J.Y. Yang, born, raised and centred in Singapore, has been a scientist, a screenwriter, an editor, and a journalist at various times, but she almost always has been a teller of tales. Some of them have been published in places both local and international, including *Crossed Genres* and Ann Vandermeer's *Steampunk Revolution*. Last year she co-edited *Ayam Curtain*, an anthology of speculative micro-fiction written by Singapore-based authors. It was fun, but she isn't sure she'll do it again soon (for her sanity's sake).

Made in the USA
Lexington, KY
28 February 2014